SANCTUARY

SANCTUARY

A THORNTON MYSTERY

C.L. TOLBERT

Author Photo Credit: Richie Arpino

Cover Art Photo Credit: Brian Swanner

First edition

ISBN: 978-1-68512-146-4

Cover art by Level Best Designs

This book was professionally typeset on Reedsy.
Find out more at reedsy.com

To Elise, Lila, and Vivienne, my three beautiful granddaughters...for whom I'm more thankful every day...

"Most people have forgotten nowadays what a house can mean, though some of us have come to realize it as never before. It is a kingdom of its own in the midst of the world, a stronghold amid life's storms and stresses, a refuge, even a sanctuary."

DIETRICH BONHOEFFER,
LETTERS AND PAPERS FROM PRISON

Praise for Sanctuary

"Brace yourself. Deadly personalities, hidden agendas, and long-buried secrets threaten law professor Emma Thornton after she agrees to defend a terrified young woman accused of murdering the charismatic leader of an oppressive cult. The dark heart of New Orleans has never felt so dangerous."—Roger Johns, author of the Wallace Hartman Mysteries

"The lies stack up as fast as bodies in this latest thriller from C.L. Tolbert. Law professor Emma Thornton returns as the tenacious and fearless defender of New Orleans' downtrodden. An enthralling mystery, *Sanctuary* explores the seedy underbelly of the Big Easy."—Bruce Robert Coffin, award-winning author of the Detective Byron Mysteries

"A shady religion, shadowy deals, and twisted family relationships come together in the atmospheric world of New Orleans to create a captivating mystery. Emma Thornton is an attorney with a heart of gold."—Liz Milliron, author of The Laurel Highlands Mysteries and The Homefront Mysteries

"*Sanctuary* explores the seedy side of the French Quarter complete with cults and drugs as Attorney Emma Thornton races to clear the name of a young runaway. Author C.L. Tolbert takes the reader along on a heart-pounding journey into the dark underbelly of New Orleans."—Annette Dashofy, *USA Today* Bestselling author of the Zoe Chambers Mysteries

Chapter One

Monday, October 14, 1996

J ames Crosby licked his index finger and thumb and pinched the flame
of the candle until it was out. His mother had taught him how to snuff
out a candle years ago, assuring him that the flame wouldn't burn him,
encouraging him to follow her example. She could be charming when she
wanted, but when he burned his fingers that day, she laughed. He was only
five.

James stood at the altar for a moment, watching the glowing ember of
incense resting on its stand, then reached into his pocket and placed a small
mirror on the smooth wooden surface. He poured a line of white powder
on the mirror, plucked a razor from his wallet, and began to cut the powder
into smaller lines. Bending over the altar, he sniffed loudly, then shook his
head, savoring the feeling. For a moment, he saw a kaleidoscope of color.
He turned around, staggering, gripping the altar, and gazed out over the
room.

James was alone that afternoon, although he was expecting the plumber
to show up at any moment. He preferred solitude, especially since he spent
all week listening to people talk about their problems. Cecelia, his wife,
had gone grocery shopping, and at his request, Mira, his assistant and the
mother of his second child, was visiting their French Quarter shop to check
on some of the sales. The spa services, offered in the back of the temple,
were closed on Monday, as were all lessons, sessions, and chanting. The

temple was open for meditation only, but no one was there.

Mondays were slow in New Orleans. Galleries, hairdressers, spas, theaters, and many of the restaurants in the city were also closed. Mondays seemed like a holiday to him. A day he could do what he wanted. It was his favorite day of the week.

James pulled back the velvet drapes of the altar room and stepped into the hallway. He breathed deeply, filling his lungs. The air was clearer there, the incense not nearly as thick. He tried to clear his head with each breath, but the drug had kicked in. He turned, catching his reflection in the mirror at the foot of the stairs. He didn't like what he saw.

He turned, stumbling, to make his way to the second-floor offices and apartments, and noticed there were still some tools the plumbers had left behind in the hallway from the work they did last week. They hadn't been paid yet and were probably expecting something soon. He'd have to remind Mira to send them a check.

The floorboards creaked from the weight of his steps, and he nearly groaned out loud at the thought of all the work that had to be done. The repairs he was having made hadn't been adequate even though workers were making their way around the place, replacing rotten boards and plumbing lines. He swept his hand along the mahogany banister. It was still a fine place, despite all the problems.

When he reached the second floor, he grabbed the knob to his office door to steady himself, then paused. He thought he'd heard steps. The front door of the house was always open for meditation, although most people knocked when temple wasn't in session. Except for the plumber. He often walked in unannounced.

James peered down the hallway toward the stairs and, seeing no one, stepped into his office. To his surprise, a window was wide open. He glanced around the empty room, confused. He hadn't opened a window in his office in more than a year. Even though it was October, it was nearly ninety degrees outside, so the air conditioner was still on. No one he knew would open a window in such heat.

Dizzy, he staggered toward the window, steadying himself, gripping the frame as he gazed out. Seeing no activity, he stepped, faltering, onto the balcony, peering out over the yard and the garconniere fifteen feet below. Then he leaned out farther still to see if the plumber's truck was parked in the front of the house.

He heard another step from behind and turned, wobbling, to see who it was, surprised by a figure in black standing in front of him. Before he knew what was happening, he felt a jab in the side of his neck, and the person backed away. He grabbed his neck, immediately feeling drowsy. He squinted at the blurred figure in the hoodie who had just attacked him, then began swinging his fists. But his blows missed. He stumbled toward his assailant, grabbing the sleeve of the person's jacket and pulling it toward him. The attacker pulled away from James' grasp and spun him around, causing him to lose his balance.

James began to lose consciousness. His vision dimmed, and his legs grew numb. He felt a hand on his back pushing him toward the railing of the balcony. Even though he wasn't fully conscious, he knew he'd lost his footing. Then he felt a hard shove and a rush of air as he plummeted headfirst toward the courtyard below.

Chapter Two

Two days later, Stacey Roberts opened her bedroom door, shocked to see two police officers standing in the hallway. Dread spread through the pit of her stomach. Nothing good ever happened when police were around.

One of the police officers handed her an official-looking paper. "We have a warrant to search some of the rooms in this house, including yours. So you're going to have to step out." The baby-faced officer rested his hand on the holster at his hip, ready to whip out his pistol at any moment.

With shaking hands, Stacey took the paper the officer handed her, but she was so frightened she had to read it twice to focus on what the words meant. They were looking for syringes and a drug called ketamine. This had to be about James' death. Why were they looking in her room?

Stacey shivered as she stepped out of her bedroom, even though, as always, it was warm on the third floor of the temple. She walked down the hall with its peeling wallpaper and water-stained ceiling, her stomach churning. The area where the spa workers lived was in poorer repair than the rest of the house. They all shared the one bathroom on the floor, which only worked part of the time. As she started her descent, her stomach lurched like she was about to be sick.

Downstairs, Stacey waited nervously while the officers searched her room, relieved only by the fact that the place was so small and her furnishings were so scant, the search shouldn't take long. Her bedroom held an iron bed, nearly as old as the house, a nightstand, and a rickety French armoire for her clothes. There wasn't even a closet. They couldn't possibly find anything incriminating, but that didn't stop the queasiness in the pit of her stomach.

She had walked into the kitchen to get a glass of water when she heard clamoring footsteps descending the stairs. With shaking hands, she placed her water glass back on the counter and peered around the door to the staircase. The officers saw her and walked down the hallway toward the kitchen.

"We need to ask you a few questions about something we just found in your room. You have the right to remain silent."

Stacey's throat closed.

"Anything you say may be used against you in a court of law. You have the right to consult an attorney before speaking to us or any police officer, and you have the right to have an attorney present during questioning, now or in the future. If you decide to answer questions now, without an attorney present, you still have the right to stop answering at any time until you talk to an attorney."

Stacey nodded. "It's okay. You can ask a couple of questions." She hardly recognized the sound of her own voice.

"First thing. How old are you?"

"I'm nineteen."

The officer nodded at his partner, a female who had pulled her blonde hair into a tight knot at the base of her neck. Her hat rested directly on top of her bun.

The female officer held up a plastic bag containing a large syringe and needle. "Is this yours?"

She shook her head. "No. I don't take any medications that require syringes." She felt dizzy and held on to the kitchen counter.

Then the female officer held up another plastic bag containing a white t-shirt.

"What about this?"

Stacey nodded. "Yes. That's my t-shirt."

The baby-faced officer pursed his lips. "How do you explain a syringe in the bottom of your armoire wrapped in one of your t-shirts, then?"

Stacey swallowed, feeling queasy. "I wouldn't know anything about that.

I didn't wrap a syringe in my t-shirt, and I didn't put it or the t-shirt in the bottom of my closet." Her heart was pounding, and she was unsteady on her feet. She walked over to the kitchen table, pulled out a chair, and sat down.

The officers followed Stacey to the table. "Well, we found them there. And how do you explain that if you don't take intravenous medications or drugs?" The officer raised his eyebrows, anticipating her answer.

"I - I can't really. I don't know why they were there. Someone must have put them there." Stacey put her elbows on the table and held her head.

"Do you know why a witness would have said they saw you walking up the stairs with a syringe like this in your hand shortly after four o'clock the day Mr. Crosby fell from the balcony?"

Stacey lifted her head and turned toward the police officers. "No! It's just not true! I didn't do anything like that. Who said that? They're making it up."

"What about these? Are they yours?" The officer held up another bag filled with small glass vials and packets of white powder.

Stacey shook her head. "No. I've never seen them before in my life."

"They were found in your nightstand. How do you explain that?" The officer pointed to the bag.

Stacey lifted her hands. "I can't. I don't know what to make of any of this. Someone else had to have put them there." She covered her face with her hands and began to cry.

"Also, we were told your father recently died of a heart attack while he was searching for you. Do you blame either James Crosby or anyone else here at this place for your father's death?"

"It's true my father died when he was looking for me, but I'd never blame anyone for his death. It was just a terrible tragedy. I don't blame anyone."

"That's not what we heard. We're taking you in for further questioning. Maybe that will jog your memory."

Chapter Three

Professor Emma Thornton grimaced. If she didn't hurry, she'd be late for class that morning. Almost dressed for work but still in her slippers, she'd followed her twins, Billy and Bobby, down the stairs to the sidewalk so she could watch them run down the street to catch their school bus. Her gaze followed the vehicle as it rounded the corner and rattled to a screeching stop, disc brakes squealing. The driver knew the boys and patiently waited for them to board. Even though they'd barely made it on time, they still turned and waved to her as they stepped onto the bus. Emma loved watching them. They'd be driving soon; she didn't have many of these days left.

The phone rang. Clenching her jaw, Emma ran back up the stairs to answer it. She was going to be even later than she'd imagined.

"Collect call from Central Lockup. Do you accept?"

"Yes." Emma was certain she'd live to regret that decision. But she could always refer a case to someone else. She might as well listen to what the prisoner had to say.

"Professor Thornton?"

"Yes, who's this?"

"It's Stacey Roberts. Remember me?"

Stacey had been one of Emma's clients at the homeless clinic she ran at St. Stanislaus University Law School.

"Of course, I remember you. That group arrest down in the Quarter. It's been about three years? I'd ask how you were doing, but I guess that's why you're calling." Emma could hear the clanging of prison doors slamming and voices yelling in the background.

"Yeah. Not so good. Obviously." She paused. "I got arrested."

"Sleeping on the streets again?" Emma moved into the bathroom and chose a color of lipstick that complimented her outfit. She outlined her lips as she listened to Stacey.

"No." She hesitated. Her voice sounded shaky, but it was difficult to tell over the phone line. "I…I've been arrested for killing a man, for murder." Stacey stifled a sob.

Emma put her lipstick down. "Oh my God! Murder? I can't imagine you being involved in something like that!"

"I'm not involved in anything. I didn't do anything to anyone." She sniffed.

"What's this all about? Who was killed?" Emma walked back into her living room.

"A guy named James Crosby. He's the Pujari of the Japaprajna order down on Esplanade."

"I don't know what any of that means. Pujari?"

"It's a Hindu religious title, I think. It means priest."

"What's the Japaprajna order? Do you belong to it?" Emma checked her watch.

Stacey sighed. "I joined right after you got me out of jail three years ago. It's a long story. At first, it was a place to sleep and eat. It seemed like a good idea to me then. I didn't want to go back to my parents. Now I wish I had." She sniffed again.

"So you went to live with the Japaprajnas."

"That's right."

"How did you find them?"

"They had some recruiters in the French Quarter. They had a shop there. They still do."

"A shop? What kind of shop?"

"They sell rolling papers, pipes, clips, candles, things like that."

"A head shop?"

"Yep."

"Hmm. That's a little unusual for a religious group. How did they go about recruiting?" Emma grabbed her briefcase from her closet and checked to make certain she had everything she needed. If she didn't get going, she'd be late for class.

"They just said that if I'd come work at the spa on Esplanade, they call it their temple, that I could live there free. I guess they could tell I was homeless." She cleared her throat. "They wanted me to get involved in some of the meditations, and things like that, too. I thought that was a good idea. And they had to teach me about massage too."

"This is when you were sixteen."

"That's right."

"And you started working there after that?" Emma walked back into her closet and grabbed a pair of shoes.

"Yeah. I moved in and worked at the spa for a while. It's really just a place where people get massages in the back of the temple. Everyone who lives there works somewhere at the place. That's how it is. You have to contribute."

"I don't mean to be offensive, but are those actual massages, or do they offer more than that, if you understand what I'm saying?" Emma stepped out of her slippers and slipped her shoes on.

"I know what you're saying. And no, I never gave a massage that offered anything extra. Some of the girls might have. I really don't know." Stacey paused. "Some weird things go on at the temple, but I think everything's okay with the massages unless some of the girls need extra money. But if they're doing that, I don't know about it. That kind of thing wasn't part of our training."

Emma hoped Stacey hadn't been exploited or treated badly. It happened so often, especially to girls. "When was the last time you spoke to your parents?"

"Not since my mom bailed me out of jail three years ago. My dad died a couple of months after that."

"I'm so sorry to hear about your father."

Stacey exhaled shakily. "I didn't find out right away because I didn't stay in touch with them. My dad had a heart attack almost three years ago when he came to New Orleans looking for me." Her voice caught. "I never even knew it happened until about a month ago." Emma could tell she was crying.

Emma heard static over the phone lines. She sighed. She was shocked that Stacey had been charged with murder. And she couldn't imagine how upset Stacey must be. She was nineteen years old now, and she sounded even more scared than she did three years ago. She was still a young girl with no home. But now, she was facing murder charges.

"They just told me I only have about a minute left on my phone call. Do you think you could meet me here at Central Lockup tomorrow? I can explain things better then."

"Absolutely. I'll be there tomorrow, after my afternoon class. You can tell me everything then. We'll get to the bottom of this." Emma picked up her keys and briefcase and flew out of the door, praying as she ran that traffic had died down and that her usual drive to the law school was at least five minutes quicker.

Chapter Four

Emma drove out to Central Lockup the next day and parked in the gravel-filled parking lot, her tires crunching as she pulled in. She showed the deputy her Bar card and was allowed through the screening device. Another deputy examined her purse, and a third led her to the interview room, where inmates were permitted to speak to their attorneys. The room was large, open, and surrounded by bars so that Emma could see down the hallway. She sat down in one of the folding chairs next to a long metal table to wait.

She dreaded this. Not because she didn't want to help. But she hated that Stacey was in circumstances that were even worse than those she'd been in before. When Emma first met Stacey, she was a bright and very pretty girl with blonde hair, sparkling green-blue eyes, and a cheerful smile. She'd shown so much promise, even though she was a runaway.

An unmistakable shuffling-clanking sound, the sort of sound a person makes when they walk with chains, preceded Stacey. She stumbled into the interview room in front of a female guard. Stacey's blonde hair was shorter than Emma remembered. Because Stacey walked with her head bowed, Emma couldn't make out her features or her mood - Emma hoped she was holding up. Jail was never easy, a fact reinforced by Stacey's hands which were shackled in front of her body, and her orange jumpsuit, which seemed ten times too big on her tall, thin frame.

The guard and Stacey entered the barred room and stopped. Stacey held out her wrists so the guard could unlock her chains. The guard nodded and walked toward the entrance, and stood to the side of the doorway.

11

Emma stood to give Stacey a hug, and Stacey clung to her for a few seconds, her hands gripping Emma's shoulders. Emma stepped back to get a good look at her as Stacey blotted the tears that ran down her face with a soggy tissue.

Her face was gaunt. Traces of gray shadows underscored her eyes which were red from crying. Her cheekbones were more pronounced, and she wasn't as quick to smile.

"You haven't changed that much." Emma smiled. "Maybe thinner?"

Stacey sniffed.

Emma sat down and placed a retainer agreement and a pen on the table. "I've brought this retainer for you to look over. I've thought about your situation. I'd be happy to represent you if you'd like me to, but on a *pro bono* basis instead of running it through the homeless clinic."

Stacey sat down and slid the document closer so she could read it. "What does *pro bono* mean?"

"It just means I'll represent you without charge. The semester has already begun at the law school, and the students have a full caseload. So, I'll handle your case by myself, privately, but I won't charge anything. All I ask is that you tell me everything. And that you cooperate as much as you can so we can develop the best defenses possible. What do you think?"

Stacey nodded, tears still rolling down her face. " Yes. That would be wonderful." She looked over the retainer and signed her name at the bottom of the page.

Emma scrambled in her purse for a tissue and found one with lipstick smudges.

"Sorry. This is all I have."

Stacey held her hand out.

"Now that we have the formalities taken care of let me say that I'm so sorry this has happened. I'll do my very best to represent you, and I'll need you to answer all of my questions to the very best of your ability. I'll need you to tell me why you think you're here. I can tell you realize that these are very serious charges. You said you didn't kill Mr. Crosby, the Pujari." Emma hesitated. "Did I get that right? And I believe you. But we will need to put the events of the evening of Mr. Crosby's death together with as much detail as you can recall." Emma pulled her notebook out of her purse.

"Yes. Pujari. And you're right. I didn't kill him." She sniffed.

"Why do you think you were arrested, then?"

"The police found something in my room that made them think I did it. So they arrested me."

"What did they find?" Emma clicked her pen and leaned in. This was going to be a long afternoon. Stacey seemed so traumatized by her arrest that she had difficulty talking about what happened.

"A syringe, wrapped in my t-shirt. They found it in the bottom of my armoire."

"Just a plain syringe? That couldn't be enough to arrest anyone."

"They found some drugs in my room too. And I've never taken drugs. Well, once I did. I'll tell you about that. But these weren't my drugs. They found vials of stuff and a bag of white powder in my nightstand, stuffed in the back of the drawer, behind a loose board.

"At first, the police thought James' death was an accident, that he'd overdosed and had fallen over the balcony. But now it looks like they think he was murdered. So, they came back a couple of days later. They did a search in my room then and found that stuff. After they brought me in, they held me overnight, and then I was arrested." Stacey pushed her hair out of her eyes with a shaky hand.

Emma jotted down notes as Stacey spoke. "It's hindsight now, but you should never have been questioned without an attorney. Did they ask you if you wanted one?"

Stacey nodded. "They did. I told them it was okay. I didn't think it was fair for them to hold me at all, but they said they could until some testing was done."

"That's right. They could have held you up to seventy-two hours. But I wish I'd known that, and I would have been there." Emma flipped a page in her notepad.

"Me too, now. But it didn't take that long. They ran the tests. I didn't think they'd find anything. That's really why I didn't think about calling.

But they said they found enough evidence to arrest me, so they did."

"Did they say what they had?"

"One of the officers said a witness saw me walking up the stairs with a syringe in my hands the day James was killed. And that's not true. So someone just made that up. The police officers told me the witness even wrote out an affidavit." Stacey pounded her clenched fist on her thighs. "That's why they searched my room. So, when they found the syringe, they suspected me right away." Stacey stood and began pacing. "They asked a bunch of questions, too. Like if I took intravenous drugs, and I don't. Then some questions about my dad. I guess someone told them about the heart attack he had when he was looking for me." Stacey stopped next to Emma and paused. "They wanted to know if my dad's death made me feel angry. They talked to me about James and the Japaprajnas, too." Stacey sat down. "I've probably already said too much."

"You've had so much to deal with at such a young age." Emma reached out and squeezed Stacey's hand. She looked through her notes. "Why do you think the police were asking whether you were angry about your father's death?"

Stacey shook her head. "I'm not sure."

"Did the police ask you if you blamed James for your father's death?"

"They just asked me if I was angry. That's all."

"And what did you say?"

"I said I was upset. Who wouldn't be? But that's all I said."

Emma nodded. "Do you know who told the police they saw you walking up the stairs with the syringe?"

"No, they just said, 'a witness.'" Stacey shifted to the edge of her chair.

"Okay. After your arraignment, I'll file a Motion for a Bill of Particulars to see if I can get any more details. If they didn't have probable cause at the time of the arrest, I'll move to dismiss. Has the judge set bail yet? Do you have an arraignment date?"

"I don't think so. But I don't really understand what's going on, and I'm scared. I don't know what to do." Stacey twisted her hands together.

"Both the bail hearing and the arraignment should be coming up pretty soon. I can call the court and get more information on it. The bail hearing could be first. The arraignment is when you'll plead whether you're guilty or not. You'll want to plead 'not guilty. We could get subpoenaed for the hearing. I'm not sure how this judge handles arraignments, but I'll find out. Have you called your mother and asked her to help you make bail yet?"

Stacey shook her head. She clamped her lips tight.

"She helped you before. Don't you want her help again?" Emma said gently. She waited a few minutes for Stacey to respond.

Three years ago, when Stacey was arrested with a group of other homeless kids, Emma was unable to talk most of them into calling their parents for bail that night. They refused, some out of stubbornness, clinging to their anger like a badge of honor, and some because their relationship with their parents was too damaged to repair. But Stacey, who seemed pretty logical at the time, realized she had no business being in jail, especially after being locked up for hours with kids who were coming down from heroin or other drugs. She opted to call her mother, who wired bail money from her bank in New Mexico, and Stacey was able to get out of jail the next day. But that was then.

Emma continued. "We'll need a plan first. Let's just say the judge agreed to set bail in your case, your mom agreed to help out, and she posted bond like she did for you three years ago. Where would you live? You wouldn't be allowed to leave the jurisdiction, so you couldn't go back to New Mexico. You can't go back to your old room at the Japaprajna temple. So, we're going to have to think of alternative places for you to stay. Would you consider accepting help from your mom for a hotel room or to sublease an apartment?"

"I'm not going to ask my mom to help me out with a place to stay or bail or anything else," Stacey frowned.

"Okay." Emma paused. "Then you'll have to stay here, and if that's what you want to do, we can make that work." Emma waved her hand toward the barred walls.

"The problem is, I don't know how my mom will react to me after all this time." Stacey suddenly sounded very young.

15

"You won't know until you call." Emma rubbed her forehead, praying that her boys would never hesitate to call her if they were in trouble. "But tell me more about you and your mom. Why aren't you speaking?"

"My mom knows I'm in New Orleans. She knows I live and work at the temple, but she's never made any effort to reach out to me."

"So, you think your mom doesn't want to talk to you?"

She nodded. "I think she blames my dad's death on me." Stacey looked down at her folded hands.

"I really doubt that, Stacey. You said he had a heart attack. That is usually caused by a physical condition. A heart condition. Is there something else you haven't told me?" Emma watched Stacey for a moment. Stacey's mother had been eager to help Stacey three years ago. But afterwards, Mrs. Roberts didn't come to New Orleans to pick up her sixteen-year-old daughter even though Stacey had been living on the streets for the better part of a year. Something didn't add up.

Stacey hung her head.

"We can discuss this again, but we don't have that much time, and we need to make plans. I'll do whatever you prefer. I don't want you to be uncomfortable about your decision. If you don't want to call your mom, that's fine, but think about it."

"Three years ago, when she bailed me out of jail, she told me she was disappointed in me and that she never wanted to see me in a situation like that again. I promised myself that the next time we talked it would be because I had gotten myself to a place where she could be proud of me, and where I was proud of myself too. But I've messed that up now. I'll never be okay in her eyes."

"Anyone can mess up. We all do, every day. And in this case, if you haven't killed anyone, and you said you didn't, you just need help. The circumstances are bad, but you and I can work together to put together a proper defense for you. I'm hopeful we can figure out what's really going on, too."

Stacey nodded.

"You've been arrested for the murder of James Crosby, and I know you're upset. I don't want to make that worse, but I'd like to explain what the

16

charges could mean. Is that something you'd like to hear now, or would you rather wait?

Stacey hesitated. "It's okay. You can tell me."

"If the DA has enough evidence, and it seems like he might, he'll most likely charge you with second-degree murder. And since a large quantity of drugs was also found in your room, I think you'll also be charged with possession of that drug with the intent to distribute. I don't believe he'll charge you with first-degree murder, which carries a much harsher penalty. But, we'll still have a lot to do to prove your innocence, and we should meet regularly to work on your case."

Stacey nodded, her face paler than when she'd first entered the room.

"First-degree murder is when you intend to kill a person while you're also engaged in another crime, like aggravated kidnapping, arson, or robbery. And if you kill someone while you're engaged in the sale or purchase of a drug like cocaine or ketamine, you can also be charged with first-degree murder. Even though drugs were found in your room, there's no evidence that you and James were involved in the sale or purchase of drugs at the time he was killed. So, you shouldn't have to worry about a first-degree murder charge."

Stacey nodded. "I guess that's good."

"It is, believe me."

"Second-degree murder in Louisiana is the intentional killing of a person. To prove intent in your case, the DA will have to look at a couple of things. One thing is the amount of ketamine in James' body. Was there enough ketamine in the syringe or in his body to have killed him? We don't know that yet. And they'll also have to see whether James fell over the balcony or if he was pushed. And, like I said, you'll probably be charged with possession with intent to distribute, and that carries a separate sentencing protocol.

"Second-degree murder carries lighter sentencing than first-degree murder." Emma paused.

Stacey's eyes grew larger at the mention of sentencing.

"Second-degree murder usually carries a sentence of about fifteen years. Unlike first-degree, the death penalty is never given in a second-degree conviction. But if you're convicted of both crimes, second degree murder and possession with the intent to distribute, the judge could run the prison terms consecutively instead of concurrently. That means you might have to serve fifteen years for the murder conviction and then serve additional time for the drug charge. Ketamine is a schedule III drug, and in Louisiana, you can get up to ten years in prison for its distribution. You may also have to pay a fine of up to $15,000."

Stacey's eyes widened. "That's twenty-five years in total! I could be forty-four years old before I get out of prison! And I didn't even do any of this!"

"We don't know what your charges will be yet. And I quoted the maximum sentences. I don't believe that's what the judge will give you. You've never been involved in a violent crime, and you haven't been involved in drug activity before. So if you are convicted of either crime in this case, I'm sure your sentence would be something below the maximum. And the judge would probably allow the terms for the two crimes to run concurrently, which means that they'd run at the same time. He could throw the entire case out, but I don't think that's going to happen here either unless we find something during our investigation to prove your innocence."

"I'm not sure I want to know all of this."

"Just know that if the DA chooses to charge you, we can fight it." Emma reached out and touched Stacey's hand, which was trembling. "But it's important for us to work together."

Stacey nodded and looked down at her hands, and clasped them in her lap. "Okay."

"Just in case you decide to speak to your mom, you should know that the bond fee could be pretty high. The average bail around here for second-degree murder is $250,000, but we don't know what the judge will do yet, of course. The bond fee is ten to twelve percent of bail. And the money your mom would pay the bondsman would be something she'd never see again."

Stacey nodded.

"Let me know your decision about whether you're going to ask your mom to pay the bail bond fee. The hearing should be coming up soon."

"Okay."

"Did you ever see any evidence of drug use at the temple before James' death?" Emma scooted her chair closer.

"I was pretty sure James took drugs and pushed whatever he took on other people too. One time he wanted me to snort a powder that I thought was probably cocaine. That's the drug experience I was telling you about. It's my only one."

"So you did take the drug."

"Yes. But I didn't like it. It made me feel woozy, and my hands and feet even got a little numb. I never did it again. But other girls did. And some of the followers did, too."

"Do you know for sure that it was cocaine?"

Stacey shook her head. "No. I thought it was at the time because it was a white powder. But I don't know for sure." She paused. "And once, when it was my turn to clean the house, I actually picked up a syringe. It was in James' office, on the floor next to his desk."

Emma stopped writing. "What? You've actually seen syringes at the temple?" Emma was stunned. Here was a syringe where not only Stacey's fingerprints could be found, she would bet traces of James' DNA were there too.

Stacey nodded. "Yes. But if I did, other girls probably did too."

"Where did you put the syringe?" Emma jotted down notes as Stacey spoke.

"In a garbage bag."

"How many times did you see syringes at the temple?"

"I think there was only that one time."

"What happened to the garbage bag?" Emma continued to write as quickly as Stacey spoke.

"I put it into a larger bag that eventually went outside in the trash."

"Do you know who took it out?"

Stacey shook her head. "I wish I did."

"How long ago did this happen?"

"I don't know. Maybe a couple of weeks ago."

Emma flipped over another page in her notepad. "Okay, let's talk about the day James was killed. Were you there at the temple that day?"

"It was a Monday. The spa was closed. It's the day I usually do my laundry and clean my room and stuff."

"Walk me through everything you remember about that day."

Stacey shoved her hair away from her face. "I put my clothes in the wash and headed out for a walk down Esplanade to City Park. That was probably around one o'clock. It's a little more than an hour to the park, but I like to stop along the way for a coffee or something to eat. I like to look at the homes and gardens along the street. It's one of my favorite things to do. I walked back around forth, and stopped by the temple to throw my clothes in the dryer. Then I walked over to the coffee house across the street and sat down at one of the outside tables. I didn't go inside to order because I'd had enough caffeine for the day. I do that at the end of the day on Mondays when the weather permits. Grab a newspaper, read under the trees, and wait for my laundry to finish. I stayed there until I noticed police cars, which was when I walked back over."

"Did anyone stop you or speak to you then?"

"Not on Monday."

"Did you see anyone at the temple when you came in at four o'clock?"

"No."

"Do you know if anyone was there?"

She shook her head. "I don't know."

"Is laundry done in the kitchen, or is there a separate room for laundry?"

"It's a separate room, but it's attached to the kitchen. You know, you can see into the kitchen through the laundry door. There's a big glass in the door."

"Where did James' body fall?"

"It landed on the fence in the courtyard."

"Could you see the courtyard from the laundry room?"

"You can see the courtyard from the kitchen window. And I could see the kitchen window from the laundry room."

"Did you notice anything unusual in the courtyard at four o'clock?"

"Like James' body? No, I didn't. But I don't recall looking into the courtyard either."

"Can anyone from the coffee shop verify that you were there until about five o'clock or so?"

"I don't think so. I was the only one sitting outside at that time."

"Do you remember anything else that happened that day?"

"I think the cops spoke to Cecelia and Mira that day."

"Who are they?"

"Cecelia is James' wife. Mira is the temple bookkeeper. She also manages the French Quarter business. And," Stacey paused. "Mira has a four-year-old boy. I'm pretty sure James is the boy's father."

"Do they also live at the temple?" Emma jotted down notes. She couldn't help but wonder why Stacey had gotten herself mixed up with these people.

"Cecelia and James live on the second floor, and so do Mira and her son. It was one big happy family."

"And you were on the third?"

"Me and the other workers."

"It was better than the street," Emma said.

"Yes." Stacey nodded and clasped and unclasped her hands.

"How many workers were at the temple?"

"There were six massage therapists who lived and worked there. Different ones would come and go."

"Did your circumstances ever change there? Did your salary ever increase or did your living circumstances change in any way?"

"No. It never changed."

"Do you know if that applied to all workers? Did anyone get pay raises over the years?"

"I wouldn't know, but I doubt it. No one really got much of a salary there. We got room and board."

"I understand. I'd like for you to be thinking about whether you know of any people who might have had a vendetta against James, or who have had problems with him in the past. But for now, decide what you want to do about getting in touch with your mom. Anyway you decide to go will be good with me. I'll go get the preliminary reports today if they're available.

21

I'll also get in touch with Cecelia Crosby and Mira at the Japaprajna temple. What's Mira's last name?

"Godfrey."

"And I'll also need to speak to the other massage therapists, your co-workers. Please write down their names for me." Emma slid her notebook over and handed Stacey her pen. "I'll see you soon."

* * *

Emma ran by the Eighth District Police Station later that afternoon. She showed them her recently filed Motion to Enroll as Counsel of Record, and asked for a copy of the homicide report and any other preliminary forensic reports in the Crosby case. The clerk gave her what was available, which was bare bones. The preliminary reports included a statement of the incident and list of evidence found in Stacey's room: syringe wrapped in t-shirt; four hundred grams of ketamine; and a preliminary autopsy report which indicated that the death was due to "impalement by rod from iron fence," and ketamine overdose. Witness statements "to be attached."

Emma drove home to her apartment in the garden district, her mind swirling with probabilities and intuitions, a jumbled mass of possibilities that would lead nowhere. What she needed were facts, and she had few. Except that Stacey was at the temple right before James Crosby was killed. But no one would be able to verify that she was at the coffee house later on that same afternoon, which was the actual timeframe of the murder.

The evidence Emma hadn't seen, the affidavits and witness statements, had to be damn compelling. Somehow Emma knew Stacey's fingerprints would be on that syringe. Even if the syringe was the one from James' office, the one that Stacey picked up and put in the garbage, with everything else the police had against her, would anyone ever believe that Stacey was innocent?

Chapter Five

Emma arrived at the temple the next day while she had a break between her morning and afternoon classes. She climbed the steps to the grand home, stopping for a moment outside to take in the stunning magenta color of the building. Closer inspection revealed that under the bold color was years of neglect. Strips of peeling paint and decay had been covered over with a thick application of the vivid hue.

She rang the doorbell and was greeted by a young woman in a jumpsuit that matched the color of the building. The door opened into a wide center hallway. Sconces flickered along the walls, and a chandelier similar to one Emma had seen hanging in a Turkish import store hung from the ceiling. The hallway had entrances into two parlors, one on each side.

She was led to the left side parlor of the former nineteenth-century mansion. A few chairs lined the back of the room. The remainder of the space was empty with the exception of a row of red and magenta-colored brocade cushions which had been placed along the floor and candles and incense burning on the altar. Emma sat down on one of the chairs to wait and immediately closed her eyes. Something about the quiet, cushion-filled, patchouli-laden room made her sleepy.

She felt a touch on her shoulder. She opened her eyes.

"Emma? Are you ready? I'm Raphael Evans."

Emma started. "Of course." She felt herself blush as they walked toward the door. "But I was hoping to speak to Cecelia today. We'd set up an appointment."

"Cecelia couldn't make it." He guided Emma with his hand toward the door. "We're moving upstairs. She wanted someone to talk to you today, and I volunteered since I know a lot about the history of the Japaprajnas. More than Cecelia, even." He smiled.

Raphael was a tall African American man. There were touches of gray in his hair. He was well-dressed. Jeans, white shirt. Each spotless. His movements were effortless, confident.

They moved down the hall, past a pair of velvet drapes also dyed to match the dominant color of the temple. The hallway opened to the magnificent curved staircase, the type of stairway you'd expect Bette Davis to descend in the movie *Jezebel* if she were expecting a visit from Henry Fonda.

The scent of patchouli was stronger there. A chandelier that appeared to be as old as the house hung down the center of the stairwell. It provided little illumination and cast odd shadows along the hallway and stairs.

"What's with all of the magenta? The place is saturated with it. It's one thing to have magenta furnishings, but you have to admit it's an unusual color for the outside of a Greek revival home on Esplanade."

"James's dad, J.R., chose the color when he first started the group way back in the 1930s. He said it represented 'universal love.' So James used it too."

"I see."

"J. R. was the real deal. He really believed in universal love. But James and Cecelia are another story. So, don't be fooled by the paint job or anything else here. They built that fancy altar in the front parlor and decorated it with candles and things, but I've always felt, as far as James and Cecelia were concerned, that they're just going through the motions. It's all for show." He turned and looked at Emma. "But let's leave that between you and me." He smiled. "Just so you know, I don't think Stacy killed James. And I'd like to help you, but," he paused, "I don't know how. I wish I did."

"Why are you telling me this?"

"I'm leaving this place pretty soon. That's why I wanted to see you today. I wanted to tell you a few things before I get on out of here."

"Where are you going?"

"Down the street. But I'll still be working as the driver here for the massage girls."

Emma looked at him curiously.

"I'll explain everything in a minute." He waved his hand at Emma. "I wanted you to know that even though James and Cecelia hosted those meditations and chants, that day spa in the back was probably the most important thing to them." He paused. "Just my two cents." He pointed down the hall. "And more clients came for those $75 stone massages than anything else, too. Nothing in the city is cheaper."

As they climbed the stairs to the second floor, Emma imagined being in another place and time. She could almost hear the crinoline skirts brushing against her legs.

"Amazing staircase, isn't it? It gets me every time." Raphael said. "They were thinking of installing an elevator in one of the unused closets, but Cecelia decided not to. I'm glad they didn't."

As she climbed, Emma turned around and scanned the bottom of the stairs, thinking about the day of the murder and the witness who said they saw Stacey walking up the steps with a syringe. To have observed Stacey that day, the witness would have had to have been standing in close proximity to the staircase, probably somewhere in the hallway.

When they reached the top, they turned to their left, and Raphael opened the first door.

"This is James' old office. He shared it with Mira Godfrey and, as you can see, their son." He nodded to the other half of the room which contained enough children's toys to fill a kindergarten classroom. "Thought you'd like to see the window he fell out of that day." Raphael looked at Emma and raised his eyebrows. "Pretty awful, huh?"

"Yes. Gruesome. I guess the police are finished with their inspection?"

"Days ago."

Emma glanced around the dimly lit space. The bookshelves lining the office were crammed with notebooks and ledgers. Emma's eyes moved down the shelf stuffed with unused product samples, bongs, and hookahs. The floor was bare, the furnishings mid-century modern spare. She walked to the window which opened from the floor. It was nearly as tall as the twelve foot ceilings. She stepped on to the balcony and looked out over the courtyard. "He fell from this window?"

"Some say he was pushed."

Emma nodded, taking notes. "I haven't seen the final reports yet."

"I was here that afternoon. He landed on top of the iron fence that's next to the garconniere. Talk about gruesome."

"I see. Was he…" Emma hesitated.

"Yes." Raphael nodded. "He was impaled." He grimaced. "There are no words."

Emma inhaled deeply and continued to gaze out the window, looking at the broken roof tiles of the small structure below. "Part of his body landed on the garden house?"

"It's called a garconniere. Bachelor's quarters. That's where the elder sons would take their ladies or have their drinking parties in the old days. And, yeah. It looks like at least part of James' body hit the roof. He was pretty much laid out over the fence when I saw him." He paused. "Like I said, it gutted him." He wiped his forehead.

"Looks like there was no way to have avoided that fence if you fell from the balcony." Emma took out a small camera from her purse and snapped several photographs from a variety of angles.

"Don't think so."

Emma moved away from the window. "I thought the spa was closed, and the temple was empty that afternoon." She took several steps away from the window and took several photographs of the window frame.

"A couple of people were here. Sort of in and out." He moved toward the door. "Maybe we should move to Cecelia's office. I'm sure you'll find it more pleasant there."

Raphael led Emma down the hall to a smaller space which also looked out over the courtyard. Painted a vivid white, with white sheer drapes, the room was bright and airy. Raphael directed her to one of the upholstered chairs in front of the lean black desk and sat down next to her.

"Before you continue your review of the temple's history, I've got a few questions for you. You are certainly not required to answer anything I ask, so if a question makes you feel uncomfortable, we'll just skip it. I'm trying to fill in some blanks about the afternoon of October 14."

He nodded. "Shoot."

"Do you remember where you were the afternoon James Crosby was killed?"

"I was up there in my room on the third floor. I'd say until early afternoon, probably around one-thirty. Then I went down to the Quarter. I came back a couple of hours later, sometime before five, because I needed to drop off one of the girls at the ETC shop to work. I fell asleep up there sometime after I came back. I like cat naps."

"What's the ETC shop?" Emma readied her pen.

"It's James' smoke shop down on Bourbon Street."

"The head shop?"

"Yeah. They sell that stuff you saw on the bookshelves in James's office. The bongs and other smoking things."

"Oh. Okay. Stacey told me about that place. Did you ever work there?"

"No. The massage girls were the only ones who worked back there."

"Do you know what they did at the shop?"

"No. I just dropped them off. And they never discussed what they did there. Not even between themselves. It was strictly forbidden."

"Can you tell me what you mean by *strictly forbidden*?" Something was going on at that place.

"All I know is that it wasn't supposed to be discussed, and as far as I know, it wasn't."

"Weren't you curious about what was going on there?"

"I've learned at this age to mind my own business, with a few exceptions. I stuck my neck out today for Stacey." He smiled. "Wanted you to know a few things, anyway."

Emma nodded. "And I appreciate that. Do you know if any of the people giving massages at the temple actually have a license?"

Raphael shook his head. "Nah. No one has a license there. I never did when I gave massages."

"How are they getting away with that?"

He shrugged. "I wouldn't know. Could it be part of their religious practice?"

Emma looked down at her notes and pointed to her last question. "Hmm. The religion of massage therapy might be taking things a little far. Doesn't that strike you as silly?"

"I just don't know the answer to that question. I don't know how they're getting away without having licenses." He shook his head.

"Okay, so you made two trips to the Quarter that day?"

"That's right. But the second trip was delayed."

"What happened? Why was it delayed?"

"Because James was killed." He rubbed his head. "I was going to take Angelina Diaz to the shop at five, but that's when everything happened. So we left a little later, after the police were gone."

"Do you know if you were at the temple when James was killed?"

He shook his head. "I don't know if I was or not because I don't know what time that happened. I didn't see or hear anything until Cecelia screamed. I know that much."

"If you'd been in your bedroom when James fell, wouldn't you have heard the sound of his body breaking the roof tiles of the garconniere?"

He shook his head. "I don't know. Maybe. If I was awake. But, like I said, I was taking a nap."

"Do you remember what happened after Cecelia's scream?"

"I ran down the stairs to see what was going on."

"About what time was this?"

"This was after Cecelia came back from shopping and after I'd come back from the Quarter the first time, so I'm guessing it was around five." Raphael swung his foot as he answered.

"And the scream woke you up?"

"Yeah. It scared the hell out of me."

Emma flipped through her notes again and checked off several questions she'd asked.

"Did you see Stacey any time before or after Cecelia's scream?"

He shook his head. "I don't recall seeing her until later, after the police arrived."

"Have the police spoken to you yet about James' death or what happened that day?"

"Yeah, they talked to me. I told them what I told you."

"Did you see them talking to anyone else on the day he was killed, or any other day?" Raphael nodded. "I know they spoke to Cecelia and Mira. I saw them. I'm guessing they talked to Stacey, but I didn't see that."

"Didn't they speak to Angelina?"

"Yeah, that's right. Angelina said they did. She was there that day, but I didn't see her until later. After the police left, she walked up, ready to go. She said she'd been there all along."

"The way I understand it, the girls here at the temple work for room and board. Are you paid a salary instead?"

"No, I work for room, board, and tips from some of the lady clients. And I make pretty good tips. I can't complain. Plus, I have a second job. That's the job I'm leaving for."

"What's that second job?"

"Well." Raphael paused, then smiled. "You may as well know." He leaned his head back and squinted at Emma. "I'm a bouncer at one of the clubs down in the Quarter."

"A bouncer?"

"Yeah. I'm a pretty big guy." He shrugged. "I make more money there than I could ever make here."

"Then why do you bother working here?"

"For the free room and board! But now that's changed. I enjoyed it while that lasted. You couldn't beat it, and I make a habit of not turning down things that are free, if it's something I need." He smiled. "But it's time to go."

"I guess that makes sense." Emma glanced at Raphael and smiled. She didn't know what he was really up to or if she could trust anything he was saying. "You were going to give me some more information on why you're leaving."

"It's just that I don't feel right being here after James's death. It feels wrong, kind of creepy. I can't get that image of him draped across that fence out of my mind. But I still want to drive the massage girls back and forth between the temple and the shop for work. That helps them, and I can keep in contact with them that way, too."

"You said you made tips. What about the girls? Did they make tips too?"

"I had a special arrangement with Cecelia. She let me keep my tips. But she takes all the girls' gratuities. Says it belongs to the temple, not them."

"Do you know why you're treated differently?"

Raphael looked down at his shoes. "Well, that's some of the problem here. Those girls aren't treated very fair. It's like Cecelia doesn't want them to have any cash so she can keep a tight leash on them, you know? I could have left at any time, and I finally walked away, except for that small job driving the girls around. James and Cecelia never had their thumb on me. But they do on those girls."

"I see. You also were going to tell me more about the history of the Japaprajnas." Emma smiled. She was confused about the group and hoped he could add some insight.

He nodded. "That's right. I'm the only one from Idaho who traveled to New Orleans with James and Cecelia. And I'd been with J.R. since I was a kid. Like I said, he was a good man who believed in what he did." Raphael crossed his leg. Emma stared at Raphael's boot. Bruno Magli. Five hundred dollars, at least. Raphael must be doing pretty well.

"But James eventually developed his own following, right?"

"Not until he came to New Orleans. His dad, J.R., made it big in Idaho. He had a lot of followers. He based his teachings in part on Hindu practices and yoga and threw in some meditation and European spa and hydrotherapy sessions, too. He died unexpectedly in the sauna in 1978 of a stroke. He was only sixty-seven." He shook his head. "Sure hated that."

"What is this Japaprajna thing?"

"It was based on the Hindu belief of mindfulness through meditation. J.R. said *japa* meant repetitive chanting. And they always did that chanting thing at the temple as a part of their meditation. And he said the word *prajna* is a Hindi word meaning wisdom."

"And he just put those two words together to make up the name of the group?"

"I guess. He didn't base the name on an actual religion, as far as I know. J.R. didn't practice any formal religion. Anyway, after his dad died, James took over the financial responsibilities of the temple. Not long after that, he hired Cecelia to teach yoga and give massages. Cecelia has some nursing training, so she was good at massage. They were married the following year in a ceremony at the temple. I was there. Her hair was all wrapped up in flowers. She was taller than James, blonde, very pretty."

"Is the Japaprajna group a cult?"

"I don't know if you could call it that. It wasn't when J.R. ran it. I'm not sure I know what a cult even is."

Emma squinted at Raphael. "Okay." She paused, trying to collect her thoughts. She'd learned a lot that day, but had any of it helped Stacey? "How long did James and Cecelia run the group in Idaho?"

"About ten years. They'd just about run it in the ground by then. So, in 1988, they sold the temple in Idaho and the hydrotherapy equipment and headed south. James said he'd always been attracted to the nightlife of New Orleans." He paused and smiled.

"The nightlife? That's just weird."

"Yeah. He was crazy." He shook his head. "But I tagged along for a couple of reasons." He stretched out his legs. "I mean, Idaho and me? Girl! I don't hike, and I don't plow. And I don't even like potatoes." He threw his head back and laughed. "Really. I never belonged there. I just happened to have been born in Idaho, and I couldn't wait to leave." He paused. "And at the time, I didn't have a job or a prospect of one either." He pressed his lips together.

"That's when James opened this temple here in New Orleans?"

He nodded. "Yeah. He and Cecelia found the building right after they got here. That was eight years ago. They'd walked down Esplanade, looking for a coffee house, and there it was. This big old three-story Greek revival behemoth of a pre-Civil War-era home. It was in bad need of a paint job and just about everything else, but James thought it was perfect. They called the owner that same day.

"Cecelia was real worried when they bought it. And even I knew it would

31

cost more to repair the place than it would cost to tear it down and build it over again."

"Did they redo it?"

"Some of it, little by little. A little plumbing here. Some painting there. It's been a slow process."

"And Cecelia started out in charge of the massages?"

"Yeah. She must have had ten or so women here at one time or another. Maybe more. Now they keep around six full-time. But there's a lot of coming and going. They all live at the temple. Cecelia personally trained most of them. She has everyone play the same music, wear identical uniforms, use the same rosemary-lavender scented oil, and everyone has to finish the massage in forty-five minutes. She's real strict."

"Do you know whether James had a drug problem?"

"I don't really want to talk about that here. Maybe somewhere else. Some other time. But I don't mind saying that James wouldn't run away from what he thought might be a good time. He was that sort of guy. I just don't want to say more than that."

Emma made a star by the comment in her notepad. *Raphael knew something about James and his drug habit, but he was afraid to discuss it at the temple.* He couldn't be afraid about losing his job. He was already leaving. Was he afraid for his life? Or was he the killer, and Emma was getting too close to the situation for him? That might be it. And that would explain why Raphael was changing jobs.

"What about Stacey? Did you ever see her taking drugs, or was she known to be involved in drugs in any way?"

"Nah, not Stacey. That's why I was so surprised when she was arrested. Something isn't right."

"What about Stacey's relationship with James? Did you ever notice any tension between those two?"

"Tension? Maybe. I guess I did notice some. Like, this past year, I guess. Not at first. At first, when she first started here, everything was good between them. Then things changed. About a year ago, Stacey stopped the work she did in the Quarter recruiting girls for the spa. Once that stopped,

32

I could sense a coldness between them."

"Wait. Stacey did what?"

"She started out as a massage therapist. But James got her to go out to the Quarter about three or four times a week to recruit other girls to work at the temple. Mostly for the spa."

"I didn't know that. Do you know why she stopped?"

Raphael shook his head. "No. I wouldn't know why. Stacey and I used to talk some when I drove her to the Quarter, but once she stopped recruiting, that stopped too. I never really knew what happened."

"That seems like a lot of recruiting."

"She only went down there when there was an opening, you know, when one of the massage therapists left. But there was a lot of turn over."

"I see." Emma scribbled a few notes in her notepad. "Did you ever see anyone else using drugs here at the temple?"

"I really can't say. I'm not sure." He crossed his arms. "I'm not comfortable talking about this."

"I understand, Raphael. I don't mean to put you in an awkward position. But at the same time, my client says she's innocent and has been charged with a crime that carries very harsh penalties. Maybe we can talk again somewhere you feel more comfortable."

Raphael nodded.

"Is there anything else you can tell me about the French Quarter business, ETC?"

"I've pretty much told you all I know, except that Mira manages the business. She and James had the only keys to their office, too. So, no one ever knew what was going on up there, or knew anything about the financial goings on of ETC except Mira and James, and they planned on keeping it that way. I mean, everyone knew what they were selling down at the store, but no one knew how much money they were bringing in or anything about that." Raphael paused. "The one thing I remember him saying over and over was, 'the best thing about this place is that it's all tax free.'"

"Is that because the Japaprajna temple was classified as a church?"

"I guess so. But I wouldn't have that sort of information." Raphael placed his fingers in a steeple position and smiled.

"Why were Mira and James the only two that knew anything about the finances of the French Quarter business?"

Raphael turned toward Emma and slowly smiled. "Now you've asked the sixty-four million dollar question."

Chapter Six

Emma drove home from her meeting with Raphael, hashing the events of the day over in her head. She knew when something wasn't right, and today she'd been played. Why wasn't Cecelia available to discuss her husband's murder as they'd planned? Maybe Cecelia didn't want to see Emma because she was upset and had asked Raphael to run interference for her. But Emma couldn't shake the feeling that it was something more.

What was it Michael Corleone told his wife in *The Godfather* when he tried to keep her from discovering the family's corruption? "Don't ask me my business." Someone didn't want Emma to know everything, at least whatever information Cecelia would bring to the table. But it was essential to interview her, and as soon as possible.

Emma pulled up to her building, a three story, narrow turn-of-the-century structure with a tiny sandwich shop on the first floor, and two residential floors above. The shop, known mostly for turning out po'boys and beer during Mardi Gras, had few customers during any other time. The owners made enough revenue from that one holiday to support themselves for the entire year. They had recently repainted the outside of the building a cheerful yellow, trimmed it in a light teal blue, and had painted the doors a terra cotta-peachy color. So many coatings of paint had been applied to the shop and the attached apartment over the past hundred and fifty years that the trim and woodwork seemed nearly an inch thicker than they should have been. It gave the place a fuller, happy look.

Emma ran up the stairs to her apartment, where the paws of the family's three-year-old German Shorthaired Pointers, Maddie and Lulu, clicked a welcoming dance on the hardwood floors. She needed to start dinner and, as usual, hadn't given it one second's thought until now. The boys' bus was due any minute. Tonight was a stay-at-home night, which meant no extra-curricular activities. Emma put up her purse, grabbed an apron, then an onion, and started chopping.

At age fourteen, Billy and Bobby were on the cusp of adulthood, but they were still kids. They liked video games, but Emma had outlawed them on school nights. They liked sports, which was great, but it interfered with homework. And they had recently begun hanging around girls. Emma occasionally dropped them off at a mall so they could do just that, but never on a weeknight. She was beginning to feel like a prison warden. But she was glad the twins had joined the school's soccer team. She attended every game, yelling at everything that looked like a goal. She loved watching everyone on the team running around the field on crisp fall nights. And she enjoyed her boys.

Emma's eyes started watering from the onions. Blinking, she grabbed a paper towel and blotted her eyes. She scraped onions into the olive oil that was heating on the stove. As they started to sauté, she decided to add tomatoes, some spices, chicken, and a little white wine. Didn't that make chicken cacciatore?

She heard the boys tromping upstairs, the front door opening, then the loud thud as their backpacks slid to the floor right by the spiral staircase which led to their room. The pungent aroma of onions and spices sauteing on the stove led them to the kitchen, where Emma stood stirring a pot.

Now taller than his mom, Bobby peered over her shoulder. "What's for dinner?" He nodded toward the contents of the pot.

"I'm calling it chicken cacciatore. Hopefully, that's what it will be. But it will take a while, so it would be a good idea to go ahead and start your homework before dinner." Emma reached back and touched his cheek with her free hand. "Did you have a nice day? And do you have a lot of homework?"

"It was an okay day. And I've got some homework."

Emma knew what *some* meant. He had hours of homework ahead of him. Ninth grade had been a big year for the boys. It was their first year in high school, and their workload had increased.

"What about you, Billy?"

"Same."

"Did you have a good day?"

Billy shrugged.

"Anything you'd like to talk about?"

Billy shook his head no.

Emma worried about Billy. He was the one who kept things to himself. "Why don't you two grab something to eat and drink and start on your homework in the next fifteen minutes. That way, you can actually finish it tonight," Emma said, pointing to the refrigerator with her wooden spoon, then to the boys' backpacks, like a drum major directing a high school band.

Billy and Bobby pulled open the refrigerator and stared.

"Go ahead and make up your minds about what you want to eat, and I'll be up to chat once this sauce is simmering." She was anxious to see if Billy would tell her what was bothering him.

Just then, she heard the ground-level door slam and someone taking the stairs two at a time. Ren was on his way.

Maddie and Lulu beat Emma to the front door, squirming in anticipation, their short tails wagging at the sound of the key in the lock. Ren let himself in before Emma reached the door.

"Hey! Three ladies! That's what I call a welcome!"

Emma's fiancé, Ren Taylor, was a detective in the New Orleans Police Department. They'd met in Georgia where he'd been a deputy sheriff. He'd investigated the very first murder she'd ever worked on, and she'd come to trust his insight and steadiness. And she loved him, even though she didn't want to admit it at first. After living apart for four years, Ren moved to New Orleans and got a job with the NOPD. That was two years ago, right around the time he'd asked Emma to marry him. They were still working on a date, or they would be if Emma would sit down and take a serious look at her calendar.

Ren had recently requested a transfer from his first position in internal affairs to homicide. He'd always wanted to be a detective. He put in for a change, took the required tests, and only a few weeks ago, learned that his request for a position change had been accepted. He was now the newest homicide detective in the New Orleans Police Department.

"I have a new case." Emma walked back into the kitchen and checked on the chicken dish. Ren followed her. "But I'm not running it through the clinic."

"Why not?"

"It's mid-semester. All of my clinic students have full dockets, and I can't give them any additional cases. Plus, the client isn't technically homeless. So I'm taking this one privately."

"Isn't that a lot to handle by yourself?"

"It is, but my workload isn't too bad this semester, so I should be able to handle it. And the Dean has okayed it. Plus, Stacey's a former client. I know her. I don't believe she's capable of murder. I've been wrong before, but I'd be surprised if she's guilty of anything here. Of course, there's still a lot of work to do." Emma grabbed a big pot to start the water for pasta.

"What did they arrest her for?"

"Murder. Of her boss. By an injected drug overdose and impalement on a fence." She paused and glanced at Ren. "For that to have happened, the guy had to have been pushed over a balcony. If you saw Stacey, you'd never think she could have done it, physically. Have you heard of the case?"

"I wasn't assigned the case, if that's what you're asking. And I haven't overheard anyone talking about it either. What sort of case did you have with her earlier?" Ren grabbed a spoon and dug into the chicken dish for a taste.

"Vagrancy. Legal Aid needed a hand in representing a group of homeless kids who had been arrested for sleeping on the streets in the French Quarter. Stacey was only sixteen at the time. You know how the city tidies up the sidewalks during conventions." Emma filled the pot with water.

"Yep."

"I'm a little worried that she's not calling her mom for bail money. She did three years ago when the rest of her angry friends refused to. She was the only one with common sense back then. I'm not sure what's changed." Emma threw some salt in the water and turned on the stove.

"Maybe she'll decide to call her." Ren threw his spoon into the sink.

"If she has any sense, she will. I really think this whole case against her is a set up."

"The police wouldn't have arrested Stacey unless they had something pretty solid."

Emma nodded. "I know. They found what they're calling the murder weapon in her room. And they said there's a witness affidavit, too. I don't know who the witness is yet or exactly what the affidavit says. I'll get all of that information as soon as I can." She nodded. "But obviously, the DA's got something."

"You're trying to be so secretive about the weapon, but you said that the death was by injection. Right? So, isn't the weapon a syringe? Did they get any fingerprints off it?"

"I only have the preliminary reports. They may have, but I don't know anything yet."

"Do you have any plans for her defense?"

Emma sighed. "I've just started to look at the case. I'm assuming the DA will charge her with second-degree murder and possession with intent to distribute. Apparently, the police found a lot of ketamine with the murder weapon. She hasn't had her arraignment yet, so I could be wrong."

"I think you need more information. What if her fingerprints are on the murder weapon? I would bet they are."

"That could be a problem. But why would Stacey kill a guy and then leave the weapon in an armoire in her room and drugs in her bedside table? She's not a druggie, for one thing. And even though she's young, she's not stupid."

"The police have to take what they find at face value. You know that. What they found was pretty good evidence against Stacey."

"Have you ever seen anything like this before?"

"We see things like that all the time. But usually, it's on the streets after a sale has been set up. The person selling the drugs gets killed, and his drugs get stolen. The opposite happens too. Sometimes the seller just takes the money offered to him and kills the buyer. The method of murder was a little unusual, though. You don't see that very often."

"But that's not what happened here. The drugs were found in an entirely different room. Anyway, none of this sounds like something Stacey would ever be involved in. At least not the Stacey I knew."

"Maybe she was trying to make the murder look like an accident. You know, jab the guy with the ketamine, which would knock him out, then push him over the balcony." Ren raised his palms.

Emma shook her head. "She didn't do this. I'm sure of it. And you'd think the killer would realize that the injection would be obvious on autopsy. I don't think whoever killed James Crosby cared if people thought it was an accident or not. They just wanted him dead. I think they were planning on setting up someone all along." Emma stirred the pot again.

"I don't think murderers always think things through that well." Ren grabbed some silverware so he could begin setting the table.

"There were some strange things going on at that temple. I think there could be plenty of suspects there." She explained to Ren about the temple and the spa in the back.

"Young girls giving massages?"

"That's weird, huh? I'm going to visit the place and interview some of the employees. Crosby also had a drug paraphernalia business in the French Quarter."

"Good God. A head shop too? Those places are right on the edge of what they can get away with, legally. Bet they make a pretty profit on all of that."

"Yeah. I'm not intimidated by Voodoo, or Hoodoo or any religion. When you grow up in Savannah, you get used to it. And I'm not judging anyone for any sort of religious practice. But the Japaprajna group seems to be outside the bounds of religion." She shook her head. "I'm not sure what it is, but it's more than a little off."

Ren nodded. "I think you're right."

"Think someone from the NOPD would be interested in looking into a church with a head shop in the French Quarter and a massage business in the back of the temple?"

"They might be. But you don't have to worry about any of that. Just worry about your client and your case. Let the police take care of everything else."

Emma tossed her dishtowel at Ren. He caught it, his eyebrows raised.

"No need to be upset."

"I'm not. I'm just running upstairs to check on the twins while dinner finishes cooking. I'll be back down in a few minutes."

Emma knew Ren was right, sometimes she overstepped. She knew she shouldn't suggest a police investigation to Ren. Especially if it could affect one of her cases. Ren didn't pull any punches with her. He was direct, getting to the heart of everything right away. She appreciated that. She understood that lines had to be drawn between his work and hers. She drew them too. But sometimes his words stung. She needed to step away for a moment - a little space helped her get perspective. Plus, she wanted to talk to Billy.

She listened to the boys chat as she climbed the staircase to their bedroom. As usual, Bobby was leading the discussion. She hoped to coax Billy into telling her about his day. Something was bothering him, and he had been reluctant to talk about it earlier.

The quiet ones, the people who didn't speak up when something hurt them, concerned Emma the most. She had a feeling both Stacey and Billy fell into that category. She wasn't going to let Billy get lost in the bustle of their daily routine if she could help it.

Chapter Seven

E mma had a break between classes the next day and drove down to Esplanade with the hope of speaking to Cecelia. She didn't call ahead. She didn't want to give Cecelia advance warning of her visit, hoping that would give Cecelia less of a chance to avoid her visit. She parked her car by the coffee house across the street from the Japaprajna temple. The Java Zone was in a triangular-shaped, art deco building. A small median, what locals called a 'neutral zone'[1], separated the traffic lanes between the buildings on either side of it, restricting parking to what you could catch on the street. As a result, most of the coffee shop's patrons were from the immediate neighborhood. Parking was so congested that day Emma began to wonder why she had bothered to drive down to Esplanade at all. But fortunately, a spot on the curb opened up.

She walked inside and chatted with the barista, verifying Stacey's conviction that he hadn't seen her on the day of the murder. Emma had hoped Stacey was wrong. But even though the barista had been on duty the afternoon of the murder, he only recalled seeing police cars at the temple that day. He had no recollection of seeing a young woman at the coffee shop that afternoon. Emma purchased a café au lait and sat down at one of the small metal tables outside where she could see the temple clearly.

Time spent with Ren had taught her that it usually paid to observe first and ask questions later. She'd already walked into the temple blindly, and it had gotten her nowhere. She'd need to spend some time watching the house to find out if there was any pattern to the people coming and going, or if anything seemed unusual.

After forty-five minutes, a tall blonde woman parked a silver Toyota in the driveway of the temple and entered through the side door. Fifteen minutes later, Raphael and a shorter, dark-haired woman pulled up and parked a pea-green vintage Mercedes behind the first car. Both Raphael and the dark-haired woman entered the temple through the same door. Five minutes later, Raphael walked back out of the temple with a young woman wearing a magenta-colored jumpsuit and drove off.

Emma waited ten more minutes, then left the coffee shop and knocked at the front door of the temple. She heard approaching steps. Then another young woman opened the door.

She smiled broadly. "I'm Emma Thornton, attorney for Stacey Roberts. I'd like to speak to Cecelia if she's available."

"She's not here right now, but I'll tell her you came by." The woman kept her eyes downcast.

"I just saw two women drive up to the temple, and I'm certain the woman with the long blonde hair was Cecelia. Please tell her I'd like to see her."

"Wait here for one minute." The woman closed the door. Emma could hear her climbing the stairs. She stared at bright pink paint chips, which were already flaking away, exposing the original white color of the front porch. A few minutes later, the door opened again.

"You can come in." She gestured toward the hallway. "The stairs are at the end of the hall. Ms. Cecelia's office is on the second floor, second door on the left."

Emma walked down the hallway and passed a corridor leading to the kitchen on her left. She could see that the side entrance opened to the kitchen. She continued down the hallway, climbed up the stairs to the second floor, and knocked.

Cecelia opened the door. Dressed in white pants and a flowing white top, she didn't look like a woman who'd just lost her husband.

Emma shook her hand.

"I'm so sorry for your loss. But you do look lovely."

"Thank you. White's the color of mourning in many Asian cultures. I thought it was appropriate to wear it now." Cecelia smiled.

43

"I see. It's beautiful. I'm not a fan of wearing black."

"Oh, heavens! I'm not either! It's so morose! But, please, come in."

"Thank you for seeing me. I'd like to ask you some questions about the Japaprajnas and about the day Stacey was arrested."

"That's fine. I was not going to see visitors today but decided to make an exception for you." Cecelia indicated that Emma should take a seat by her desk. "Didn't the police find the murder weapon in Stacey's room?"

"It's my understanding they found a syringe in her room. But I'm not convinced it was the actual weapon."

"I see. Would you like to ask your questions as we walk through the house? That way, you can see the entire place, which should help you with your investigation. James loved the place so much it's given me comfort to stroll the halls since he died. I feel like a part of him is still here."

They walked down the stairs and hallway and outside to the front of the house. Emma touched the deep carving on the mahogany door.

"It was once a magnificent home, wasn't it?"

"Yes. Even though we've been involved in so many repairs, we really enjoyed living here, especially James. The original owner was a merchant and had two families, one in the uptown area and a second one here. The family that resided here was Creole, like many of the families on Esplanade."

"When was the house built?"

"1852. The family were free people of color and, after the merchant died, owned the house outright."

"I read that many of the houses built during that time contained hidden passages or rooms. During the Civil War, homeowners would use those places to hide their silver or jewelry from Union soldiers because of the looting. It was rampant."

"I've never heard of that, and I certainly haven't found anything like that here. And you'd think I would. We've been here eight years."

Cecelia opened the front door and motioned for Emma to enter the left parlor.

"James held the chanting and meditation sessions here," she said as she motioned with her hand toward the altar. It was an elaborate wooden structure with gilded wooden carvings that looked to have been patched together from several antique pieces. The legs were cylindrical and painted gold. A shelf behind the altar was covered in silk fabrics and flickering candles.

"Raphael told me a lot about J.R, but not that much about James. How was James' practice here different from his dad's in Idaho?" Emma pulled a small notebook and a pen from her purse.

"James had a different outlook from his dad. But, J.R. was important to us. He established a creed and codes of discipline. And because of that, we were able to meet the governmental guidelines for a church, which means the temple got a tax break. So we owe J.R. a lot.

"James might not have been as disciplined as his dad. But he tried to maintain some of his ideas." Cecelia looked around the room.

Emma paused for a moment, stunned by Cecelia's frank admission. Emma pretended to scan her notes while she gathered her thoughts. "I'm a little confused. If I understand correctly, you consider the temple a church or a holy place, but it's also a residence. You and your family live here."

"The Temple of the Japaprajna People owns the building. James and I never have. The people who come to the temple are believers. And after Mr. Zubowitz's experience here, there's no doubt that it's become a religion to our followers. But no lines are blurred. We live on the second floor. Temple sessions are on the first floor only."

"So, the second floor is considered the rectory for the Japaprajna priest and his family? And you and James lived there rent free?"

"I guess you could say that. And yes, we all live there rent free, including Mira and Jimmy."

"You said the people who come to the temple are believers. What do they believe in? James, or the mind-body connection? And who's Mr. Zubowitz? What happened to him?"

"Craig Zubowitz was a follower who suddenly stopped breathing during a massage one day. It could have been a small heart attack. I'm not sure. One of the massage therapists, it may have been Stacey, shouted for help, and James came to see if he could offer any assistance. James laid his hand

45

on Mr. Zubowitz's head, and he started breathing again.

"After that, word spread, and people started thronging to the temple to see James for help with all sorts of problems. They'd chant and meditate in this room. They'd bring their own yoga mats or cushions. That's why the room is empty. We never knew how many people would show up. Then they'd move from this room to the next, one by one. James would have sessions with them and ask them about their troubles or illnesses. He was very charismatic. To answer your question, I guess people believed both in James and in his philosophy. A little of both."

"Did he charge for these sessions?" Emma scribbled furiously to keep up.

"No. But people donated money to the temple if they had it. People are grateful when they feel better. When they're grateful, they're generous."

"Are you going to handle the sessions now?"

Cecelia lowered her head and brushed away something from her face. "I'm not sure. I can conduct meditations and chants. I have before. But I'm a yoga instructor, and I run the massage center in the back. I've been able to put my nurse's training to use that way. I'll have to see what the people want. I'm just not sure yet."

"How many followers do you have?"

"Right now, we've got about five hundred. But only about one hundred regular followers. Our religion was spreading to other states, too. People drove from Alabama and Texas to come to James' sessions, to get healed."

"Do you mind talking about the day James was killed?"

"No, that's okay. I knew you were going to ask those questions."

"Were you the first person to see him that day?"

She nodded. "Yes. And I wish I never had. It's not just that he died that makes me sad. It was the way he died. So gruesomely. And we actually believe in karma. So, the manner of death matters to us. No one deserves a death like that. It was awful." She put both hands over her face. Her voice was raw.

"I'm so sorry." Emma reached out and touched Cecelia's hand. "I have a few more questions, though. It might be better if we could sit down somewhere. Are you okay to continue?"

"Yes. It's okay. There are a couple of chairs in the other parlor." She straightened her shoulders.

Emma and Cecelia walked across the hall and into the next room. A large, ornately framed photograph of James, Cecelia, and Mira hung on the north wall above the mantle. Emma glanced at the photo as she and Cecelia sat down in two wingback chairs in front of the fireplace.

"Let me know if you'd like me to stop."

Cecelia nodded.

"Can you tell me what you saw that day?"

Cecelia hung her head. "I walked into the kitchen and could see him through the back door, the one that leads to the courtyard. This is so difficult to talk about." She drew in a long breath and exhaled in a short shaky little bursts. "I ran into the courtyard, and there he was, lying across the fence, impaled." She shut her eyes.

"I think James was pushed off of that balcony. The top of the balcony hit him at about waist level. He wasn't a very big man. You can't just fall over a balcony, unless you're drunk, and James didn't drink. So someone had to have shoved him off, " Cecelia said.

"I believe the police think so too, or there wouldn't have been an arrest."

"And I don't think Stacey could have done it. She's not a very big girl - tall, but small boned, you know?"

"I appreciate that you're trying to help Stacey out, but it's best if we just stick to the facts. Do you remember if you saw Stacey that afternoon?"

"I remember seeing her going up the stairs. I think it was right before I saw James. So that would have been a little before five. She was carrying something in her hands, but I couldn't see what it was."

"Where were you when you saw Stacey?"

"I think I was in the hallway."

"Why were you there?"

She shook her head. "I don't remember. I think I was just walking down the hall. Does that really matter? I know I saw Stacey, though. I'm sure of it."

"Did you pass through the kitchen to get to the hallway?"

"I'm not sure. You can enter through the front door and bypass the kitchen altogether."

"Is that what happened? It's so important to get these facts exactly as they happened. Do you remember which door you entered when you brought in your groceries the day James was killed? It makes sense that you would have entered through the side door, which opens into the kitchen. That way, you could have easily put your groceries on the kitchen counter."

Cecelia shook her head. "I'm certain I entered through the front door."

"Alright." Emma didn't believe her. She flipped a page in her notepad and smiled at Cecelia. "You said James didn't drink, but drugs were found in his body at his death, and he owned a head shop, which sells drug paraphernalia. Do you know whether James had a drug problem?"

"No. James did not have a drug problem." Cecelia's face flushed.

"Does anyone who lives here at the temple have a drug problem?"

She shook her head. "Not that I know of."

"What about James' friends? Did he have any friends in the drug business? I'd think that anyone who owned a head shop might acquire a few friends from that part of the world."

"If he did, I didn't know anything about it. And I didn't have anything to do with that business."

"It's clear from the preliminary reports that James was injected with something before he was pushed from the balcony. Have you ever seen syringes or drugs in a white powered form anywhere at the temple?"

"No, never."

"Did you notice that James had been more irritable lately?"

"Maybe."

"Was he having a hard time sleeping?"

"Perhaps? Why?"

"It could be a symptom of a drug addiction, particularly an addiction to ketamine."

"Ketamine addiction? Well, it could be a symptom of other things too, like drinking too much coffee."

"That's certainly true, Ms. Crosby. I didn't mean to offend you with this line of questioning."

"I refuse to believe he had anything to do with drugs."

"I understand. Have you ever known Stacey to be involved in any way with drugs, ketamine, or any other sort of drug?"

"Not to my knowledge."

"On the day you discovered James' body, did you notice anything else that stood out to you as unusual, either around James' body, or was there anything unusual in the area where his body was found?"

Cecelia nodded. "I noticed his lips." She dabbed her eyes.

"What about his lips?"

"They were sort of blue."

"Do you remember what time Mira arrived that day?"

"I think it was right after I found James. Right after I screamed, I think."

Emma paused. "I couldn't help but notice that large photograph over the fireplace. What was the nature of Mira's and James's relationship?"

Cecelia looked at her hands for a moment, then glanced up. "First of all, the photo is something James wanted to have done for the temple. It has nothing to do with us as a family. James, Mira, and I were the three top officers of the Japaprajnas. We were called the Principals. Commanders come right under us. James also called himself the Pujari, which is a Hindi word for priest. But I always thought that was silly since we're not Hindu. I think he just wanted to be thought of as a priest. Commanders were followers who made large financial contributions.

"But I know you're asking me this question because James and Mira had a child together. A little boy. He's four now. His name is Jimmy, so he's named after James. They never bothered to hide either Mira's condition when she was pregnant or that fact that it was James' child." She looked down at her hands again. "I can't have children. We knew that when we got married. But he married me anyway." She looked up. Her mouth quivered at the corners.

"Jimmy's in preschool right now and stays there until five when Mira goes to pick him up. It's right around the corner. He started out at an uptown preschool, but Mira couldn't handle the commute. And, I hate to say this, but Mira has been far more irritable, forgetful, and anxious lately. Does that fit in that symptom list of yours? Maybe she's the one with the drug problem." She glanced at her wristwatch. "You can see for yourself. They should be here any minute."

Chapter Eight

Within five minutes, Emma heard a car pull up in front of the temple. She looked out of the side parlor window as a pea-green Mercedes with a broken headlight parked across the street. Raphael and the woman with dark hair, the same person Emma had seen him with earlier, emerged. The woman opened the back door and unbuckled a small child from his car seat as Raphael walked ahead and unlocked the side door to the temple. Clomping footsteps echoed throughout the house as they ascended the stairs to the second floor.

"Would you like to meet her?" Cecelia raised her eyebrows.

Emma nodded.

Emma and Cecelia followed Mira and Raphael up the stairs until they reached the wide second-floor hallway.

"I'll be next door if you need anything." Cecelia smiled and walked toward her office.

Emma rapped on the door. She heard a rustling of papers inside and the high-pitched tone of a small child talking.

"Come in," Mira cleared her throat.

A toddler with dark hair was playing in a miniature kitchen when Emma walked into the room. She introduced herself to Mira.

"I represent Stacey Roberts. I was so sorry to learn of James' death, and I apologize for bothering you so soon afterwards, but I'd like to ask you a few questions if you have the time today."

"Honestly, my first inclination is to throw you out of that door and all the way down that pretty staircase." Mira Godfrey nodded toward the door

51

Emma had just entered. "But my better nature usually wins." She paused and gestured toward a chair that was close to her desk.

Emma sat down. She could feel her face flush. She hadn't anticipated open hostility. But she'd dealt with worse. She should have realized that Mira might be as upset about James' death as his wife, Cecelia. Mira's anger could be nothing more than a symptom of her grief.

She detected a subtle Brooklyn accent. Mira was probably in her mid-twenties. She had jet-black wavy shoulder-length hair. The opposite of Cecelia, she was stocky and muscular where Cecelia was slender and willowy. Unconcerned with common courtesies, she was abrupt and to the point, in stark contrast to Cecelia's almost self-deprecating politeness.

"Well, I'm glad to hear about your better nature. I'm sure you won't mind getting right down to business, so I won't waste your time. Or, if you'd prefer, we can schedule this for another day."

Mira continued to flip through the papers on her desk. Her face had begun to turn red. Emma noticed an occasional tremor in her hands and wondered if it was related to anxiety or the drug use Cecelia alluded to.

"We can get it over with today."

"Thank you. I'd like to ask you a few questions about the day of James' murder. I apologize if I ask anything which is uncomfortable for you or causes you any pain. If you don't want to answer a question, we can reserve it for later."

Mira nodded. "It's a tough time. I knew it would be, but it doesn't make it any easier." She inhaled a shaky breath.

"What can you tell me about the day James was killed?" Emma clicked her pen.

"It was a regular Monday. The temple's always closed on Mondays. It happened at the end of the day. I was running errands. James always said our family worked 'like a John Deere tractor.' Cecelia prepared the morning meal; I cooked all the evening meals. We took turns trading extra chores on the weekends. Except for James. He didn't have chores, with the exception of the organization of labor, which he enjoyed. But then, he brought in most of the money with the healing work he did. That, and the business in the

French Quarter we ran together."

"And there was also whatever Cecelia brought in from the spa." Emma scribbled down a few notes to herself.

"Yeah. That too."

"I thought the spa business brought in the most money."

"Who gave you that idea?"

"It's just something I heard."

"I don't actually know the spa numbers. But I doubt it."

Emma pursed her lips and nodded. "Okay. I'd like to know more about the shop in the French Quarter, but first, let's get back to the day James was murdered. You said it was a Monday, and you'd been running errands."

"I'd been down at the shop in the Quarter for a couple of hours, checking on the merchandise and sales, seeing if I needed to order anything. Then I ran by the pharmacy to pick up a few things for Jimmy." She nodded toward the toddler. "After that, I picked up Jimmy and came home."

Emma got the name of the pharmacy from Mira.

"What time did you get home?"

"I pick up Jimmy at five o'clock because his daycare closes then. So I picked him up and got back to the temple around five-fifteen."

Emma noted the time on her notepad. "When you got here, what did you do?"

"I ran up here with Jimmy. I needed to enter some sales information in the books. Then I heard a scream. I looked out of the window in the direction of the scream and saw James' body lying over the fence. Then I ran downstairs to see what had happened."

"Was your window open? How did you know where the scream was coming from?"

"No, my window was closed. But I knew the scream was coming from downstairs, and it sounded like it was coming from the courtyard. I opened the window to look out, and that's when I saw him.

"When I got downstairs, I could tell that James had fallen from a window on the second floor. One of the fence prongs had gone all the way through his body. I didn't think it was possible to survive an injury like that." She clenched her fists.

"Did you notice anything else?"

"Just that I didn't think he was breathing. But I didn't get very close to the body."

"When you got home that day, which door did you enter?"

"I don't remember. Probably the side door."

"Wouldn't you have seen James through the kitchen window if you'd entered the side door?"

"Maybe, if I'd looked. But I didn't. I didn't see him."

"Did you see Stacey that day?"

"I think she came up later and asked what was going on. But I don't know anything about how long she'd been there or what she'd been doing."

Emma jotted down Mira's remarks. "What about Raphael? Wasn't he there?"

"I'm not sure. Maybe. He was there later, for sure."

"What about Cecelia? You said you heard a scream."

"Yeah, I heard a scream. I didn't see her at first, but when I got down there, she was in the courtyard."

"Did the police speak to you?"

Mira nodded. "They did. I just told them what I told you. And they asked me if there was a witness at the business in the French Quarter, someone who could verify I was really there. So I gave them her name."

"Who was that?"

"Moonstone Carville. She's a great employee. I don't know what I'd do without her." She nodded.

Emma checked her notes, scribbling in the margins. Mira seems to have calmed down. "Can you tell me about your relationship with James? Something about your child-raising responsibilities, your home, and work relationship?"

"I already told you that we operated the same as any family. Cecelia and I split chores, although the massage girls had weekly house cleaning responsibilities, too. I did the bookkeeping and managed the shop. Cecelia managed the spa. James didn't do much except hold sessions at the temple.

Somehow Cecelia and I were okay with that." She bit her lip.

"Tell me about your business in the French Quarter. Let's start with the name of the shop. What is that?"

"We incorporated it under the name ETC Shop and Smoking Supplies, Inc. We liked that because ETC stood for *etcetera*, and could mean just about anything."

"What was the purpose of that business? What do you do or sell there?"

"We opened it for the purpose of selling souvenir items; you know, mugs and t-shirts. But that didn't work out."

"Why not?"

"There are too many places in the French Quarter that sell those things. One on every corner. We needed something different. So we hit on the idea of selling stuff needed for smoking, especially when you're rolling your own. But we also got in hookahs, and sometimes we'd get in some apple concoctions or flavored tobaccos. We don't sell actual drugs, of course, but we sell items someone might need to smoke weed. Papers, bongs, hookahs. And it works. We've made pretty good money at it."

"How did you know where to find the suppliers?"

"One of my high school friends back in Brooklyn has a store like that. He gave me the name of a few of his suppliers. We took it from there."

"So James had the idea, and you had the names of the suppliers."

"I had the idea and the names of the suppliers. But James had the money to buy the merchandise."

"I see. Did you share in the profits with James?"

"No. But I don't pay rent here at the temple. And Jimmy and I share one of the larger bedrooms on the second floor. So my kid gets to live and eat free too. And I get a salary." She glanced at Jimmy, who had hopped on top of the fire engine and had begun pushing it across the wooden floor with short, sturdy legs, much like his mother's. "He's happy here. He loves this place and this yard. And he loved his dad." She began to cry. "That's the worst part of what happened. Jimmy really loved his dad. I still haven't figured out how I'm going to tell him." She reached into her desk, pulled out a tissue, and blew her nose. "His dad and I didn't have a great love affair or anything. One night, we just got together, and that was it. Jimmy happened, and Cecelia has been pretty good about it." She sniffed. "I stayed on, and we agreed to raise Jimmy together because that was the best thing for him. I've really been pretty lucky." She started crying again. "But James share profits? That's funny." She rolled her eyes and shook her head. "No."

"What's going to happen now? Will you stay on or move?"

"The day after James was killed, Cecelia let me know that it was okay for Jimmy and me to stay here. But I'm starting to think we'll need to move on. It seemed okay when James was alive because he was Jimmy's dad. But now it doesn't seem right." She sighed and blew her nose again. "I was thinking of getting back in touch with my mom in Brooklyn. Maybe pay her a visit soon. But I'm not sure what I'm going to do yet."

Emma nodded. "Do you know if the police ever spoke to Moonstone?"

"They did. A couple of days after the murder, they came by and verified that I'd been there in the late afternoon on October fourteenth. I don't know what else they talked about, but she was in tears when they left."

"Do you know if James had a history of drug abuse?" Emma turned a page in her notepad.

"If he did, it wouldn't have anything to do with his death, would it?" Mira crossed her arms across her chest. She clearly didn't like the question.

"What do you mean?" Emma said.

"I heard he was jabbed in the neck with enough ketamine to kill a horse." Mira sniffed.

"Who told you that?"

"That's the talk around here. But whatever was in that syringe, there was a lot of it. James was out of it, or he couldn't have been pushed over that balcony. So it wouldn't really matter if he'd had a drug problem or not, right?" Mira flushed.

"I don't see it that way. A drug problem could affect his tolerance. Or if he already had a drug in his system and then someone gave him something else, the effect of the drug could be exaggerated."

Mira stared at her desk, saying nothing.

"What about James and Stacey? Did they get along?"

Mira shrugged. "I guess so."

"Did you ever notice any animosity between them?"

"No. none of that. But maybe the typical tension between a boss and an employee sometimes."

"Can you recall a specific incident when there was that type of strain between the two of them?"

"I don't think she liked going to do the work in the French Quarter after she'd done that a while. I say that because she just stopped going."

"You're talking about the recruiting work she did?"

"I wouldn't call it that, but yeah."

"Do you know why?"

"We never really talked, so that would be a guess on my part."

Emma paused. "Since I'm here, I thought I'd also speak to some of the girls at the spa. Do you know if that can be arranged today?"

"I wouldn't know. You'd have to see if Cecelia would talk to you again and if she feels like taking you down there."

Chapter Nine

Emma rapped on Cecelia's open door.

"Come in." Cecelia frowned over a pair of horned-rimmed glasses.

"Hi, Cecelia. I'd like to run down to the spa and meet some of the massage therapists, especially Angelina Diaz. I won't be long. She could be an important witness." Emma smiled, hoping she didn't seem too anxious.

"What do you want to know from Angelina and the others?" Cecelia motioned for Emma to come in. The small crinkle between her eyebrows grew larger.

"I'll need to ask questions similar to those I asked you, like where they were on the day of the murder and something about their relationship with James and with Stacey. Their schedule at the spa could be important, too."

Cecelia nodded. "I see. It looks like you're doing a very thorough investigation."

Emma backed toward the door. "If I've got your okay then, I'll head on down to the spa. I'd like to start interviewing the girls who are working there today. When they're available, of course."

Cecelia shook her head. "I can't let you do that without me. For one thing, we have clientele here now, and their privacy is a concern. And for another, the girls are all so young. But you can speak to them with me."

"If they're over age eighteen, they're old enough to talk to me by themselves."

"Ms. Thornton, this is private property, and not only that, it's a religious establishment. I can and will prevent you from speaking to these girls. If you're going to talk to them, it will be with me."

"Okay then. No problem. I'd like to get started with everyone who's working today." Emma was getting frustrated with Cecelia and her damn roadblocks.

"That's not possible. I couldn't spare more than thirty minutes for this today."

Emma sighed and followed Cecelia to a door marked 'SPA' at the end of the hall. They entered a small darkened chamber filled with the aroma of rosemary and lavender. Emma couldn't help but breathe deeply a couple of times. She felt calmer, clearer, if only for a moment.

The faintly lit room was sparsely furnished. A pitcher of water with ice and several fresh cups had been provided for clients on a narrow glass table. A tall chair stood like a sentinel next to a padded wooden bench. Soothing music played in the background.

Cecelia motioned for Emma to take a seat on the bench. She pushed through another door to the rooms in the back.

Seconds later, Cecelia returned with one of the masseuses who was dragging a chair behind her. The girl was young, small in stature, and had dark shoulder-length hair.

Cecelia directed the girl to place her chair opposite the bench where Emma was sitting while she pulled the other chair over and sat down.

Emma introduced herself. "I want to ask you a few questions about the day Mr. Crosby was killed. But before we get started, please tell me your name."

"This is Angelina Diaz," Cecelia said.

"Cecelia, I'd prefer it if you'd allow Angelina to answer these questions for herself."

"Like I said, Angelina is young."

"How old are you, Angelina?"

"She's only nineteen. Isn't that right?"

Angelina nodded.

"Then she's old enough to answer anything I need to ask her. And she has a right to do so."

59

"We do things my way here at the temple, Ms. Thornton."

Emma pulled her notebook and pen out of her purse. She looked directly at Angelina. "Please tell me where you live."

"She lives right here on the third floor, just like Stacey once did."

"Angelina." Emma maintained eye contact. "Were you living here at the temple on the day Mr. Crosby was killed?"

"She was." Cecelia shifted so that she sat deeper in her chair and crossed her arms.

Emma controlled her urge to snap at Cecelia. "If the DA were asking the questions in court, Angelina would be required to answer. I've already spoken to you. I need to speak to Angelina because we have to know what she would say, not what you would say. This meeting is pointless otherwise." Emma smiled at Cecelia, hoping she was hiding her irritation. She turned toward Angelina.

"Angelina, please answer to the best of your ability. If you don't know the answer to any of my questions, that's perfectly acceptable. Where were you at four o'clock on Monday, October fourteenth? That was the day Mr. Crosby was killed."

Angelina looked down at her hands which she'd folded in her lap, then glanced up at Cecelia. "I think I'd already gone down to the other place, the store, you know. The one Mira runs."

"I think we need to cut this session a little short, Ms. Thornton. I'm sorry. I've completely forgotten about a client that's coming in the next few minutes." Cecelia started to stand up.

"Just a few more questions, please, Cecelia. We've only just begun." Emma turned her attention back to Angelina. "You sound unsure of the time you left. What time do you usually go down to the store to work?"

"I usually get there around five."

"What makes you think you got there around four o'clock that day?"

"I just thought we got there early. I seem to recall we did."

"Can anyone verify that you left the temple at four?"

"I don't know."

"Who took you down to the shop?"

"Raphael."

"I don't believe Raphael remembers things quite the same way you do. He recalls that you waited until the police left that day before driving down to the shop. So that would have been sometime after five."

Angelina shrugged. "I don't remember it like that."

"What do you do at the shop?" Emma asked.

Angelina was still looking at her hands, her eyes downcast. "We take turns working there on Mondays when the spa is closed. We usually work there at night or late afternoon until about ten o'clock."

"Who is *we*?"

"Me and the other girls. We work at the back of the shop, not up front. But only one of us can be there at a time. And no one works there every week. It's staggered, so we only have to work every few months or so."

"Do you know if Stacey ever worked at the back of the shop?"

Angelina shook her head. "No. She didn't. She spent a lot of time down in the Quarter trying to get other people to come work at the spa. We had a lot of turnover. Girls would come and go. And then she worked at the spa too."

"Did anyone resent the fact that Stacey didn't have to work at night behind the shop?"

"I didn't. And I didn't hear anyone else say anything. Her job was just different."

Cecelia reached out and touched Angelina's shoulder. "We need to go. Our client will be here any minute. I'm so sorry I forgot about him. Maybe we can schedule something later?" She stood up. "Thanks so much for all of your work on this case, Ms. Thornton. Angelina, you need to prepare your room for the next person."

"But Angelina didn't really answer my question about what she did at the shop. And I have a couple more questions, too. Angelina should be able to answer these quickly."

Cecelia, face flushed, nodded and sat back down. "Please make it quick."

Emma nodded at Angelina. "Explain to me what your job was at the back of the ETC shop."

"I did whatever I was told to do. If it was time to make boxes, I did that. If it was time to count boxes, I did that."

"Do you have a massage therapy license?"

Angelina shook her head. "No, I don't."

"She doesn't need one." Cecelia glared at Emma. "A massage therapist is a person who engages in the practice of massage therapy for compensation. That's written into the law, the statute. I've got a copy at my desk. Angelina doesn't receive money or anything from any of our clients. She receives full room and board here, but not for giving massages. As a devotee to the Japaprajna order, she donates her time and her work. Whatever she brings in from the massages she gives goes back to the order. And that includes tips."

"That's interesting. How do you feel about that, Angelina?"

Angelina hung her head.

"Where is your home town? I'm curious about how you came to the temple, how you heard about the Japaprajnas," Emma said.

"That's enough, Ms. Thornton. I'm so sorry, but we really need to go." She smiled.

Cecelia and Angelina stood up simultaneously. Cecelia gave Angelina a tiny push toward the back door.

Cecelia turned around. "I'm sure Stacey couldn't have had anything to do with James' murder. I can't imagine who'd want to kill him. He was such a sweet and thoughtful man. Everyone loved him. Absolutely everyone."

Cecelia led Emma down the hall toward the front door. Emma waved goodbye and walked down the sidewalk, thinking about Cecelia and the spa.

Even if the spa was legitimate, something wasn't. Cecelia was controlling and seemed anxious to keep Emma from learning about the girls who worked there. Emma doubted the validity of the entire spa setup, even if licenses weren't required. And she didn't buy Cecelia's argument about that for a minute. The girls were underage, but they still needed to be paid a wage. What a strange place.

Since it was the weekend, Emma thought she'd start afresh at the beginning of the next week with a visit to ETC Shop and Smoking Supplies. But when she got back to her office, she had a subpoena on her desk. Stacey's arraignment and bond hearing was set for Monday.

Chapter Ten

T he Orleans Parish criminal court building was clustered with Central Lockup and the Orleans Parish Prison, a collection of buildings that had overseen the parish's criminal justice system for more than half a century. Built in 1931, the criminal court building was a drab, art deco structure designed to invoke the solemnity of justice. Instead, it incited fear.

Arriving fifteen minutes early Monday morning, Emma scanned the courtroom for Stacey. She was already there, seated in the first row on the left side of the courtroom with a few other prisoners. Guards were standing watch. Her orange prison uniform had been replaced with a pair of nice black slacks Emma had brought over to the prison earlier, and a black and white striped shirt. The occasion called for respectful attire.

They were assigned to Judge Harvey, who had a reputation for fairness. Emma walked up to the clerk seated next to the judge's bench to check the docket. She and Stacey were first up.

Seconds later, the clerk called the court to order, and the judge entered the courtroom. When Stacey's case was called out, the guard released Stacey to stand by Emma.

Judge Harvey was a seasoned jurist, the lines on his face revealing the burden of thirty years of criminal cases. His robes seemed heavy on his shoulders, as if he were weighed down by the responsibility of his position. He frowned as the clerk read the Bill of Information, his finger tracing each charge.

As Emma had suspected, Stacey was charged with Second Degree Murder, and the lesser included Manslaughter. It was no surprise that the charges included possession of ketamine with intent to distribute. The hearing was brief.

"How do you wish to plead?" Judge Harvey asked.

"Not guilty, your honor," Emma said.

"Bail has been set at $250,000. You may see the court clerk to make arrangements for payment. Also," he scowled at Stacey, then Emma. "These are serious charges. If and when you are released, you are not allowed to leave the jurisdiction of this court before the trial date. You are also required to check in, on a monthly basis, with a probation officer who will be assigned to you. The clerk will take care of all of these details." He glared at Emma. "Make sure you visit with the clerk, Ms. Thornton, is it? Get the trial date and all of the information on reporting to the probation officer. You need to make sure your client is fully aware of this. Failure to comply with the reporting requirements will land her back in jail. If that happens, the bail bond fee will be forfeited. Your client will be returned to jail today until payment arrangements have been made."

* * *

Emma pulled into the Central Lockup parking lot for the third time in a week. She'd received another telephone call from Stacey that afternoon, after the arraignment. Her mother had posted bond, and she was about to be released. She asked Emma to pick her up in a couple of hours since it would take that long for the clerks to process her paperwork.

Emma had been at work since receiving Stacey's call, trying to find her shelter. She was curious about Stacey's conversation with her mother. What had made her change her mind and make the call?

Emma walked into the jail and sat down in the waiting room. The large space, constructed of poured concrete, had never been painted. The lighting was poor, with two lopsided florescent fixtures dangling by a couple of chains from the ceiling. The room was filled with rows of folding chairs, several of which were occupied by people scattered about the room. Like

Emma, they were waiting to pick up loved ones being released. Across the room, clerks worked behind glass-covered caged windows.

A young man appeared at a doorway in the back of the room. A group of people rose, surrounded the young man, and began hugging him. Some had tears in their eyes. Emma heard "...Praise Jesus!" from an older woman she suspected was the young man's grandmother. A middle-aged man dressed in navy blue work clothes murmured to the young man who gave him a fist bump, then a hug. They all left smiling.

Emma shuffled her feet and moved her hips to rearrange herself in the cold metal seat. She was thankful when she finally saw Stacey appear in the rear doorway. She was dressed in street clothes, jeans, and a t-shirt. Emma stood and walked over to greet her.

"How are you? I have to say, I was surprised you called your mom."

Emma hugged Stacey and in that moment could feel her shoulder blades underneath her shirt. Stacey's clothes hung loosely on her body, and her skin was pale and blotchy. Her eyes were downcast.

Stacey nodded. "Okay. Let's get out of here."

Emma and Stacey walked out into the parking lot toward her car.

"Do you have any ideas about where you'd like to stay until the trial is over?"

"I've thought about a couple of options. But I've got to get my stuff at the temple first."

Emma unlocked her car, and they slid in. Emma headed towards the French Quarter.

"What places are you thinking about?"

"I know this guy who said I was welcome to stay at his place. And I thought I could also find some of the girls who left the temple and see if I could also stay with them."

"Those don't seem like real safe options to me, but we can explore them. In the meanwhile, I know of several shelters where you'd be safe. A couple of them would let you stay there through the trial date. They're more like homes or apartments instead of shelters. It's really not as bad as you might imagine. There are several throughout the city, and a few across the river.

There are openings, and you can get in for tonight."

"Well," Stacey paused and sighed. "After I get my stuff at the temple, we can decide."

"Are you okay? You seem a little down. Is there anything you'd like to tell me?"

"I don't want to talk about anything."

"Did something happen?"

Stacey shook her head. "No."

"Are you upset about calling your mom?"

"Maybe. Yeah, I guess. I didn't want to have to do that."

"That doesn't make you a failure, you know. We all need help sometimes."

"I guess it's the whole thing. Being charged with murder. It's all so awful. I can't believe this is my life."

Emma looked at Stacey. She was slumped over in the seat with her head down. "For one thing, you're only nineteen. You've got a lot of life left to live. And even though I know it seems terrible, we'll get to the bottom of it. We're going to figure out what happened to James, but we have a lot of work to do. And we need to work together. It just takes a little time." Emma turned a corner. "Here's what we'll do tonight. I've got to go get the twins. They stayed late at school today. I called the temple earlier and spoke to them, so they're expecting you, but I can go in with you now to make sure everything's okay. Then I'll run get the boys, and call one of the shelters—the nicest one—to confirm that you're coming tonight.

"That will give you time to gather your things. I'll come get you in about an hour and a half after I drop off the boys. Think you'll be okay there for that long?"

"Sure." She looked down at her hands.

She handed Stacey a ten-dollar bill. "Here's some cash in case you finish packing before I get back. If that happens, go across the street, get a cup of coffee and something to eat, and wait for me there." Emma pointed to the coffee house across the street.

"Okay." Stacey took the money.

"There's one more thing, before I forget." Emma pulled into the turning lane. "The judge emphasized how important it is for you to show up every month for your appointment with the probation officer. And you've got to be on time, too. One misstep and you're back in jail, and your mom's thirty thousand dollars will have been spent for nothing. I'll keep reminding you, but I wanted to tell you again, right now, to make sure you understood." She paused. "Did your mom say anything about coming down for the trial?"

Stacey shook her head. "She said she wanted to come down sometime, but I didn't ask when." Stacey turned to look at Emma. Even though she tried to smile, there was a sadness in her eyes.

"Well, that's good."

Stacey shrugged.

"I know you and your mom have had a difficult relationship, and it's hard to change the dynamics of a situation like that when it's gone on for a long time. My mom and I never got along, and still don't. I'd be happy to talk to you about it."

"Maybe. Some day. I've just never been convinced that she loves me."

"Well, I'm here."

Stacey nodded. "Thanks."

"Mother-daughter relationships can be challenging. You may never figure it out." Emma smiled at Stacey as she checked traffic. "I'm going to check in with you on a weekly basis, at least, unless something specific comes up. And I'll take you to your monthly appointments with the probation officer."

Stacey nodded. "Okay."

"Do you have any questions?"

"Yeah. What do we need to do to get ready for trial?"

"I was going to get there." Emma smiled again. This was a good sign. Or she hoped it was. Stacey had a lot of worries for a nineteen-year-old, but she should be concerned about her trial. Her question indicated that she was willing to be a team player. And that was all Emma could ask for in a client. "I'll need to interview a few more witnesses, and as I gather information, I'll have some questions for you. I have a couple right now, if you don't mind."

Stacey nodded. "That's fine."

Emma stopped at a light. "You're going to have to tell me more about

68

what happened the time you took drugs. Was it at the temple?"

Stacey nodded. "Yeah. During a session. James made a line of the white powder and gave me a little tube, and told me to sniff it in. Like I said, I assumed it was cocaine. It made you feel sort of out of it. Other girls said he gave it to them too."

"Okay. Did you ever see James take anything like that powder?"

"No. But I heard he did."

"But you never saw him?"

"No, I didn't."

"Do you know of anyone who actually saw him taking drugs?"

"I think maybe Natalia did once. I'm not sure."

The light turned green. Emma made a mental note to get in touch with Natalia. She wondered whether James had a secret place at the temple where he indulged his drug habit.

"Did you ever notice scatterings of white powder in any of the rooms at the temple?"

"Maybe a few times in the altar room."

"Did you ever see people who were not followers at the temple? "

Stacey shook her head. "Not that I know about. But there could have been."

"Do you know a girl by the name of Moonstone? Moonstone Carville. She works in James and Mira's store in the French Quarter."

"She's the one with the tattoos?"

"I wouldn't know about that."

"I think that's who she is. I've seen her around."

"When? How do you know her?"

"She came to the temple a couple of times. Kind of hard to forget that name and those tattoos."

"Do you know why she came to the temple?"

"I think she saw Cecelia. Not sure why."

"You told me you liked James at first, then you changed your mind about him. But you didn't say why. Why did you stay so long at the temple if you didn't like James?"

"That's a good question." Stacey cocked her head to one side. "I think part of the reason is because I didn't have anywhere else to go. I'd started saving money, but only a small amount. Hardly enough for a bus ticket to Biloxi. But I was planning on leaving. I was working on a plan."

"Why did you change your mind about James?"

"It's a long story. Maybe for another day."

"You've been accused of his murder. I'm going to have to know that story."

Stacey looked out of the window at the passing traffic.

Emma parked in front of the temple.

"Well, we're here. Like I said, I'm going to go in with you to make sure you're welcome. Then you can gather your things and I'll get back as soon as I can."

"Please don't do that. I'm nineteen; I'm not a kid. I can handle this. And thanks for everything you've done for me. I know I'm not paying you, and you're doing a whole lot for me for nothing."

"It was my choice, Stacey. I wanted to represent you because I believe in you. We'll get to the bottom of everything."

* * *

Emma drove away from Esplanade toward the twins' school. She was worried about Stacey. She'd lost a considerable amount of weight during the time she'd spent in prison and was more distant, troubled, even depressed. The situation was taking a toll.

Billy and Bobby were waiting outside the school when Emma arrived. Billy was still moodier than usual. He'd finally told her that a kid had been picking on him, and she was glad to know what had been bothering him. The twins were approaching the days when bad habits began to develop, when kids stopped talking to their parents and started to withdraw. She was doing everything she could to keep the conversation with her boys flowing. Stacey was only a couple of years older than the twins when she ran away from home. Emma couldn't imagine how frightened she'd be if Billy and Bobby did that.

The boys tumbled into the backseat of the car.

"How were basketball tryouts?"

"Okay," they said in unison.

"Do you know if you made the team yet?"

"No," Again, in unison.

"How about pizza tonight?"

Billy and Bobby looked at each other and nodded.

"Pizza it is, then. We'll go after I get back. I've got to drop off a client somewhere." They pulled up to the apartment, and Emma walked inside to place a call to the most reliable shelter she knew of for women and children. She verified Stacey's spot within seconds, making sure they knew she might cancel. Stacey still hadn't approved the lodging.

* * *

Within fifteen minutes of dropping off the boys, Emma pulled up in front of the temple, circling for a few minutes until she found a parking space, hoping that Stacey had been able to locate her belongings. Thanks to a brief cold snap, it was one of those crisp fall evenings before the sun sets where colors were crystalline clear. The sky was a bright, deep cornflower blue, and the air was so clear it almost hurt to breathe. She felt pretty good about the evening she had planned with Billy and Bobby. It was hard not to be in a great mood. She ran up to the massive front entrance of the temple, lifted the heavy brass knocker, and dropped it twice against the door.

In a few minutes, she heard the sound of footsteps. A girl in a magenta jumpsuit opened the door.

"I believe Stacey Roberts is here. I came to pick her up." Emma smiled at the girl.

The girl frowned. "I haven't seen Stacey."

"Are you sure?" Emma peered around the girl. Her heart was beginning to beat rapidly. Stacey didn't have her keys. Someone would have had to have let her in through the front door.

The girl raised one eyebrow. "I think I'd know if she'd been here."

Emma looked down the hall. "You've got to be mistaken. I dropped her off at the front of the temple about an hour ago. She was only going to pick up her things. I guess she could be at the coffee shop across the street. But I'd like to speak to Cecelia before I go."

The girl paused. "Wait here." She gestured toward a small bench in the hallway.

Emma sat down to wait for Cecelia. It was a Wednesday. The spa was open for business. She could hear low, soft music in the background, and the hushed tones of people talking.

Emma was surprised by Cecelia's sudden appearance. Her rubber spa shoes must have silenced her steps. Concern was etched into her face.

"We haven't seen Stacey! When did you drop her off?"

"About an hour ago. She was just going to pick up her things. Are you sure you haven't seen her? Could we go up to her old room and take a look?"

"Absolutely. Follow me."

Cecelia led the way up the stairs to the third floor and down a narrow hall to Stacey's small bedroom. She wasn't there. The room was no larger than a walk-in closet. Bare, except for a small twin bed which was crammed in one corner and a narrow armoire which was in the other. A tiny table stood next to the bed.

"Would you mind if I looked inside the armoire to see if Stacey has taken any of her things?"

"Of course. Please do." Cecelia nodded.

Emma opened the armoire. It had been cleaned out. She pulled out the drawer of the nightstand. It was also empty.

"Okay. Well, it looks like she's either been here or her things have been moved."

"I can assure you, Ms. Thornton, we have not moved Stacey's possessions. We haven't found a replacement for her yet, so no one's been in this room since she was arrested."

"Okay. Well, maybe she's across the street at the coffee shop. I'll check."

Emma walked out of the temple and crossed the street to the coffee house. The barista was cleaning the machine, and his helper was sweeping the floor.

The shop was preparing to close. Other than that, it was empty.

"I'm looking for a young girl, nineteen, tall, thin, sort of dirty blonde hair. Has anyone of that description been here in the past hour?"

"No, ma'am. No one's been here at all in the past forty-five minutes, and the guy that came in before that was a regular. He sure doesn't fit that description."

Emma walked back to her car.

You've really messed up if you've run away again, Stacey.

And I so have I. I should never have left her on her own at the temple.

Chapter Eleven

Emma drove back to her office. *Stupid, stupid Emma. What are you going to tell the probation officer? And the judge?*

She needed to regroup. And she should call Stacey's mom just in case Stacey had contacted her. It was unlikely, but possible. What could have happened? She dismissed kidnapping immediately and didn't see any other signs of foul play. With Stacey's history, it seemed pretty clear. She'd run away again. Emma was upset with herself for failing to anticipate that. At nineteen, Stacey was still a kid. It was obvious she was depressed at the time of her release. Emma wasn't sure what would make someone run away. The urge didn't seem to be part of a logical process, so it could be difficult to predict. But, in Stacey's case, it was definitely within the realm of possibilities. She sighed.

She drove into the faculty parking lot and parked. She walked up the steps to her office, dreading the call to Stacey's mother.

She wasn't surprised that she still had Leah Robert's information. Emma never threw away anything.

"Mrs. Roberts? This is Emma Thornton. I hope I'm catching you at a good time. I'd like to thank you for posting bond for Stacey."

"It's good to hear from you, Professor Thornton. I'm so glad you're helping Stacey with her case. I had to do what I could for her. I can't believe all this has happened. She could never hurt anyone."

"Yes. It was important to get her out of jail. Central Lockup's not a great place for anyone, that's for sure. I'd like to ask you a few questions if you have a minute. I also have some news to share."

"Of course."

Emma explained that Stacey appeared to have run away from the Temple after being released from jail.

"Strangely, her clothes and other personal items were gone, but no one had seen her. It looked as if she'd grabbed her things and had run off. I don't know where she is and don't know where to begin looking for her. I was hoping she'd contacted you."

Emma could hear Leah's sharp intake of breath over the phone.

"Oh no! I can't believe she ran away again!" Emma heard a long sigh, then a sniff. "No. She hasn't called me. What can we do? I haven't heard anything from her. Until she called and asked for bail, I hadn't heard from her in years." There was a pause, and Emma could tell Mrs. Roberts was pacing. "But I know she liked staying in the French Quarter. That's where she was arrested three years ago. It's not a very big place, but she has to be found before dark. New Orleans streets are so dangerous at night." She paused. "Do you think that's possible?" Mrs. Roberts' voice quavered.

"I'm worried too. I'll call within twenty-four hours to report her as missing. I hope to hear from her before that. Needless to say, that's a complication since she's been released on bail. Let's hope we find her way before she has to report to her probation officer. You're probably right about the French Quarter, but, if she doesn't want to be found, there are plenty of places to hide, even there.

"I know the homeless population here pretty well. I think I can call on them to help me out. First, I wanted to ask you a few questions about why Stacey ran away in the first place, back in 1993. She was only sixteen years old at the time, right?"

"Yes. It seems like much longer ago than that. More like a lifetime. Stacey wasn't a very happy teenager. It all started when she was twelve. There were mean girls at school, girls that bullied her, called her names. I wanted to move to another school district or put her in a private school. But Randy, Stacey's dad, didn't think the name calling was that much of a problem and thought Stacey should ignore it. The truth was that he didn't want to spend money on the move or the private school. So Stacey stayed where she was, at the mercy of those girls. The longer she stayed there, the unhappier she became until, eventually, she started taking it out on us. She'd fight with all of us, especially her father."

"I know Mr. Roberts died after Stacey ran away. She's afraid you blame her for his death."

Mrs. Roberts exhaled. "I'd never do that. None of it was her fault. Randy blamed himself for the fact that she ran away. He felt so guilty. That could have contributed to his heart attack, but he was also overweight and didn't take good care of himself. The stress of everything probably was a factor in his death. But if I were to blame anyone, and I don't, I'd blame those mean girls. If they hadn't bullied Stacey, none of this would have happened. Cruelty is so destructive."

Emma paused. "I'm so sorry for the loss you and your family have suffered. Stacey hasn't helped herself or her case by running away, but I blame myself for this. I should have anticipated that this might have happened. She seemed depressed when I picked her up from jail. I was hoping she might have reached out to you, but I knew that was a long shot."

"Don't blame yourself. I don't think anyone would have expected this. Just like I didn't think she would have run away three years ago. I was shocked she called and asked for help with bail."

"I don't think she had many friends at the temple, but I can check to see if any of the girls who left the group have offered her a place to stay, or if they know where she is." Emma paused. "Stacey mentioned you were planning on coming down to New Orleans sometime before her trial. Do you have a date for your trip yet?"

"I think I should come down now. I'm worried about Stacey. I want to join in the search."

* * *

Emma was late for dinner and had to meet Ren and the boys at Gino's, their favorite pizza restaurant. They'd already ordered when she arrived, which was fine since they always ordered the same thing, two large pepperonis.

Ren always got a beer. White wine was Emma's drink of choice, and Cokes for the boys. They finished off the evening with gelato at an ice cream parlor next door. She and the boys had been celebrating the same way for years, and now Ren was in on it.

The restaurant was dimly lit. Emma suspected its ambiance hid years of grease-caked walls and grimy floors. She didn't want to think about it. It was an old place, decorated with nostalgic photographs from Italy and dripping candles planted in old wine bottles centered on red and white checkered tablecloths. It was charming, but she never wanted to see it in the daylight.

She leaned back for a moment and gazed at Billy and Bobby as the waiter brought the pizzas to the table. They were handsome young men. Their faces were changing, becoming more angular, masculine. She'd noticed the other day that each of them had blonde peach fuzz on their upper lip and chin. She'd have to speak to Ren about getting them some razors. She wasn't ready for this.

"So, congratulations, again, guys, on getting through basketball tryouts and doing your best. That's what really matters. We're proud of you." Emma lifted her wine glass.

They both picked up their mugs and clinked her glass half-heartedly.

"Yeah. Me too, guys," Ren said. "It's always good to try out. If you make it, good. If you don't, then you just try again. But it's always important to keep trying for what you want in life. No matter what." Ren tipped his glass against Emma's and then the boys' glasses.

"It's just that we don't know if we made it on the team yet or not," Bobby said.

"That's the whole point. It doesn't matter. What matters is that you tried your best." Ren grabbed their plates and handed slices across the table to everyone.

* * *

That night after the twins had gone to bed and Ren was watching *Seinfeld*,

Emma pulled out her notes and reviewed Angelina and Cecelia's statements. There was no doubt Angelina was nervous. Cecelia was pretending to be protective, but it was clear that she didn't want anyone to look too closely at the spa services or the girls who worked there.

She slid her notes back in her briefcase. She was worried about Stacey, too distracted about her to think about the spa or the massage girls. She'd call the jail anonymously tomorrow to see if Stacey'd been arrested. And before bed, just to be on the safe side, she'd call the local hospitals. She couldn't afford to ignore the possibility that Stacey might be injured. For that matter, there was also the chance that someone had assaulted her, or worse. Stacey should be street savvy by now, but she was young. She could easily be overpowered.

* * *

The homeless community of New Orleans, the band of homeless veterans, the mentally disabled, the angry kids, the otherwise disenfranchised was surprisingly structured. They had occasional meetings and a half-baked network, but it worked. Messages were passed by word of mouth, and they kept their collective ear to the ground.

Raymond Collier was their self-appointed leader. He had charisma and a talent for command and organization. He was tough, as evidenced by the scar that nearly circumscribed his neck, earned one night while he slept under the overpass on Rampart Street. His appeal and his authority were undeniable and were made even more remarkable by the fact that he hadn't had a bath or brushed his teeth in months. Emma had first met Raymond at a City Council meeting, protesting the arrests of the homeless in the French Quarter during conventions and high tourist seasons.

These days, Raymond slept under the I-10 overpass near Claiborne and could usually be found there early in the morning and during most evenings. Homeless for nearly fifteen years, he considered it his duty to represent the dispossessed. If the topic of homelessness was on a local governmental agenda, he was there, whether it was a city council meeting, a state legislative gathering, or a town hall get-together. Raymond was relentless and usually articulate. He'd been instrumental in increasing the intake of city shelters and had recently begun an unsuccessful bid for public showers in the city.

The next morning, Emma headed toward Raymond's spot under the overpass. The area was crowded with makeshift tents made of blankets, jackets, or sheets flapping in the breeze, as well as sturdy camping tents provided by one of the local charities. Campfires were prohibited, but Emma could see the remnants of several. Some people were trying to sleep on top of muddy bedrolls or worn quilts, but others were smoking, propped against whatever they could find. Some were milling about. Everyone who was awake stared at her as she walked past. She spied Raymond and waved. Raymond motioned her over to his red tent overflowing with canned goods and stacks of blankets. The floor of the tent was lined with newspaper.

"What's up? Is somethin' going on with the city? Was someone arrested or shot?" Raymond stood up, thrusting his hands out to his side with a stiff, jutting motion. His hair, which stood out on all ends, was matted. Dreadlocks had formed, and debris was embedded in several of his tangles. His eyes darted about as he spoke in staccato bursts. He swallowed hard.

Emma wished she'd thought to bring some water. Something to help him, calm him down a little. He was a Vietnam War veteran and had never recovered from the post-traumatic stress caused by fighting there. He couldn't conform to social norms upon his return and didn't like taking his meds from the VA. He couldn't hold down a job or even sleep in a house, but none of that prevented him from advocating for the homeless. He would know about Stacey if she visited any of the local camps. And Emma knew he'd keep an eye out for her once he knew she was missing.

"Everything's okay, Raymond. I just need to know if you've seen a young girl, about nineteen years of age, who goes by the name of Stacey. I have this one small photo of her." Emma pulled out a tiny two-inch-square photo she had of Stacey from the first time she had represented her, three years ago. "She's been missing since last night. She's run away before and was homeless for a while too. But that was three years ago. We haven't reported her to the police yet, but we're about to. She used to work at the Japaprajna Temple on Esplanade. I called last night to see if she'd been reported as injured at any of the local hospitals, and she hadn't. She also hasn't been arrested."

"Why are you trying to find her? What'd she do?" Raymond extended a leathery hand toward a pile of clothes next to his tent that he seemed to be using as a makeshift chair.

Emma shook her head, refusing the seat. "She's just missing. At least I hope nothing's happened to her."

She told Raymond how Stacey managed to slip away. Emma put her hand up over her forehead to shade her eyes and looked out over the group of folks under the underpass. There had to be at least two hundred people there. And that was only one area in the city where the homeless gathered. There were thousands of homeless in New Orleans. It was going to be tough to find Stacey.

"Yeah. Okay." Raymond looked down at his feet. "Well, I'll do what I can to help you. But I don't want no troublemaker here in our place. That's how I got this scar." He pointed to his neck.

"I know, Raymond. She's not like that."

"Yeah. Famous last words. If she ran away, you gotta ask why. Makes you wonder, doesn't it? What are you going to do if you find her?"

"I've found a shelter for her, like I said. I'll move her there so she'll be safe. Nothing complicated about any of that."

"Ever think that some people just don't want to be in a shelter, or a home, or apartment? I don't. I'd hate it."

"I guess we'll just have to find out if she's one of those people. Maybe you're right. But I'd still like your help in finding her. Can you help me?"

"Yeah," Raymond nodded. "We're having a meeting here later on today. I'll tell everybody then. We'll do what we can to keep an eye out for her."

Chapter Twelve

The French Quarter was home to Stacey. She could relax there. She loved the winding streets, the ancient buildings, the ironwork on the balconies, and the festival-like spirit of Jackson Square. Plus, it was easy to blend in. With at least as many tourists as native New Orleanians, no one stood out more than anyone else. The exceptions - the homeless, the street performers, and artists - were part of the scenery. They blended into the background in a multicolor splash.

She needed money and had been watching the tarot card readers in the square. They made thirty-five dollars a read, plus tips. She could do that. She'd been taught the Celtic spread years ago and still had her deck tucked away with the rest of her stuff. It had taken her a few days to get squared away. Yesterday, she'd found a discarded chair on the street in one of the residential areas of the Quarter. She knew someone who worked at a pizza place right off of Pirate's Alley, a small street next to St. Louis Cathedral. She'd asked if she could stash the chair behind their dumpster, and he'd agreed to it. That was helpful since she could store her things close to the place where she'd be reading. Now she just needed a small table or a box and a second chair, and she'd be ready.

Even though the city required a license and permit for the artists who painted in Jackson Square, there were no such requirements for card readers. But, every once in a while, the Jackson Square artists proposed an ordinance to the City Council to remove the fortune-tellers. So far, they'd been unsuccessful, and recently the readers had come back in full force. They added an ambiance to the area, especially when they burned their incense.

She liked the way it smelled.

Stacey glanced at her reflection as she walked by a shop with a large plate glass window. She still wasn't accustomed to her new look. She'd used some of the money she'd saved to purchase hair color and had dyed her honey blonde hair a dark brown. She'd also cut it much shorter with a pair of cheap scissors in hopes of disguising her appearance. She'd done it herself, and not very well. She didn't like the jagged ends. But overall, it worked. She had to admit she looked like a different person and thought it was possible to sit in full view in the middle of Jackson Square, conduct tarot card readings, and not be recognized. At least not by the likes of police officers or others who might be looking for her.

She crammed her hand in her pocket, making sure that the wad of dollar bills she'd neatly folded and covered with several rubber bands was still there. One of the problems of not having a place with a door to lock was that you had to carry your valuables with you. She still had some of the money she'd saved from working at the Temple. She was frugal, eating only one meal a day, and that was a cheap one. But she'd been on her own for four days, and her money would run out soon. She hoped her plan to make more money in Jackson Square was a good one.

Stacey avoided shelters. Emma knew everyone in the city who ran them and would look for her at women's shelters before she'd look anywhere else. But Stacey had found the perfect place to stay about three miles away from the Quarter—a small chapel in the middle of a cemetery in the Bywater District. It was called St. Roch's and was named after the patron saint of dogs, invalids, and the falsely accused. The cemetery, the street, and the surrounding community were all named after the saint. Locals mispronounced the chapel's name, calling it St. Roach's. Even though the structure was crumbling, it still provided the shelter Stacey needed.

St. Roch's had been built in 1867 by a priest who had prayed to St. Roch during the yellow fever pandemic in New Orleans, asking the saint to spare his community. Ten years later, when no one from his parish had succumbed to yellow fever, he made good on his promise, built the shrine, and dedicated it to the saint. It was a small chapel comprised of only two tiny rooms. One room contained a statue of St. Roch and his loyal dog, and the other room was filled with human prostheses, braces, glass eyeballs, glasses, false teeth, and praying hands, rosaries, and religious figurines, all offered to St. Roch as thanks for healing. Bricks on the ground in that room were inscribed with the word *thanks* and littered with coins. Over the years, a dusty haze had settled over the various prostheses at the shrine. The walls were crumbling, and a statue of Mary had started to disintegrate. Most people considered the chapel creepy, so creepy, that they avoided it at night, although tourists occasionally visited during the day. Rumor had it that voodoo ceremonies were carried out in the cemetery after dark, although Stacey never saw anything like that. She slept in the tiny room with St. Roch and his dog.

It took between forty-five minutes and an hour to walk to the French Quarter from the chapel, depending on whether Stacey stopped for anything. She woke up early in the morning and left the chapel well before any tourists might arrive. She usually walked to Decatur Street, then down to the Riverwalk Mall, avoiding Esplanade Avenue entirely. She liked the restrooms at the mall. They were clean and usually unoccupied early in the morning. She washed up and brushed her teeth. Once, she'd even shampooed her hair. She carried her bag of dirty laundry with her and would occasionally rinse out her things in the sink. What little makeup and toiletries she needed were easily picked up from department store samples. She walked back to the chapel before dark. At night, the same laundry bag served as her pillow.

By Friday, Stacey had found the second chair, a wooden box tall enough to use as a table, and an interesting scarf someone had stuffed in a Goodwill box along the side of the road. She'd decided to throw it over the makeshift table to give her fortune-telling booth some panache. She was ready for business.

On Saturday morning, Stacey walked to the Quarter, freshened up, grabbed her table and chairs from behind the dumpster at the pizza place, and set up her tarot stand, all before ten o'clock. She was pleased with the location. Only five feet from the steps of the St. Louis Cathedral, it was a prime spot. Tourists swarmed to the cathedral at all hours of the day and were already beginning to mill about. Within fifteen minutes, a middle-aged woman wearing a baseball hat, a neon green bandana, and pink tennis shoes, approached Stacey.

"How much do you charge?"

Stacey stood, her hands behind her back, and smiled. "Thirty-five dollars."

"How long's the reading?"

"It's for fifteen minutes."

"Okay." She looked around the square. "Looks like that's the going rate. But you need a sign. Let's go."

She sat down across from Stacey, perched on the tiny seat, and waited for Stacey to shuffle the deck.

Stacey mixed the cards a couple of times, then set the stack in front of the woman.

"Cut the cards into three smaller decks." She'd noticed a man staring at them from a distance. He was too far away to see clearly. Perhaps he was staring at someone else.

The woman cut the cards.

"Now pick one of the three decks."

The woman chose one.

Stacey fanned the cards from the chosen deck out in front of the woman and removed the other cards. She thought the man looked familiar. He started to walk toward them. As he approached, she could tell who he was. Raphael. He stopped on the stairs of the cathedral to watch.

"Choose fourteen cards." Stacey glanced up at Raphael. He hadn't budged.

The woman carefully chose fourteen cards and handed them to Stacey, who began laying them out in the traditional Celtic cross. The woman had chosen the King of Pentacles as card one, crossed by the Tower. The King of Pentacles, which represented business acumen, was in the position of present influence. And the Tower, which was a card of catastrophic or shocking change, and chaos, crossed the King, indicating the nature of his obstacles. The third card, placed under the cross, was the Death card. Death also represented change, and even occasionally, but rarely, death. Stacey froze. Had the cards picked up on what had happened to James instead of the woman's situation?

Stacey sensed movement and glanced up. She flinched when she saw Raphael walking toward their table. Raphael stopped about a foot away from where she was reading, stopped, then crossed his arms.

"This is a private reading." Stacey stopped laying out cards. Her heart was pounding.

"Interesting that you got the death card, don't you think?"

"Sir, please leave. This isn't any of your concern." She didn't want him drawing attention to her. She just wanted him to go away.

"I'll leave. Sorry I interrupted." He nodded toward Stacey's client. "Thousand pardons, ma'am."

"If you haven't cut into my fifteen minutes, I'm fine."

"Of course not." Stacey smiled at the woman. "You'll get your full reading." She stood and turned toward Raphael. "We have nothing further to discuss."

Raphael shrugged. "I've been worried about you, and so are a couple of other people. And just in case you thought that new hair color was a disguise, let me just tell you it isn't. If I know who you are, so will others. They'd be very interested in knowing where you are now and what you're doing." He nodded toward the cards in her hand. "Good luck with that."

"You need to leave immediately."

Raphael started backing away. "I'll be back." He put his hand to his forehead in a farewell salute. "You can count on that."

Stacey didn't know if Raphael was threatening or warning her. But she knew she didn't want him to come back to the Quarter to see her anytime soon.

Stacey glanced back at her client. "I'm so sorry for the interruption. Where were we?" She sat back down. "Oh yes." She examined the cards. "Has a man in your life undergone a significant change, the end of a relationship, or even a death?"

"No, not that I know of."

"Alright, well, let's proceed." Stacey watched as Raphael retreated across the square and took a right at Pirate's Alley.

She continued to lay out cards for the woman.

The fourth card, the card of past events, was the seven of swords, the card of deception. As far as she was concerned, that card certainly applied to James. He'd deceived her from the very beginning. She'd fallen for his tricks. She couldn't see through his deception at first, but she caught on, finally. The fifth card, the card of the present, was the Chariot, the card of courage and movement. She smiled. She was hoping to do something about the mess she'd gotten herself in. At least she wasn't sitting in jail like a scared rabbit. For the final card in the cross, the card of the near future, the woman had drawn Justice. She held the final card in her hand for a couple of seconds before laying it down in front of the woman. Even though she hadn't drawn the cards, Stacey still believed they were telling her story, not the woman's. Justice, the card of fair decisions, gave her comfort.

"The final outcome, Justice, relates to karmic justice. It refers to legal matters as well, but generally, it's telling you that all actions have consequences. Have your own actions contributed in any way to any of the circumstances you find yourself in today?"

The woman nodded. "I can see that they have. I'm not sure that a man in my life has met any sort of catastrophic end, though. Maybe something's coming up. I hope not." She shook her head, reached into her pocket, and handed Stacey three tens and a five. "That was fun. I love getting tarot readings."

Stacey watched the woman walk off and thought about the consequences of her recent actions. She'd been trying to avoid that for months. It was so easy to blame others. It was also easy to turn a blind eye to what was going on in front of you. She was young, but she wasn't stupid.

That day she had four other readings, making a total of $175.00. She was stunned. She'd made money at the temple, but they held on to it for her rent and food. So, she'd never had much cash, even though the temple made seventy-five dollars per massage. She packed up for the night, brought her table and chairs back to the pizza restaurant, stashed them behind the dumpster again, and tipped the manager. She was glad she knew the guy. That was the thing about New Orleans. If you knew how to get around, you could make things work for you, even though it could be a dangerous place.

She was starved and decided to treat herself to a shrimp po' boy from Felix's on Bourbon. She hadn't had one in forever, and she felt like celebrating. And now that she had enough cash to last a few days, she could afford it. Plus, she wanted to walk by ETC to talk to the girl who was working in the back of the shop. She didn't know who it was, and she didn't care. But she hoped she could work out a deal with her. Pay her a little cash and get her to leave the back door open so she could start sleeping there at night instead of St. Roch's. The chapel floor wasn't comfortable, and the cemetery wasn't safe at night. An option would be nice. It was worth a try.

Chapter Thirteen

Emma lingered in bed. It was almost nine on a Saturday morning, but she didn't want to face the day. The twins were still asleep too. They'd never get up if she'd allow it, even though they had things scheduled all day long. Weekends were so busy. Both of the boys had basketball practice at three-thirty, and then she had to run Bobby down to the natatorium for swimming at six. Somehow, she had to manage to get Bobby fed in between.

A jangle of keys and the creaking front door let her know that Ren was home and was trying to be quiet. She turned over and pulled the covers over her head. Ren's boots fell to the floor in the living room with two muffled clumps. Then Emma heard soft padded steps down the hallway to their bedroom.

The bed sagged as Ren sat down next to her. She could smell the aroma of coffee and fresh pastries wafting through the air, even through the covers. He pulled the blanket down enough to kiss the top of her head. She peeked one eye out.

"Do I have to get up?"

"No, not right now." He kissed her again.

"Oh, take off those pants and get in here."

He slipped his pants off, nearly tripping in his haste, hopped in bed, and scooted under the covers. He snuggled close and gave her a kiss. "Now, this is what it's all about. I thought you'd be happy about the coffee and sweet rolls, but not this happy." He snuggled even closer.

Emma smiled. "Let's just say the day is getting better." She wrapped her arms around his neck and kissed him, then stopped.

"Wait a minute. Why are you only now coming home?" She sat up. "I expected you home last night around midnight. Then I fell asleep. What happened?"

"Right." Ren sat up and fluffed the pillows behind her back, then his. "I thought I'd get back then too. I was called in about nine on that homicide down by the river, the one I told you about. And we wrapped it up in about three hours, as usual. But when I was about to finish up my paperwork, something else came in. I was the only detective in the office, so Chief Simpson asked me to run down to the Quarter to check it out. This one took us by surprise, so I did some research on it. I thought you might be interested in what was going on."

"Something about Stacey? She's been gone since October twenty-first. Five days. I'm really worried about her."

"No. No Stacey sightings yet. A girl was found behind a restaurant in the French Quarter. Looks like an overdose; her lips had a slight blue tint. There was an injection mark at the side of her neck, which means this whole thing, her appearance, and the method that was used looked a lot like Crosby's murder. Of course, no tests are in yet on the girl. I looked up the preliminary report on Crosby, but the full autopsy report still isn't in yet. I'm guessing it'll be another week before it's ready."

Emma nodded. "Yeah, I knew the report wasn't ready." She wrapped her arms around her knees. "Do you have a name or any other information on the girl?"

"We know her name was Angelina. The last name was Diaz, I think. She worked at that smoking store you were telling me about, ETC. The one that sells drug paraphernalia."

Emma inhaled sharply. "Oh my God! I interviewed her the other day! She's one of the masseuses at the temple on Esplanade. She's so young! I can't believe she's dead." She shook her head. "Where did they find her? Which restaurant?"

"A pizza shop off of Pirate's Alley. There were some signs of a struggle. Some mild bruising. But they don't think she was killed there. They think she was dumped." He paused. "Sorry to spring this on you." He reached out and pulled her close to him.

Emma leaned on Ren's shoulder. "It's okay. I need to know, and I'm glad you told me." She sat back up. "Who told you Angelina's name?"

"Someone who worked at the pizza place. Maybe the manager. Yeah, I think it was the manager."

"Did you get that person's name?"

"Yeah. I think it was Lenny."

"Okay. I need to get by the temple and speak to a few people. But I can't today. Too much to do with the kids."

"I can take the boys wherever they need to go."

"Would you? Maybe you should get a nap first. I don't have to go right away."

"Go ahead and go." He squeezed her hand. "And I don't mind. I know you need to figure out what's going on in your case. Maybe tonight we can celebrate that the boys made the team. Pizza again, unless you've got a better idea?"

"No. Pizza's always the best idea."

"Okay. What time's practice? I'll set my alarm and then get up and take them around wherever they need to go. See you later on tonight with the boys. Let's surprise them."

"Thanks, babe. Practice is at three-thirty." Emma edged closer and kissed his mouth. "I don't deserve you."

Emma watched Ren set his alarm. She'd come to rely on him. Even the twins had come to depend on him as much as she did. Six years ago, when she met him, she would never have guessed they would have been together so long, or that they would have become so important to each other. She was lucky, and she knew it. But sometimes, she was afraid it would all fall apart, and her hopes for a happy life would be dashed. She found it difficult to believe in good things. And she couldn't seem to come up with a wedding date. She knew it was because her first marriage had been so awful, which was unfair to Ren. He was patient with her, and she was thankful for that. But his tolerance couldn't last forever.

90

CHAPTER THIRTEEN

* * *

Emma checked the street for a parking space, surprised to see the street lined with cars. She had no idea the temple would be so busy on a Saturday. She parked a few blocks down the street, then walked back, and entered the building with a group of people. She followed them into the left parlor.

The room was jammed with followers seated on their knees or crossed-legged on the large Oriental rug that covered the floor. All were in various poses of prayer, chanting, their thumb and index fingers touching. A few older people had tiny cushions that they sat on. Emma tried to get a count of the numbers, but gave up after failing to get an estimate for the number of people in any given row. There had to be more than fifty people crowded into the space. Cecelia was at the front of the room, behind the altar, dressed in magenta silk robes, lighting incense.

Cecelia stepped in front of the altar and began leading the group in a chant. The room was filled with deep, rhythmic sounds. Several minutes later, a young woman dressed in a simple robe interrupted the chanting for a moment by striking a wooden mallet against a gong. Cecelia stepped down from the altar and eased out of the room. The chanting continued as the girl began leading people out of the room, one by one, in ten-minute intervals.

After the first of the followers began leaving the room, Emma ducked into the hallway, and watched as people were taken across the hall to the right parlor, the room where James had held individualized 'spiritual enlightenment' sessions. She tried to peek into the room as they entered, but her view was obstructed by followers who were beginning to form a line.

Cecelia was new to this. She must be taking too long in her sessions, which caused the backup.

Emma walked down the hallway where a young girl stood monitoring the stairway and the entrance to the spa. She was tall, blonde, and fine boned, with porcelain skin. Her features were perfect, her eyes, icy blue, her cheeks, rosy pink. She looked like a towering, animated china doll.

"Hi. Would you mind telling me the time the service in the front parlor will be over?"

"The chanting might go on all day. But Cecelia said she'd do the guidance sessions for two hours. That's what James usually did too." The girl shifted her feet and glanced down the hallway, toward the parlor where Cecelia was conducting sessions. People continued to gather behind the door, waiting to get in.

"Oh. I see. This must be a difficult time for everyone. Is this the first time Cecelia has done a guidance session since James' death?"

The girl nodded.

"Is she the new head of the church?"

"She's the new head of the temple." The girl looked down at her feet.

The people lining up in the hallway were quiet since they were still in a meditative state, but the chanting in the other room echoed down the hallway. Emma had to raise her voice to be heard above the clamor.

"I didn't even introduce myself. I'm so sorry! I'm Emma Thornton, Stacey Roberts' attorney."

The girl nodded again and put her hands in the pockets of her jumpsuit, keeping eye contact at a minimum.

Emma wondered whether the young women who worked at the temple had been trained not to make eye contact. Or were they frightened by their circumstances? "Do you know Stacey?"

The girl nodded.

"Do you remember the last time you saw her?"

"Not since she was arrested."

"You didn't see her a few days ago when she came by to pick up her things?"

The girl shook her head. "I don't know anything about that."

"What's your name?"

"Natalia."

"Where are you from, Natalia?"

The girl shuffled her feet and looked behind her toward the spa entrance, her face flushed. "I grew up in Moscow."

"What's your last name?"

"Andreev"

"Did you know Angelina Diaz?"

She nodded.

"Did you ever work with Angelina down at the ETC shop?"

She nodded. "Well, not with her. But we both worked there."

"What do you and the other girls do there? It's such a small place. Do you help with inventory or sales?"

Natalia raised her eyebrows. "No, not inventory. We..."

The door to the right side parlor opened, and Cecelia walked into the hallway.

"Emma, I thought I heard you!" She walked up and shook Emma's hand warmly. "What brings you to our temple today?"

Emma squinted at Cecelia. "You're looking well today. But I'm afraid I have some bad news to share. It's about Angelina."

"What kind of news? I was told she hadn't shown up for work this morning. I was worried about her."

"That's right. I'm so sorry, but last night she was found behind a shop in the French Quarter. She was dead. Right now, it looks like an overdose by injection, like James."

Cecelia's knees buckled, and she collapsed on the stairs. "I can't believe it. I can't believe she's dead, too! Why poor Angelina? How awful!"

"It seems strange that she was killed in the exact manner as James. Do you know of any connection between Angelina and James? Why someone would want them both dead?"

"No. Nothing. I couldn't imagine who would want to harm James, but Angelina. She was so young and innocent. Who would want to kill someone like that?"

Emma looked at both women. Cecelia, sitting on the stairs, clutching her robes in distress. And Natalia, who stood behind Cecelia, pressing her lips together.

What was it that she wanted to say?

* * *

Emma pulled into a multi-storied garage off of Bourbon Street, close to the smoke shop. She didn't like to leave her car on the street in that part of town. Over-indulgence was a competitive sport in the French Quarter, and Bourbon Street was a street carnival of adult temptations, open twenty-four hours a day. She grabbed a ticket from the attendant and walked out of the garage into the daylight.

The shops and clubs along the block were a mixture of New Orleans-themed gift stores, shops with garish sex toys, nightclubs with gifted musicians, and various themed strip clubs, some posh, some seedy, all sordid. Bars were open, one selling a high alcohol content, fruit-punch-colored drink in a tall hurricane glass that was known to make you sick, especially on a warm day. Most clubs were open, even in the middle of the day, although the nightclubs came to life later in the evening. She recalled passing pictures of naked ladies on Bourbon Street as a young girl when she and her family were on vacation in New Orleans, and how her mother kept her eyes straight ahead, not looking at the posters. Her mother's message had been clear. These things existed, and they were to be ignored. But it was hard to ignore the shops with pulsating dildos in the front window.

Although called a smoking shop by the folks at the temple, ETC was a head shop, and the only one on that section of Bourbon Street. Its sign was peeling behind the neon lights, and the paint on the storefront was chipped and had oxidized. It, like everything else James had been in charge of, was in need of attention. Emma pushed on the faded front door.

"Good morning. Can I help you?"

A heavily tattooed young woman with long jet-black hair greeted Emma. Her cool blue eyes were surrounded by a heavy, coal-black outline, giving her an exotic, Cleopatra-like appearance. When Emma walked in, the girl was cleaning the case at the front of the store which held glass pipes, roach clips, and rolling papers. The dark wood-paneled walls were lined with shelves holding hookahs and bongs. The room was tiny, about the size of a small bedroom. Fluorescent lights hung overhead. Emma noticed the floors had been covered with linoleum that had worn through in several places.

Emma introduced herself. "I represent Stacey Roberts and was wondering whether you've seen her recently."

"I'm Moonstone Carville." She extended her hand. "You've lost your client? That's not good." She smiled. "I know who Stacey is, but I haven't seen her lately."

"I agree. That isn't very good, is it? If you have a minute, I'd like to ask you a few questions."

"Sure."

"What are your duties here at the shop?"

"I just work the front. Ring up sales. Keep the counter and the shelves clean. It's not too complicated."

"What about the other girls? The girls who come over from the temple? What do they do here?"

"They do some work in the back. I'm pretty sure it's inventory. But I never see them. I'm just guessing about what they do." She put the glass cleaner behind the counter and threw away the paper towel.

"Before we get into that in any more detail, I also wanted to ask you about your visit with the police after James' death. I was told they came to see you, and you found the visit upsetting. Would you mind telling me why?"

Moonstone clenched her hands. "They asked me to verify that Mira was here the afternoon of the murder. And that was easy. She was. She always comes in a little before five and checks the cash register, takes out most of the big bills, leaves me enough fives and tens to make change for the remainder of the evening.

"But they also had a few questions about the murder. It was upsetting to me. I didn't want to talk about it at all. I mean, I wasn't anywhere around the place when James was killed. But when they searched his office, they found a letter I'd written to him some time ago.

"I'd gone to one of his sessions. He often asked people who attended his sessions to prepare a confession, to write down something they'd done in their life they knew was wrong. He said if you wrote it down and gave it to him the thing would be cleansed or erased from your soul. So I told him about something I'd done that I wasn't very proud of and I gave it to him. He had the paper on his desk. The police found it and wanted to ask me about it. That's all."

"Would you feel comfortable telling me what you confessed to?"

"No." She shook her head. "I wouldn't."

"Did James ever try to use that knowledge against you?"

"Funny you should ask that. But yeah. He did once. He tried to use it to have sex with me. It didn't work, because even though he was a creep, I knew he was an addict and a coward. Whatever he had against me, I had even more against him. But I avoided him after that. It was easy enough. He never came down here. I was one of the lucky ones. Others weren't so lucky. I have my own apartment. I never lived at the temple like the other girls. I like Mira and like working for her. But I could move on if I needed to."

"Do you get an actual salary?"

She nodded. "I do. And that's different too. They pay me an hourly wage. This place is a legitimate business." She made air quotes with her fingers.

"Have you ever known Stacey to take drugs, specifically ketamine?"

"No, but that doesn't mean she doesn't."

"Do you know if Stacey ever worked in the back of the shop?"

"No. I don't think she ever did. I'm pretty sure Stacey was either doing massages at the spa, or when they had an opening in the spa, and that happened a lot, she was down in the Quarter, usually around the Jackson Square area, trying to find more girls to work back there."

"She seems to have been treated differently than the other girls who worked at the spa. Do you know why?"

Moonstone shook her head. "I wouldn't know, but I agree with you. From what I can tell, she had a different job description. Maybe that's all there was to it."

Emma nodded. "Maybe. Have you ever seen drugs being taken or used by anyone else at the temple?"

"I'd rather not say."

Emma sighed. Who was Moonstone protecting?

"Stacey's been charged with murder and with the possession and distribution of ketamine, but she's never been involved in drugs, and she certainly didn't kill James. Anything that goes on at the temple that's drug-related might be connected to her case. If you know something that might help us, I hope you'll let us know what it is." Emma pressed her card into Moonstone's hand.

Moonstone slipped the card into the pocket of her jeans.

"You said you never saw any of the girls who worked in the back. Does that mean there's a separate entrance?"

"Yeah. There's a back door. There's a key, but I never use it. Mira is always here before I am in the morning. She opens the shop, unlocks the front door, and fills the cash register. She leaves once I get here, but she'll come in and out throughout the day. I always enter through the front door to start my work day. I have a key to the front if I need to close for lunch."

"So you work open to close every day. What if you're sick and need to take off? What about vacations?"

"Mira and I coordinate that. She'll come in for me when I'm sick or on vacation. We've never had a problem."

"There's a door in the back of this room, just there." Emma nodded toward the back wall. "Does that lead to the back room?"

"It opens into a short hallway where the bathroom and storage rooms are, and at the end of the hallway is another door. I've always thought that must lead to the backroom, but it's locked, and I don't have a key to that door." Moonstone opened the cash register, took out the twenties, counted them, and returned them to the same space.

"Have you ever seen anyone unlock it for any reason?"

Moonstone shook her head. "No, I haven't, not from either side."

"How do the girls who work in the back get in?"

"They must have their own key."

"Have you ever walked around to the back so that you could see them working in the back room?"

"No, I've never done that. I can't leave except for lunch, and they're not back there then. I usually hear them in the evening, around five."

"Is that once a week, or more often than that?"

"I hear them pretty often. More than once a week anyway."

"So, not on Mondays only?"

"No, I think I hear people on other days too. But I don't keep a diary." She smiled. "I'm not being a smartass here, but I can't tell you any specific day other than Monday. I don't really pay that much attention to it."

"I understand. I know my questions must seem picky. How late is the shop open?"

"We usually close around nine or ten, depending on business. If the place is busy, especially on weekends, we'll stay open later."

"Do you recall if you hear people in the back at closing time?"

She nodded. "Mira closes up so she can deposit the money the next morning. We're always talking, and she's usually counting money, so I don't pay that much attention. But, yeah. I'm sure I've heard people back there at closing time."

Emma waved goodbye to Moonstone as she closed the door. She shook her head as she walked down the street to the garage. It was obvious Mira and James were trying to keep what was going on in the back of the shop a secret from everyone. Emma thought it was pretty safe to bet that whatever they were doing was illegal. And since she already suspected James of drug use, and pushing drugs on others she had to think that's what it was. There must be a drug operation going on in the back of the ETC shop. Stacey wasn't the drug dealer as the police suspected. James was.

Chapter Fourteen

Stacey turned the corner at Royal, crossed Canal, and headed toward the Garden District. She remembered Emma lived somewhere off St. Charles, above a shop. She thought she'd recognize it when she saw it. She'd seen the place a few years ago.

She'd been moving at a pretty fast clip for about thirty minutes. Her breath was jagged, shallow, coming in short bursts. She slowed to a walk, but her breathing was still uneven. She tried slowing down, holding her breath for five seconds before letting the air out of her lungs, but nothing worked. She was beginning to see spots of light in her field of vision. She came to the end of the block, sat down on the curb, and put her head on her knees.

"Do you need help?" A shopkeeper stepped out of her door.

Stacey shook her head and stood up. She realized she had panicked. But she was okay. She wiped the perspiration from her forehead with her shirt sleeve, hoisted the bag containing her clothes and toiletries onto her shoulder, and continued her walk down Magazine Street. She felt lucky to have gotten away last night. Her decision to play detective hadn't worked out so well.

New Orleans was a walkable city. Anyone in average shape could walk the distance between Bourbon Street and the Garden District in an hour. Stacey took a deep breath. Emma lived further uptown, by several blocks. It wasn't that far away.

* * *

Emma pulled into the parking space to the side of her apartment building and turned off her car. She sat for a moment, collecting her thoughts. It had been a long, complex day, especially for a Saturday, but she hadn't accomplished anything in Stacey's case. Talking to Moonstone and Natalia hadn't really gotten her anywhere. Plus, Stacey was still missing, and she had no idea where to look for her. It was all so frustrating.

She slipped out of the car and made her way to her apartment. Ren and the boys should be home in about an hour or so. She looked forward to seeing them, and to their pizza surprise tonight.

She rounded the corner and approached the steps to her three-story building. A young dark-haired girl, who'd been sitting on the stoop, rose and waved.

"I'm sorry to come to your house like this, but I thought it was important. I need to talk."

Emma squinted in the sun. She didn't recognize the girl at first. Then her breath caught. "Stacey? Is that you?" She felt a flood of relief, rushed over to Stacey, and gave her a hug.

"Yeah. I changed my hair." She touched the top of her head and smiled.

"You sure did! My goodness! You've given us a fright! Where have you been?" She nodded toward the door. "Let's go on up." Emma gave Stacey another hug then unlocked the ground-level door. "You have no idea how happy I am to see you!" They walked up the first flight of stairs to the apartment. Maddie and Lulu greeted them, prancing, with wagging tails.

"We've been looking all over for you! Would you like something to eat or drink?"

"Water would be great."

Emma got a closer look at Stacey, then put her purse down and walked to the kitchen. Stacey's face was flushed. Droplets of perspiration lined her hairline. "You don't look so great. Have a seat on the couch and tell me what's going on. Don't leave out anything. Start with why the heck did you run away?"

"I'll get there, but, I'm here because, um…" She hesitated. "I think I saw Angelina Diaz, one of the girls from the temple, get killed last night. If she's not dead, she was hurt very badly." She put her bag down and fell onto the couch. She put her hands over her face and leaned over. Her elbows were on her knees. Her hands were trembling.

Emma grabbed a water glass and walked back out to the living room, stunned that Stacey had witnessed the murder. And, since Angelina was killed in the same way as James, this could be a problem since Stacey might now be a suspect in Angelina's homicide too. Emma needed to get as much detail from Stacey as possible about last night.

"Oh no! I can't imagine seeing something like that. Are you okay?" Emma sat on the couch next to Stacey and handed her a glass of water.

Stacey took a sip and shook her head. "It was terrible. I keep seeing it over and over again in my mind. And I'm scared." She grabbed her arms and bowed her head.

"I'm here for you, and I want to help you, but you've got to tell me what happened." Emma squeezed Stacey's hand. "Someone told me about her murder this morning. Can you tell me why you were there? How you happened to see this?"

"I saw Raphael earlier in the day yesterday. He said something about people being on the lookout for me. I've been staying at a chapel in a cemetery in the Bywater district, but it's pretty exposed. I get wet when it rains, and anyone could see me there. So I thought I'd scope out some other places, like the back of the smoke shop. I thought if I got there late at night and left very early in the morning, no one would know I'd been there. I knew that girls worked back there, but they didn't stay all night. I just wanted to check it out, and"—she hesitated, picking at her thumbnail—"I wondered if I could figure out a way to stay there. Maybe even talk to one of the girls. Pay them a little something and get them to let me in, maybe leave me a key. Use it as a place to sleep."

Emma shook her head. "That wouldn't have been the best plan, Stacey. And it looks like you were at the wrong place at the wrong time." Emma was concerned about Stacey. How was she coming up with some of her ideas? She was impulsive, but more than that, her decisions seemed to be those of a much younger adolescent.

"Yeah." She nodded and looked up at Emma. "When the killer left, he pointed at me as he drove away."

"Oh my God! That seems like a threat, and it's something to take seriously. But let's stop here." Emma paused. "You said 'he pointed.' Do you know it was a man? Did you see his face?"

"I'm guessing it was a man. The car was dark inside, and it looked like he or maybe she was wearing a hoodie. The hands were kind of small, but not real small."

"Okay. Can you tell me what happened? Step by step."

Stacey took a deep breath. "After I finished up at Jackson Square for the day, I walked down to Bourbon Street to get a po' boy. That's also where the head shop is located. When I got there, I didn't want to see Moonstone or Mira, so I sneaked down the side alley to the back of the place."

"Did you knock on the door?"

"I was going to watch for a while, and if someone I knew was working back there, I was going to knock. If I didn't know the person, I was just going to leave.

"When I walked down the alley, I could tell someone was in the room, because the lights were on. There were blinds in the windows, but they were cracked a little. I could see the glow from the window that faced the side alley."

Emma walked over to her desk and pulled out a piece of paper and a pen. "Can you sketch what you can recall about the back part of the building for me? That will help."

Stacey grabbed the paper and drew a map of the building, indicating where the shop and the room were, where the windows and the door were located, and included the surrounding side and back alleys.

"Even though the window had blinds, I could see what was going on inside when I got up close. But I was careful. When I looked into the first window, I saw Angelina. The room was small, but not as small as my bedroom at the temple. The place was empty, except for a large folding table, a folding chair, some pizza boxes, and some stuff that had to have been drugs. Angelina was lining up and counting plastic bags of stuff like white powder, pills, and little bottles of clear liquid. Then she wrote everything down in a notebook.

"When she finished, she put everything inside those pizza boxes, taped them down, and stacked them. Powder was in the large pizza boxes, pills were in the mediums, and the bottles of liquid were taped down in the smallest boxes."

Emma nodded. This only confirmed what she'd suspected all along. But she was worried. If Stacey left fingerprints on the outside window ledges or frames, Emma was afraid there was a possibility Stacey could be looking at another arrest warrant.

"What about the other shops in the area? Couldn't they have seen what was going on back there? Maybe someone even saw you?"

"I don't think so. There were no lights on in the back of any of the other shops. All the action was in the front of all those buildings along that block of Bourbon Street. "

"Could you tell what type of drugs were going inside the pizza boxes?" Emma scribbled into her notebook as Stacey spoke.

Stacey shook her head. "I don't know anything about them. Except the powder looked like the stuff James used in his sessions. That was the stuff I took that one time."

"We'll get back to that in a minute. Tell me what happened next."

"Then headlights flashed down the alleyway behind the shop. I sneaked down to the edge of the building and looked around the corner. A guy parked his truck and knocked on the door. I thought that maybe the man and the truck looked familiar, but I wasn't sure. The truck was a Toyota, I think, and it had a camper top. The driver was wearing jeans and a baseball cap. I couldn't get a clear look at his face. Angelina let him in."

"About how long had you been there by this time? Seems like you'd been standing outside for a long time."

"Not really. Angelina was almost done with everything when I got there. The guy pulled up just a few minutes after I showed up. I didn't want to knock on the door when I saw the drugs, and really didn't want to knock once he showed up.

"After Angelina let the man in, I tiptoed back around the corner and watched him gather up all the boxes and start loading them into his truck. There weren't that many, so I don't think that took longer than about ten minutes. Then he took off.

"Angelina turned around to lock the door, and another car came down the alley right away. It stopped at the back door. Angelina locked up and got in.

"Wait a minute. Let's stop here for a second. You said there were fluorescent lights. When the guy picked up the pizza boxes, wasn't he under those lights? Didn't you see his face, or at least part of his face?"

"I saw the side of his face, you know, the profile. I'm not so sure what color his hair was, because he had that baseball cap on, and I'm not so sure what color his eyes were, because he was so far away. But, I did see the side of his face. And I know about what size he is, and what color his skin is."

"What size man was he?"

"I say he was a little taller than me, and a little heavier. I'm five foot seven. So I'd say he's about five foot eight. He wasn't a very big man. "

"What about the color of his skin?"

"Pale skin. Very pale."

"Okay. What happened next?"

"After the other car stopped to pick up Angelina, it didn't immediately take off, like I thought it would. I couldn't see inside very well, so I couldn't tell what was going on, but the car started to shake a little. Then Angelina's back pressed against the passenger car window, like she was fighting against something. Then she disappeared for a few seconds. I thought she was probably pulled down. Then she popped back up. She was struggling in the front seat. I couldn't see what was going on clearly, but she had to be struggling with the driver. Then she collapsed. I rushed into the alleyway to help when the car took off. It spun off down the alley and turned on to Bourbon Street, almost hitting a couple of people walking by."

"What did this car look like?"

"It was big and black and sort of square. It had a hood ornament, and I think it only had two doors, but I'm not sure about that. It might have had little oval windows in the back, too."

"Did you see the driver?"

"No. It was too dark, and there were reflections on the glass windshield. But when they passed me, that's when the driver lifted a hand and pointed an index finger at me, like I was next." She put her head in her hands. "That's really what scares me." She mumbled into her hands. "I hid out in the Quarter for hours, and when the sun rose I started making my way here. It took me a while to figure out where you lived. I saw your place a few years ago. You pointed it out to me, remember?"

Emma nodded and put an arm around Stacey's shoulders. "I'd be scared too. I'm sorry you saw all of that. And I'm so glad you found your way here. But I don't understand why you were looking for another place to stay, and I don't understand why you ran away after I brought you to the temple. I found a very nice, safe shelter for you."

Stacey clasped her hands. "I wanted to get away from the people at the temple as fast as I could. Someone there set me up to take the blame for James's death. And after my mom bailed me out of jail, I knew she'd want to be involved in my trial and in my life again, too. It was great that she paid for my bail, but I don't want her to be involved in what I'm doing. It sounds ungrateful, but she takes over." Stacey squeezed her hands even tighter. "Everything has to be her way. It's best if she doesn't know where I live or what I'm doing. If the police knew how to find me, then my mom could always find me too. So that's why I left. I didn't want anyone to know where I was. And I wanted to be by myself. And I'm old enough to do that."

Emma reached out to Stacey. "You seemed frightened, and I'm sorry for that. I don't know what happened between you and your mom. Just know my invitation to you to talk about it is always open. I would never insist that you do anything you didn't want to do. But instead of running away again, I hope you'll tell me what you're thinking and let me help you instead. And we still need to find shelter for you."

Stacey nodded. "I know."

"Also, running away while your case is pending for trial is the last thing you'd want on your record. You already know you could have been put back in jail. But it's also irresponsible. It makes you look guilty. If you could explain to me what's gone on between you and your mother, or why you ran away when you were sixteen, I might be able to use that as a mitigating factor during the sentencing phase of your trial, if we get there. I hope we don't, but we need to prepare for it. I need to be able to show the court some of the hardship in your life. It looks like some of your decisions are governed by your desire to avoid your mom. And that doesn't always lead you down a good path. We can talk about that more when you're not so exhausted.

Emma paused, holding her gaze on Stacey. "I hate to say it, but right now, things aren't looking so good for you. Angelina was killed while you were out on bail. It was also during the time you'd run away and were unaccounted for. It looks like she was killed the same way James was. So, you could be a suspect in her murder, too. I'm certain that the police will want to know where you were when she was killed. Will you be able to prove that?"

Stacey shook her head. "I don't see how. I don't think anyone, except maybe the killer, saw me last night."

"Think about whether someone else, anyone, may have seen you then. And, just so you know, your mom is in town now. She came to New Orleans to look for you because she was worried. Do whatever you want to do about that. What's important is to make certain you're protected and are sleeping in a safe place. Your mom could help with that."

"I've got a place to sleep."

Emma sighed. "You've already admitted that it isn't safe and that it's out in the open somewhere. We need to find something else for you. Perhaps a women's shelter."

"I can't. I really can't do that."

"I'm not sure why. They're pretty nice places, and like I said, a lot of them are for long term stays. That could be ideal. An apartment would be nice, too, but unless your mother rents one for you, it's out of the question for a couple of reasons. I hate to say it, but most landlords wouldn't want to rent to someone who's going on trial for murder. And most leases require at least a six month term. Your trial is in less than four months."

Stacey screwed up her face.

"I'm sorry you don't like it Stacey, but you've been threatened, and shelter is important."

"I don't want my mom to do anything else. I already feel like I owe her since she posted bond. And I told you I might know someone who would be willing to help out."

"Okay. Does this person have an actual house or apartment? You need safety. And I need to be able to have regular access to you."

"I'll work on it and let you know."

"It could be too late to get you in a shelter tonight, but since I've already spoken to these ladies about you they may make an exception."

Stacey stared at Emma, saying nothing.

"You could stay with your mom or stay in a shelter tonight. Seems to me those are your only options."

Stacey patted the couch. "I'd be very happy if I could sleep right here."

Chapter Fifteen

The raucous tromping outside Emma's apartment door could only mean one thing. Ren, Billy, and Bobby were making their way up the stairs. Billy was complaining. Loudly.

"More stairs! All we did was climb bleachers at practice! What's the point in that?"

"I get it. But it will make you stronger, give you endurance." Ren chuckled. "Those are good things, but I remember feeling the same way you do when I was your age."

They stopped in front of the door. Keys jangled, then the lock clicked. Emma walked to the kitchen and poured herself a glass of wine, fortification to explain Stacey's presence. She'd been dreading Ren's arrival. And what about their plans to take the boys out to celebrate?

"We're home!" Ren closed the door behind the boys.

Stacey rose from her seat on the couch.

"Well, hello," Ren said as he walked toward Stacey to shake her hand.

Emma stepped out of the kitchen into the living room, a firm grasp on her glass. "Ren, this is Stacey Roberts. And Stacey, this is Ren Taylor, my fiancé. He's a detective with the New Orleans Police Department."

Stacey flushed as she took Ren's hand. "Nice to meet you." She nervously brushed some hair out of her face.

Billy and Bobby moved toward Stacey like they were drawn by a magnet. She sat back down, patting Maddie and Lulu on their heads.

"Are you one of my mom's students?" Billy asked as he plopped down next to her.

Bobby sat down on the other side of Stacey and smiled. His cheeks flushed a bright crimson which stood out in stark contrast to his pale blonde hair, bleached out from year-round sports.

Ren took the boys' dewy-eyed attraction to Stacey as an opportunity to follow Emma into the kitchen.

"What were you thinking when you invited Stacey here? She'll be trouble, and you know it. Plus, we had a family celebration planned tonight."

"I didn't invite her. She just showed up. I need to run into the bedroom to call one of the women's shelters again to see if they'll take her tonight. If they can, I'll run her down there after dinner. We'll have to do our celebration tomorrow night. I know school's the next day, but we can make it an early night." She hesitated and glanced up at Ren. He was scowling. "I'm really sorry. And I appreciate your taking the boys around today." She walked over to Ren and wrapped her arms around his neck. It was like hugging a tree. She hated it when he was irritated with her.

Ren loosened his stance and put his arm around Emma's waist. "Just because you've got me wrapped around your little finger doesn't mean you're right. But, sure, we can do the celebration tomorrow. The boys don't know about it anyway." He stepped back. "But Stacey shouldn't be here. I know you try to help people out, but she seems like a loose cannon to me. And what if the shelter can't take her?"

"I think it'll be okay. I'm pretty sure they still have that opening."

"But you're still not sure what Stacey's going to do next. Admit it." He peered at Emma. "By the way, I got a call while I was at Bobby's swim meet. I sent a crew to search the back room of the ETC shop since that was Angelina's last known location before her murder. Guess what they found?"

"Drugs?"

"Yeah. How did you know?" He squinted at Emma. "Want to order pizzas in?"

"Nah. I'll cook something. We can go out tomorrow night. And I was just guessing about the drugs. Let me run down the hall and place that call to the shelter, then I'll start dinner."

Emma walked to her bedroom to call the women's shelter. She was relieved to learn that they still had a room available for Stacey. They typically took in mothers with children. The untaken room was tiny, too small for a family, but perfect for Stacey. She quickly reserved the space.

She walked back into the kitchen, pulled out some onions, and started chopping. She didn't know what she was going to cook, but she always started with onions.

Ren pulled out a beer from the refrigerator and opened it.

"I meant to tell you, they did a screening and presumptive test on some of the residue found in that back room of the ETC shop and found ketamine on the table and floor."

"They did a presumptive test because Angelina was killed with an overdose of ketamine?" Emma sniffed and blotted her eyes with a paper towel. Onions got to her every time.

"Yeah. We thought it might be there somewhere. Apparently, it was everywhere. We're going to get the narcotics unit to stake it out, watch the place. Did you ask Stacey if she knew anything about drug use at the temple?"

"She said she thought there might have been some, but she didn't give me that much information."

"You might want to ask her more about that. But I have to say, things aren't looking so good for Stacey right now. She's not officially a suspect yet, but I consider her a person of interest in Angelina Diaz's murder. She was out on bail at the time of the killing, and Angelina was killed the same way James was. And I know you didn't even know where she was last night. But at the same time, her travel has been restricted. I don't think she's much of a risk for travel to another jurisdiction at this point unless she runs away again." He frowned. "And that is a concern."

"I know things look bad. But I don't think she's going to take off again. I'll talk to her tonight, and we'll come down to the precinct in the next day or two. She has some information relevant to the Diaz case. She should make a formal statement, though. Chatting with you here wouldn't be appropriate."

Ren took the hint and walked back into the bedroom, not to be seen again until Emma came to get him for dinner.

* * *

Emma poured herself a glass of wine and watched her boys try to carry on a conversation with Stacey.

"Billy and Bobby, it's time to get on upstairs and get ready for bed. I've got to speak to Stacey about a few things."

She couldn't hear what they were saying, but the twins clearly had no intention of moving from the couch or Stacey. She didn't want to humiliate them, but enough was enough. She walked into the room and approached the trio.

"Boys, make sure you take a shower, and Bobby, you'll need to wash all of the chlorine out of your hair tonight before you go to bed, too."

"Mo-om." Bobby glared at Emma.

"Get on up the stairs, like I asked you to." The boys stood up and trudged up the winding metal staircase without glancing back, their cheeks flushed, this time from embarrassment. Emma knew they'd be angry with her for a while. But some things were necessary.

She glanced at Stacey. "Want to join me on the balcony?"

The sun was beginning to set, and the sounds of traffic below on St. Charles always lulled her into a quasi-meditative state. She loved this time of day.

"Are you feeling calmer now that you've been here a while?" Emma took a sip of wine from her glass and smiled at Stacey. She sat down in her favorite wicker chair.

"I'm feeling better, although I may never forget seeing Angelina being attacked and how that guy pointed at me from the car." She shuddered. "It was a scary night." Stacey sat down in the metal chair Ren usually sat in and scooted it toward the balcony so she could look over the side.

"This is the second time you referred to the driver as 'that guy.' I know you've said you weren't certain, but do you have a sense the killer was a male?"

Stacey shrugged. "Maybe. I still can't say for sure."

Emma watched Stacey for a few seconds. "Do you think your fear has interfered with your ability to recall what happened?" She took another sip from her wine glass.

Stacey shrugged. "It's possible, but I don't think so."

"Okay." Emma paused. "I need to talk to you about a couple of things." She turned toward Stacey. "They found a drug, ketamine, in the room where Angelina was working last night."

Stacey raised her eyebrows.

Emma watched Stacey's reaction to this information. "That's the same drug they found in your room. It's the drug that may have killed James, and now it looks like it was the drug that was being packaged behind the shop the night you were there."

Stacey nodded.

"Did you ever see the sale of drugs at the temple?"

She shook her head. "No. I never saw anything like that there, except for what I saw the night of Angelina's murder."

"Why didn't you work at the smoke shop like the other girls?"

"My main job was bringing in other girls, like me."

"What do you mean by that?"

"When you've been on the streets for a while, you can tell when someone else is a runaway, or homeless. There's a look. I'd talk to them about the Japaprajnas. About how they could live with us for free. It always sounded pretty good. Especially to the girls with no families, or the girls who were illegal immigrants. Girls like that."

"Vulnerable girls."

"Well, James didn't put it like that."

"But is that who you recruited?"

She nodded. "Yes."

"Do you know where they came from? You said some of them were runaways."

"I know a couple are in the country illegally. Natalia is for one. Her visitor's visa expired, I think. I think Mariana's parents were here illegally, but she's a citizen. I'm not sure about the others."

"On the night of Angelina's murder, do you remember whether you touched anything behind the shop, like a door frame, or a window ledge?"

"I could have. I wasn't thinking of protecting myself. I was just thinking of trying to save Angelina."

"Then there's a possibility you could have left fingerprints in the area. We may need to explain your presence at the scene. When we do that, you'll also need to describe what you saw last night." She glanced at Stacey. "You told me about Angelina's assault and that she put drugs in pizza boxes. Is there anything else about last night that you haven't told me?"

Stacey shook her head. "No, I told you about everything I saw."

"Do you remember what the pizza boxes in the back room of the shop looked like?"

"They were red and white. There wasn't a name on the box, but there was a design."

"Could you draw it?"

"There was a starburst on the right side of the box. I can show you." Stacey grabbed the paper and pencil Emma handed her and drew the design.

Emma nodded. It was a unique design. "Have you seen these boxes before last night?"

"Maybe. But I don't know where."

"You said you thought you knew of someplace you might be able to stay through your trial date other than your mother's hotel?"

She nodded. "There's a guy who used to come to the spa all the time. He said he had a carriage house, a place above his garage, that was empty. He said if any of the girls at the spa ever needed to get away, for any reason, the place was ours. I'm not sure why he was so generous."

"It's always good to question things that look too good to be true. There could be strings attached. Or worse."

"I think he's okay. He made a lot of money in his day and doesn't have anything else to do. I don't think he meant anything bad when he offered his place. He lives down by the race track. It's not that far from the temple. His name is Binh. I've heard his horse skills are magic. He can make a horse do anything. And I also heard he was a good guy."

"We need to be careful in choosing a place for you to stay for the next ninety days. Maybe we can go take a look at Binh's home tomorrow. I called the women's shelter, too. They confirmed that they do have a place for you tonight. I can drop you off there in the next hour, and then pick you up in the morning so we can speak to Binh."

"But I don't want to stay at a shelter."

"It would be much better for everyone if you stayed there tonight. Believe me, it's a nice place. It's a house, a lovely brick house with bedrooms, a kitchen, and a living room. You'd have a room all your own tonight, and you'd have nothing like that here. Plus, you'd be safe."

Stacey lowered her head. "Alright."

"I think you'll be glad you're there come morning, and you're not stuck on my stiff couch. We'll get an early start tomorrow, and if Binh's place works out for you, maybe you'll only have to stay at the shelter for one night.

* * *

When Emma walked back into the apartment after dropping Stacey off at the shelter, she was surprised to see that Ren was sitting up in bed, still awake.

"What are you doing up?"

"Sitting here, trying to think what I could do to talk some sense into you about that Stacey girl."

"I don't know what you're talking about." Emma put her purse down and began taking off her shoes and hanging up her clothes to get ready for bed. She was in no mood for a lecture, especially about Stacey.

"This is going to be one of those situations that blows up in your face. A girl from the temple was killed last night. I have a feeling this isn't going to end well."

"Sometimes you're Mr. Doom and Gloom, Ren. That's not always necessary, you know."

"I'm only trying to help."

Emma glanced at Ren and knew, instantly, his feelings were hurt. She walked over and sat down next to him. "I'm sorry. I know. We'll figure it out. At least I got her to a shelter tonight."

"That's just the point. Didn't you say her mother made bail? I think the mother should be finding her someplace to stay, too. Not you. Or she could stay with her mother, or somewhere, anywhere else. You're her attorney, not her mom. You don't have the responsibility of finding shelter for her."

"You have a point. I'm not making light of the situation. Stacey and I will find housing tomorrow. I'm not sure where yet, maybe with someone Stacey knows. Maybe she'll even like the shelter she's in tonight."

Ren held out his hand to Emma. "And I'm not trying to be a hardass. I'm just worried about you and the boys. And you can't spend days finding the right place. She needs shelter right now. She should stay with her mom. It makes the most sense."

Emma pulled back from Ren and looked at him. "There are some problems there, and I can't force her to accept help from her mom. Stacey is the client. Not the mom."

"Why do you care so much about that? I don't see that she has a choice. You don't need to jeopardize our family to suit her quirks. This could be a very dangerous situation for us. She could have murdered two people."

Emma sighed. "Okay. I really don't think so, but I understand where you're coming from. Hopefully, we'll find what we need tomorrow."

Ren seemed satisfied with Emma's proposed compromise, but she knew he was right. Even though she couldn't force Stacey to stay with her mother, Emma was afraid of the choices Stacey might make if she were by herself.

* * *

Before she went to sleep, Emma looked out of her bedroom window onto the side street to check for unfamiliar cars, as was her nightly habit. Most of the people who left their cars on that street at night lived in the area and parked there on a regular basis. She'd come to recognize their cars and knew when a new vehicle was parked in the area, especially after dark. She didn't notice anything out of the ordinary that night.

She heard a noise from the front of the apartment, possibly from somewhere on St. Charles Avenue. She walked to the front window, which she opened, and then stepped out onto the balcony. She looked down onto St. Charles and noticed, parked across the street, right in front of the Episcopal church, a black two-door Lincoln sedan covered with beads of water. It hadn't rained in days, so the car must have recently been run through a car wash. She hesitated. It fit the description of the car Stacey told her she saw the night Angelina was killed. But so would a thousand other cars in the city. Shrugging off her concerns, Emma closed the window and walked back to her bedroom, more than ready for a good night's sleep.

Chapter Sixteen

Emma had been awake for hours, and it was only eight in the morning. She planned on picking up Stacey around nine. Billy and Bobby had awakened even earlier, tiptoed down the stairs, and walked to the nearest coffee shop for breakfast. Ren joined them, and, a few minutes ago, had brought pastries and coffee back to the house for Emma.

She was shocked. She'd never known the boys to wake up so early on a Sunday morning and knew they thought Stacey was still at the apartment. They were in awe of the tall, pretty nineteen-year-old. Emma was glad she took Stacey to a shelter last night. Her household needed to return to normal.

She was showered, dressed, and out of the door to pick up Stacey within forty-five minutes. Fifteen minutes later, Emma was at the women's shelter, a lovely stucco bungalow surrounded by oaks and palm trees in the Fontainebleau district.

Emma walked to the front door, her heart pounding. She was so afraid Stacey wasn't going to be there. She knocked.

A matronly woman answered the door.

"Can I help you?"

"I'm here to pick up Stacey Roberts. We have a few things to do this morning. I'm her attorney, Emma Thornton."

"Hello, Ms. Thornton. We've been expecting you." She waved Emma in, and there, sitting in the living room, dressed in her finest, was Stacey.

"You have no idea how relieved I am to see you!" Emma said. "Okay. Let's get going."

Emma unlocked her car, and she and Stacey slid in.

"So, where are we headed today? Didn't you say Binh's place was close to the Fairgrounds?" Emma handed Stacey one of the coffees Ren had purchased.

Stacey nodded as she took a sip. "Yes. And his place is across the street from a small bayou. I believe City Park is on the other side of it. So, wherever that is."

"That sounds like Bayou St. John. Do you have an address or a street name at least?"

"No. I used to, but I lost it as well as his phone number. But I walked to Binh's house during Jazz Fest once. That was the only time I ever visited. It's close to that famous home. I think the name of the place is The Sanctuary."

"Oh. I know that place. Two-story Greek columns and a wrap-around porch, built in the eighteenth century."

Stacey nodded. "Sounds like it. But that also sounds like about a hundred other homes in the area." She laughed.

Emma smiled. "Do you think you'd recognize Binh's place if you saw it?"

"I think so."

"Okay. Get whatever else you need, and we'll get going."

* * *

Nestled snugly at the center of City Park, the New Orleans Art Museum, Bayou St. John, and the Fairgrounds, the Bayou St. John District was the most verdant, lush, and tranquil in the city, except during Jazz Fest. Then it was abuzz with so many tourists, parking was impossible, even for residents. Homes in that area were some of the oldest and most charming and included Eastlake-style shotgun doubles, side hall shotguns, raised center halls, and plantation-style mansions painted in various sherbet-colored peaches and teals, roses, and lavenders. Wisteria, hostas, boxwoods, and peonies graced front yards and courtyards alike, often billowing out from the iron fence work, unable to be contained.

Emma pulled over in front of a restaurant on Esplanade. The restaurant,

Café Boisseau, was closed. It was a quiet time of the morning, with little traffic. Huge oak trees shaded the area; their branches and leaves made a rustling sound overhead.

"I think The Sanctuary is up there, to the left, on Moss Street." Emma nodded in the direction of the bayou. "When we get there, keep an eye out for Binh's place." She paused. "Are you sure you'd feel safe staying with this Binh guy?"

Stacey nodded. "I took him up on his invitation and walked down there one day when I was feeling down. It was Jazz Fest, and the streets were so crowded I could hardly make my way through the streets.

"When I got there, we talked for a while. I told him I wanted to leave the temple. He told me I could stay at his carriage house rent-free until I got on my feet. Then he asked me if there was anything I needed to report to the police. And he offered to call them. But I didn't think there was a need to talk to the police at the time. That's probably why I trust him. He wasn't afraid to get the cops involved."

"Did you stay there?"

"No." She shook her head.

"Why not?"

Stacey shrugged. "I panicked. I couldn't do it. I guess I wasn't quite ready. I'd been at the temple since I was sixteen. I didn't know what I was going to do if I left. I didn't know the next step."

"You were afraid to start over?"

"I guess so. And maybe I was afraid of change. Afraid I couldn't get a job someplace else. Just afraid. Also, the temple had become home to me. It wasn't great, don't think it was. But I could walk into that room on the third floor and shut the door. No one bothered me there. I know James bothered other girls, and I had a problem with that. But he left me alone."

Emma nodded. "Can you tell me why you didn't ask Binh for a place to stay earlier instead of living on the streets this past week? Seems to me that would have been much safer for you. You wouldn't have witnessed Angelina's murder, and you wouldn't be a person of interest in another murder now, either."

119

Stacey picked at a ravel on her shirt. "I was afraid that he'd probably seen something about James' murder on television and that he knew I'd been arrested for it. I didn't think he'd want me staying there." She sighed. "And then, I'd already turned him down once. I thought maybe he wouldn't want to offer his place again."

"So you were embarrassed to ask?"

Stacey nodded.

"What changed your mind?"

"It helps that you're going with me and that you believe me. I'm not alone."

Emma started the car. Stacey looked out of the window as they took a left onto Binh's street. The narrow strip of Bayou St. John was to their right, sparkling in the sun.

"I'm glad you feel that way. When did you start to realize things weren't right at the temple?"

"Probably about the time I walked down to see Binh."

"I guess that was in April, at Jazz Fest? What made you do that? Did something happen?"

"Not really. Maybe it was that James started pushing me to get more and more girls in. And he wanted more from me, and other girls too. And when I backed off, he started using things I'd told him against me. But I still didn't really want to admit anything was wrong when I spoke to Binh, even though it clearly was." She hung her head.

"I see. Okay. Here's The Sanctuary." Emma stopped and pointed out the magnificent home to Stacey. "Can you find Binh's place from here?"

"Yeah. It's up a couple of houses. Right over there." Stacey pointed to a house that faced the water a few doors up. "That's it. I'm sure of it."

Emma drove to the front of the house and parked.

Binh's home was a white, turn-of-the-century raised center hall with stairs that led to a front door that had to have been at least twelve feet tall. It was elegant but warm and welcoming.

"I can see why you'd want to stay here. Want to go on up?"

"Sure." Stacey led the way.

* * *

The door was opened by an Asian man who was hardly larger than a ten-year-old, and a very thin one at that. Binh, who was 'magic with horses,' must have been a retired jockey. His stature had to have been a bonus in his world.

Binh was perfectly attired, his jeans and white shirt flawlessly tailored. He wore a pink plaid belt; his hair was impeccably groomed.

When Binh saw Stacey, his face lit up with one of the biggest smiles Emma had ever seen. Thousands of tiny wrinkles and crinkles surrounded his eyes and mouth. Emma knew why Stacey trusted him. He smiled from the inside out. It was like sunshine.

"Come in, come in! It's so good to see you again, Stacey!"

Emma was startled by the resonance of Binh's voice. His deep baritone and lack of accent reminded her of TV announcers and radio disc jockeys. She wondered if he'd ever done work in either field.

Binh motioned for Emma and Stacey to sit down in his living room. The bay window at the front of the house overlooked the bayou, framing a snapshot of the beauty of the shoreline and surrounding waters. Sunlight captured by the bayou sparkled and played on the ceiling of the living room like a living piece of art. A tufted jade green velvet couch fit perfectly into the bay window, and two identical turquoise club chairs faced each other on either side of the sofa. Binh was not afraid of color. Foo dogs guarded the entryway.

"Stacey has told me great things about you."

Binh smiled. "Stacey is a good girl. I offered my carriage house to her earlier. It's still available if she needs a place to stay. No cost to her. I have no need to make money from Stacey. And I don't want renters, but it would be helpful to have someone up in the place to keep the air conditioner and other utilities running so that it doesn't deteriorate. If she decides to stay, it would benefit both of us."

"Thanks, Binh." Stacey clenched her hands. "I might just take you up on that." She cleared her throat. "I don't know if you know it, but James was killed, and the police arrested me for his murder." She leaned back on the couch and began swinging her foot. Then she sat up and leaned forward. "They let me out on bail, and I do need a place to stay." She swallowed. "I could stay with my mom, because she came down here, but I don't want to. So, your offer is really appreciated, if you still want to board a person who's been charged with murder." She tried to smile, but failed.

"I heard about the murder. Did you kill James?" Binh asked.

"No, I didn't."

"I didn't think so. So you're okay by me. You can stay here as long as you'd like."

"The trial is in about four months," Emma said. The man seemed almost too good to be true. Kind. Benevolent.

Binh turned to look at Emma. "If she needs to stay here that long, that's no problem. She can stay longer if necessary."

Emma cleared her throat. "Do you mind if I get your full name and phone number in case I need to get in touch with you for some reason?"

"My name's Binh Nguyen. Kind of rhymes, huh? Binh means peaceful." He bowed his head. He wrote down his phone number for her.

"What a nice name. It's Vietnamese in origin, right?"

"Yes, I came over here with my family in 1975, at the end of the war. My father had been a colonel in the South Vietnamese Army, and my mother had a degree in flower arranging, if you can believe that. She loved to make beautiful things. We had a happy life in Vietnam - at least we did before the war started. But my father was a high-ranking officer in the South Vietnamese army, and after a while, it became obvious that our side was not going to be as successful as we'd hoped. We knew we would be treated badly afterwards. So we got on the very first boat we could and escaped to the United States."

"Your family settled in New Orleans?"

Binh nodded. "A church sponsored us. There's a big Vietnamese community here. There are beautiful Vietnamese gardens down by the river. You should go see them."

"I've heard about the gardens. I'd love to visit. When did you start working with horses?"

"As a kid, to make a little money. Actually, not much money at all." He laughed. "There aren't many horses in Vietnam. But I had to make money when I got over here. I didn't speak English then. I started cleaning stables and doing general go-fer work around the barns. Then I realized how much I loved the horses, and I'd have just about have done anything to have been around them. Literally anything. I'd have shoveled horse shit for free." He shook his head. "And I picked up English listening to the announcers at the racetrack." He laughed.

"When did you start riding?"

"That took a while. I started as a trainer, but that took time too. It all takes time, training, and patience. I applied for my jockey apprenticeship license, which I received after a few years of working as a trainer, and that was it."

"You may not know this, but ketamine played a role in James' murder. Isn't ketamine used on horses at the Fairgrounds?"

Binh paused. "That's a broad question. For one thing, I can't tell you what's used on all horses at the track. I'm sure ketamine is used by vets when they're treating sick horses, but its customary use is as an anesthetic. It knocks out the animal if they have an injury or if they need surgery."

"So a vet would administer the drug?" Emma jotted down notes as she spoke.

"Usually. Sometimes trainers will give it to the horses. The vets prescribe the medication, and the trainers can administer it. But vets do too. It just depends."

"Do you know anything about the illegal distribution of ketamine at the racetrack or anywhere else?"

"Whoa! That came out of left field!" He steepled his hands and was quiet for a minute. "I know that animal tranquilizers are misused. I know they're sold as recreational drugs, and I know that in the wrong hands they can do some harm. It's been obvious to me that there has been some drug use at the temple, if that's where you're going. But I have no proof."

"Why do you think that?"

"Some of the people there seemed high to me. And I noticed it after they got out of a session. Also, once I was asked if I'd like to try some dust to help 'awaken the spirit.' I said no. What else could that be? I mean, I knew it was a drug of some kind. I just didn't know what."

"Is that why you visited the temple? To check on drug use or illicit activities?"

"No, not at all. I wanted to speak to my daughter."

Chapter Seventeen

"Your daughter? Who's your daughter? Do we know her?" Emma said. She sat up on the edge of the sofa, startled and suddenly more alert. She hadn't expected this.

"Probably. She's worked at the temple ever since it opened. I've tried to get her to leave just about as long as she's worked there, but she won't. I don't know if she believes in the line of rubbish they try to sell there, or if she just had a thing for James. But she has a little boy, my grandson, who's there with her. It's not a good place for kids. So I started going there at least once a week to let her know that we care about her. I think it's important to do that."

"Oh! Mira! Mira's your daughter." How could this friendly, kind man be the father to someone so grim and soured on the world? "I never would have thought that. For one thing, her last name is Godfrey. And for another, I assumed she was from New York. Brooklyn, maybe." She paused. "I understand your concern, though. I'm not sure what I'd do if I were you."

He nodded. "It's difficult to know. She's an adult. But..." he shrugged, "it's hard to sit by and see her in a bad situation. By the way, your ears weren't playing tricks on you. Harry and I raised her until she was about twelve, then she went to live with her mother in Brooklyn for a few years. So that's what you're hearing. And her mother's last name is Godfrey."

"You raised Mira during her early years?"

"Yep. Her mom left when she was a baby. You know..." he paused. "We were young. We only got together briefly; we weren't married. The pregnancy was a surprise. Her mom, Angie, only listed her name on the

125

birth certificate. That's why Mira's last name is Godfrey. She didn't even put my name down as the dad, which I've asked her to change several times. Anyway, Angie had always wanted to live in New York, so she moved there when Mira was little. I was racing at that time, but I knew some really great people I could trust to stay with Mira. So I told her to go. Then I met Harry. We raised Mira together. She practically grew up at the tracks. She got to know everyone down there and is a pretty good rider herself. I know she had a happy childhood. Then, when she was about twelve, she decided she wanted to get to know her mother. By that time, her mom had a real job and could get an apartment with two bedrooms in Brooklyn, in a family neighborhood. It was good for Mira."

His face lit up as he looked down the hall. "Harry, come on in." Binh gestured with his hand, and a towering man with a smile larger than Binh's entered the room with his hand extended toward Emma.

"Nice to meet you."

Harry, tall, muscular, and blonde, had a twinkle of humor in his eyes. Emma could tell the two men shared a common kindness and gentility.

"Harry's my better half. And I do mean better." Binh gleamed.

Emma stood to shake Harry's hand, surprised by the gentleness of his grasp.

Harry sat down in one of the turquoise club chairs across from Binh.

"Like I said. I've been trying to get Mira to leave the temple for years. She refuses, but I won't give up either. James has influenced her, or has some kind of hold on her. He's been able to manipulate her into staying for years. It's not money. I told her I would take care of her and the baby. But she won't leave."

"Mira's a grown woman. You can't do anything about her choices, unless someone can prove that something's going on at the temple that could shut the place down. Something illegal, perhaps.

"A few minutes ago, I asked you whether you knew anything about the sale of ketamine from the racetracks, and you said you thought there was drug use at the temple. That really wasn't an answer to my question. But do you connect the sale of drugs from the Fairgrounds to drug use at the temple? I wouldn't put you on the spot about this except for the fact that Stacey is facing serious charges for something she didn't do. And drugs are at the heart of the case."

Binh inhaled deeply. "I didn't realize I did that." He paused. "I guess I do connect the two. You should know the names of a couple of guys at the tracks. Bradley Adcock, and Theodore Cook."

Emma scribbled down notes furiously as Binh spoke.

"Why do you connect the sale of drugs from the Fairground to the drug use at the Temple? And who are those two guys?"

"Adcock and Cook are well-known trainers, but they often have their hands in illicit activities. And they've been known to deal in drugs. Rumor has it it's ketamine. One thing you need to know is that large quantities of any drug, but especially ketamine, couldn't be coming from supplies kept at the tracks. Quantities large enough for street or recreational sales would have to be coming from somewhere else." He paused. "I've heard it comes from Mexico. They break into the pharmacies there and bring the stuff here to sell. But you'd have to verify that with someone else. I'm just telling you what I've heard. And I've heard rumors connecting some sales to the temple. That's about it."

"So, this is just rumor, then?"

"Word gets around. People love to talk. But you need to follow up. Talk to people who actually know what's going on." He paused. "I'm making no promises, but I'll see what I can do for you."

"That would be fantastic." She paused and looked down at her notes. "Are you and your daughter still close?"

"No. Not since she joined the Japaprajnas."

"Would you mind telling me how the temple has come between you?"

"No, I don't mind." He sighed. "I guess I'd say that Mira has become more remote since she joined that group. And even though she has Jimmy, her four-year-old, she doesn't come by to visit at all anymore. I have to go there to see Jimmy. I have suspected that she might be involved with drugs too, but I haven't actually seen them. It's just a sense I have based on the way she acts and looks. She's angry a lot. Doesn't have any patience. And I've noticed her hands shaking, too. But I hope I'm wrong."

Emma tried to write down every word. "I'm sorry. I hope you're wrong too. That's all I have for now. We appreciate your time and your offer to let Stacey stay here through her trial date more than you'll ever know."

"My pleasure."

"Stacey, what do you think?"

"Sounds like a perfect fit. I really appreciate it."

"Then, I think we have a deal."

* * *

Emma walked up the steps to the carriage house with Stacey. They unlocked the door and looked around the studio apartment. Decorated in shades of white and off white, it felt clean and welcoming. There was a bed and an old bleached pine dresser in one corner and a small kitchenette with a tiny washer and dryer in the other, all contained in one room. Stacey walked over and opened a couple of drawers in the pine cabinet.

"This should do. I didn't bring that many things with me."

She threw her bag on a chair next to the cabinet and closed the cabinet drawer. Then she flopped on top of the down-filled comforter covering the bed.

"I could get used to this." She smiled.

"I don't blame you. It's pretty nice."

Emma poked her head in the bathroom. Just as she thought, it was lovely. A claw-foot tub. Marble tile. Fluffy towels. Who wouldn't want to live in a place like this? And for free? Why wouldn't Mira take her dad up on his offer?

"Did you see the tub? You could practically go scuba diving in there."

Stacey looked around the small space.

"Nice. This is quite a change from the prison bathroom and my days on the streets."

"I'm sure it is. I think you've found your own sanctuary, for now. It may not be as grand as the one next door, but it's all yours. There's a phone there on the nightstand. Call me if you need anything or if there's a problem. We'll need to get together soon to discuss some strategies, but take the day off, have a bubble bath, and relax. I'll be in touch."

* * *

From her upstairs window, Stacey watched Emma walk to her car and pull out into the street. There was a black two-door sedan parked across the street along the bayou. Otherwise, it was quiet. Stacey needed food since the carriage house wasn't stocked with supplies. The only grocery store within walking distance was Taconi's on Esplanade.

The walk to the store only took about fifteen minutes. Taconi's was the sort of place that made her wish she knew how to cook. Even though the shelves of the store were dusty and the floors were encrusted with grime, the food was beautiful and bountiful. She spent far more time than was necessary looking at the cheeses, cold cuts, and vegetables on display, even though she only needed the basics. She piled things she could easily make and eat in her basket—milk, eggs, bread, peanut butter and jelly—and checked out.

On the way back, she noticed the nose of a large black sedan in the lane next to her. It seemed to slow down for a while as she walked back. She turned to get a better look, but as soon as she did, the car sped up and passed her, then took a left on Moss, the street where she lived. The vehicle had a similar size and shape to the car she had seen earlier in the day. It sped by before she could verify whether it was a two-door. She felt her heart race as she quickened her pace and crossed the street. But when she rounded the corner, the road was clear. No cars were parked on either side of the street.

* * *

When Emma pulled away from Binh's place and drove toward the temple, she was satisfied that Stacey had found a safe place to stay through her trial date. But that's all that was clear after their meeting with Binh. Nothing was exactly falling into place like perfect pieces in a puzzle.

It would be interesting to see whether Mira would actually leave the temple now that James was dead. And where was Raphael? He seemed so much a part of things when she interviewed him right after James' death.

Emma stopped in front of the temple and slid out of the car. It was still early afternoon. With any luck, Mira would be available.

Chapter Eighteen

A young woman Emma had never seen before opened the door to the temple and stood staring, tight-lipped, not speaking a word.

"I'm Emma Thornton. I'd like to speak to Mira Godfrey if she's in."

The girl nodded and opened the door wider, gesturing for Emma to step in as she turned and ran up the staircase. A few minutes later, Emma heard the percussive sound of someone descending the stairs. She looked down the hall and saw Mira approaching, dressed in jeans and a striped t-shirt.

"Good to see you again." Emma extended her hand, which Mira took. "Can we go somewhere private to talk?"

Mira squinted at Emma. "Follow me." Mira led Emma back up the stairs to her office and closed the door. "Say hi to Miss Emma, Jimmy."

Mira's son looked up from his dump truck, which was about to crash into the wall, and waved. "Hi!" He picked up his toy and flung it into the air, pretending his truck was an airplane.

Mira smiled and gestured toward a chair in front of her desk. Not much had changed since Emma's last visit, unless the stack of papers on her desk had grown even higher. And something smelled like rancid grease, or old French fries, stale fried chicken, or some forgotten lunch in the garbage can. One of those odors one gets used to and shouldn't. Emma sat down and pulled out her notebook and pen, trying to ignore the stench.

"I've met your dad."

Mira's facial expression didn't change. "Okay."

"He's a nice guy."

Mira nodded. "I agree. He is."

"I came here today to ask you a few more questions about the Japaprajnas. I also have a couple of questions I'd like to ask about your relationship with James. But this shouldn't take long." She paused and glanced at Mira. She seemed calmer today. "Your dad told me that he's been trying to get you to leave the organization for a while, but he said you don't want to. What makes you so inclined to stay here, especially after James' death?"

Mira sat back in her chair, her eyebrows raised in surprise, her hands extended. "Why wouldn't I stay? I like it here. It's home to me and Jimmy."

"When I spoke to you earlier, you said you were thinking about going back to Brooklyn to stay with your mother. What's changed?"

"A few things have come up with James' estate. So I shouldn't leave now, and I've changed my mind about going back to Brooklyn."

"What are the estate issues?"

"I'm the executrix. I need to be here in New Orleans to make the filings, do what I need to do."

"Can you tell me who inherits under James' will?"

"That is absolutely none of your business. I need to get back to work. You took up too much of my time with your questions the other day. I don't have time for this too."

"I'm not trying to be difficult, but the person or persons who will inherit under James' will is relevant in a murder case. So, I can ask you that question. And I can subpoena you for trial. DA will want to know the answer too."

Mira held her head in her hands for a moment. She pulled her hair away from her forehead, making a ponytail with her hands. Then let her long hair go with a toss.

"James and I both made wills at the same time, right after Jimmy was born. We wanted to make certain he was provided for in case one or both of us died."

"So who inherits James' estate?"

"Everything was split between Jimmy and Cecelia. But everything will automatically transfer into a trust. I'm the trustee. Jimmy won't inherit his share until he's twenty-one. I'll manage his half of the trust until then.

We're in the process of getting everything filed right now. I've applied for the death certificates but haven't received them yet."

"So you'll manage Jimmy's money until he's an adult."

"I will once everything is transferred into my name as trustee."

"Can you tell me how much Jimmy will inherit?"

"Not really. I haven't done an accounting yet. There's an insurance policy. Jimmy is the primary beneficiary. The Esplanade property belongs to the Temple of the Japaprajna People, for what that's worth. There's still a huge mortgage on it. But of course, James had a few business interests."

"What business interests?"

"Well, ETC, and the spa."

"Anything else?"

"Yeah, probably."

Emma sighed. Probably? "Anything that's illegitimate?"

Mira smirked. "I can't think of anything right offhand."

"Has Cecelia contested the will or the trust or objected to the way the assets are divided?"

"I expected her to, but she hasn't yet."

"Why did you expect her to?"

Mira shrugged. "I just thought she would. When we drew up our wills and the trust, she was upset. She made it clear she didn't like splitting the estate with Jimmy, but James didn't care. He had his lawyer draw it up the way he wanted."

"I see. It's quite likely you'll be asked to prepare a witness affidavit in Stacey's case or be subpoenaed to serve as a witness at trial. I'd appreciate it if we could discuss a few other issues in an amicable manner. Some of my questions might be difficult for you, but the same questions might be asked at trial."

Mira nodded.

"I've heard that James has manipulated young girls, maybe even underage girls, to have sex with him. Do you know anything about this?"

Mira shook her head. "Absolutely not."

"You never saw him bringing girls into that small house in the courtyard, the garconniere?"

"I don't believe I did."

Emma didn't believe her. "You didn't, or you're not sure?"

"I may have seen him walking to the back with some of the girls who worked at the spa. That's true. But I didn't know what was going on there." Mira's hands began to shake more noticeably. She looked like a cornered animal who was trying to figure its way out of a trap.

"You didn't even have a suspicion?"

Mira clenched her hands into fists and stared at Emma.

"Who recruited for James after Stacey?"

"I wouldn't use the word *recruit* for what Stacey was doing. And I'm not sure. I don't think they have anyone who talks to people about joining the Japaprajnas right now. I'm not sure if they had anyone right after Stacey quit."

"You don't think Stacey recruited? James asked her to look for young women who didn't quite fit in for some reason. She knew how to spot them and went after them. They needed a place to stay. Or they needed food. Or they needed the support of a family. Something. She knew it, and she promised them everything they needed. They bought it, and James exploited it."

Mira pursed her lips, opened her desk drawer, pulled out a fingernail file, and began filing her nails. "I don't know what you're talking about."

Emma paused. "Okay." She flipped a page in her notepad. "Let's talk about you for a minute."

"Let's not, Ms. Thornton. I have work to do."

"This shouldn't take long. Why do you think your dad is so keen on having you leave the temple?"

She stood up and walked to her bookshelf, frowning. "I know he thinks the Japaprajnas are a cult. And he's worried about me, but he shouldn't. Everything's fine here." She sat back down at her desk chair.

"But is it? Stacey has told me a few things that have made me wonder about it too. James seemed to want a lot of attention from the young girls who worked here, young girls whom he seemed to have exploited. That seems a little strange for a place that promotes mind and body healing, doesn't it?"

"James believed that human touch was restorative, a good thing, you know? Sometimes that included sex. A lot of people believe that."

"So you're admitting that James abused and manipulated young girls?"

She frowned and shook her head. "I'm not admitting anything like that."

"Then who did James believe human touch helped? The girls he took to the garconniere, or did he find it personally healing?"

"I can't answer for James. He's dead. But I suppose he believed it was good for everyone."

"I see. Even the girls who were underage?"

"What makes you think any of these girls were underage?"

Emma rubbed her forehead. "Do you have their birth certificates or any other proof of age? Do you know where these girls came from or even if they are all in this country legally?"

Mira adjusted herself in her seat. "Why are you asking me these questions? Shouldn't you be asking Cecelia?"

"Did you require identification or proof of age to work at ETC?"

Mira leaned forward. "I relied on the information Cecelia gave me." She nodded toward the ledgers stacked on her desk.

"Could I see them?"

"Sure." Mira handed the ledgers to Emma, who flipped through several pages.

"So Cecelia didn't give you social security numbers on anyone?"

"She just gave me the girls' names and said they were okay to work here."

"In your mind, if it was okay with Cecelia for a girl to work here, that was good enough for you?"

She nodded.

"And you never made social security payments on the workers."

"No, James said not to."

"Why not?"

Mira paused. "He said they'd make more money that way."

"So, you didn't issue 1099s or W2s to any of the girls."

Mira sat back in her chair and crossed her arms. "What does this have to do with James' murder? This isn't any of your business."

"I think Stacey was set up. And several people had a reason to kill James."

"That could be true."

"Including all of the massage girls who didn't get paid a salary."

"I can't respond to that."

"What can you tell me about Cecelia's and James' relationship?"

Mira shrugged. "I don't know. I guess it was pretty typical. I've never been in a marriage, so I wouldn't know, really. They had their moments. Their good days and bad days."

"Did Cecelia resent Jimmy or you?"

"If she did, she didn't show it. Except I know she was unhappy that James' trust left half of his estate to Jimmy. And she didn't like that I was appointed trustee." She paused. "I think she knew I didn't really love James. But she wanted everyone else to know she was the wife. She made sure that was clear. She was the wife. I was the smoke shop business partner. And that was fine with me."

Chapter Nineteen

Emma walked back to her car and threw her purse in the seat next to her. She looked forward to the drive back to her office on campus. She never tired of the city. The architecture in even the most rundown areas of New Orleans had a beauty and a grace she found soothing. The drive through the Quarter and Central City would help clear her head.

She turned off Esplanade onto Royal, driving slowly to avoid pedestrians, passing multistoried townhomes, wrought-iron balconies dripping with ferns, and pastel-painted creole cottages. Traffic slowed, and she could see that a few blocks ahead, a garbage truck loomed. The large vehicle slowed progress on the narrow street almost to a standstill and fouled the air with the mingled odors of rotting chicken, decaying vegetation, shrimp shells, and spoiled milk. Emma took a right turn on Bourbon to avoid it all and found herself ten feet from the door of ETC.

A rare, early afternoon parking space was close by, so she pulled in, taking advantage of what she decided had to be fate. She fed the parking meter and walked the few steps to the shop.

Emma pushed the door open and was immediately hit by a rush of icy air and the pungent aroma of creole cooking. She realized she hadn't eaten lunch.

"Can I help you?"

As Emma's eyes slowly adjusted to the dark interior of the shop, she realized no one was behind the counter.

"Hello?"

"We're over in the corner. To the side of the counter. Sorry." Moonstone stood up, holding a paper plate of food. "We're having a late lunch." She nodded at Raphael. "He brought this over kinda late. But it was worth the wait."

"Smells wonderful. What is it?"

"Jambalaya. Place down the street makes it every Friday. It's really good. Want some?" Moonstone grabbed a paper plate and a plastic fork and scraped a little mound of jambalaya together for Emma.

Emma dug in. "Oh my God! This is wonderful."

"Yeah. One of their cousins makes the andouille too. It's pretty fab."

"You may have just saved my life. I think I was starving." She paused for a moment to eat the savory treat, then glanced at Raphael as she scraped up the last remnants from her plate. "I've been looking for you."

"Really? I thought we'd already had our talk."

Raphael, dressed in black jeans, a navy and black striped shirt with cuffs rolled in the style of the day, every hair on his head precisely groomed, was the picture of perfection. Emma stared at his shoes. How could he have so many beautiful pairs?

"I told you we needed to get together to talk again, privately, remember? The more I learn, the more questions I have. You know how it goes."

Raphael nodded. "Makes sense."

"But we need to go somewhere private." She threw her paper plate in the garbage can behind the counter.

"We could step outside, or we could move into that back room," Raphael said.

"Mira wouldn't like that, Raphael. I think y'all should walk to one of the bars down the street and talk there," Moonstone said.

"We wouldn't have enough privacy at a bar. Plus, it would be too loud anyway. And it's too hot outside. So I opt for the back room. Raphael, do you have a key?" Emma said.

"I don't, but Moonstone does." He held out his hand for the key.

"The only other key I have is to the backdoor, and I'm only supposed to use it for emergencies. I've never used it. And I don't think I should give it to you." Moonstone frowned.

"We won't be long, and Mira doesn't need to know about our being back there." Emma raised her eyebrows. She wanted to get a look at the room.

Moonstone reluctantly handed Raphael the key. "The lock is an old warded lock with a skeleton key which never was that safe. So there's a padlock on the door that's used instead. The skeleton key was lost a long time ago."

Emma and Raphael scurried out of the shop before Moonstone could change her mind, walking down the side alley toward the back entrance. Emma was glad she was able to see the layout of the building and Stacey's actual perspective of the night Angelina was murdered, first, before they made the trip to the police station.

Emma and Raphael passed the first window. There were iron bars over the casements. Stacey hadn't mentioned that. Then they rounded the corner to the rear of the building and stood at the door that faced the alley. She noticed the back window also had burglar bars.

The door was held shut by weathered strips of metal, each with loops at the end and was secured by a padlock. Raphael tried to open the rusty padlock, which wasn't cooperating. He jiggled the key back and forth in the lock.

"Hmm. This seems to be a bad copy." Raphael struggled with the key.

"Here, let me try." Emma tried twisting the key around the inside of the lock. She was an expert at badly cut keys, but this one seemed impossible.

She glanced down the alley as Raphael took another turn at the lock. The alleyway was narrow, barely wide enough for the large sedan Stacey had described earlier. Emma was certain it was too narrow for garbage trucks and larger public utility vehicles.

"It just doesn't want to open." Raphael jiggled the key, then finally opened the door. He grabbed the padlock and key and closed the door behind them. "Don't want anyone to come behind us and lock us in, thinking someone forgot to lock the door. Not that anyone's back here or anything."

Once they were in, Emma flipped on the switch to the one fluorescent light which hung overhead, pulled a couple of folding chairs up to the table, and glanced around the room. She grabbed one of the empty pizza boxes

139

from a stack in the corner and brought it back over to the table.

"I feel like if I'm about to be interrogated. You sure you aren't with the police?" Raphael grinned.

"I promise I'm not. Remember the first day we spoke? You said you didn't feel comfortable talking about some things, especially about people taking drugs at the temple. But drugs were found in Stacey's room right before she was arrested. One of the charges against her was for possession with the intent to distribute. She says the drugs aren't hers, and I believe her. So, I need to know what you know about drug use or drug sales at the temple."

Raphael nodded. "I remember saying that. I didn't want to go into all of that drug talk there. But, yeah. I've seen people that were definitely high at the temple, like when they were leaving their sessions with James. And James and even Mira got high a lot too. Sometimes Mira hasn't been able to drive to pick up Jimmy from daycare, and I've had to drive her to go get him. I've had my suspicions about what it was. I knew that some of the massage girls had taken drugs, then after that, had sex with James. They'd talked to me about it a few times. So, I think the drug they took was one of those that loosens you up or knocks you out."

"Like what?"

"I'm guessing something they call a roofie, Rohypnol, or maybe even Ketamine. Something like that. But I'm only guessing. The girls said they couldn't remember much afterwards." He shook his head.

"Have you ever seen a white powder, or syringes, or vials of anything at the temple?"

"I've seen empty packets with some of the powder still inside. You know, a little residue. And sometimes, there was white powder all over the altar. So I knew something was up when I saw that."

"When did you notice this?"

"It had been going on for a while."

"Do you know anyone who sells drugs to the people at the temple?"

Raphael shook his head. "No. I don't know anything about all that."

"Do you know what goes on here, in the back of the shop?" Emma pulled her notebook and pen out of her purse.

"You mean what the girls do once I drop them off?"

"Right. Have you ever stayed and watched to see what goes on?"

"No. Mira and James didn't want anyone to, and I was happy not knowing. They only let one girl at a time work, too. I got the impression they didn't want the girls talking about work at the shop. They tried to keep them separated. But you can't prevent something like that. People talk."

"Did you ever hear from the girls about what was going on at the shop?"

"I didn't really want to know, and I told them that. But sometimes I'd overhear them talking about packing up boxes, but they never said what was inside."

"Have you ever seen pizza boxes like this before?" Emma held up a cardboard container.

"Sure. I get their pizza sometimes, and I see a delivery guy on a bicycle delivering them all over the Quarter. There's no name on the outside, but I think it's the only shop around that uses those boxes. The restaurant's close to Pirate's Alley. I can't remember the name of the place."

"Thanks, I'll look it up." Emma made a few notations on her pad. "Let's talk about you for a minute. What can you tell me about your new job?"

"One of the girls who used to be a masseuse at the temple started working at The Wiz, one of the clubs down the street. She told me they needed someone out front to be a barker and one of the bouncers. I thought I'd be good at it. So, I'm actually both, a barker and a bouncer. " He smiled.

"Who's the girl?"

"Mariana. Mariana Hernandez. She left the temple a few months before James was killed. Several of the girls have left, and some of them are on Bourbon Street in the clubs. They make more money there, and they don't have to put up with James."

"I would guess they still have to put up with men bothering them."

He nodded. "That's true."

"You just said some of the massage girls had sex with James. What was that all about?"

Raphael rubbed his forehead. "I think it happened a lot. James brought the girls off the streets, promised to take care of them, and then did everything he could to have his way with them. Of course, the drugs didn't help. I think he slipped those girls a little more than he gave his followers.

"He also took photographs of a couple of them. Not the good kind. Once Mariana told him during one of James' sessions that her mom and dad were undocumented. Later, James threatened to call the INS on her parents unless she went to the garconniere with him." Raphael paused and shook his head. "Another girl said he threatened to publish the photographs he took of her if she didn't sleep with him. He was a creep. All he cared about was serving himself."

"I would think those girls would have hated James."

"I'm sure they did." He paused. "I know they did."

Emma nodded. "Why did you continue to work there, driving the girls back and forth between the temple and the shop if the place was so awful?"

"The girls have been talking a lot more since James died. It's almost been two weeks now, and I know a lot more. But I always did what I could to help before all this happened, and I still am."

"Do you know if Cecelia knew anything about James' liaisons with the girls from the spa?"

"I don't know, but she isn't stupid."

"Did she ever mention anything to you about it?"

"Not a word."

"You still haven't told me where you're staying these days."

"I crash at friends' places, usually."

"Which friends?"

"Lately, I've been staying at the place where Mariana lives. It's a shared space. But I don't want you to get the wrong idea." Raphael put both of his hands up. "I've only stayed on her couch. The girls from the temple are very young. I'd never have anything to do with any of them. They're just kids. I kinda watch out for them."

"I understand."

"I'm a man of discriminating taste." He smiled. "I've been in love before. I admire beauty, but I admire a good heart more. And a good heart is harder to find."

"If shoes are any indication, I have to say you're quite discriminating. Those are very nice." Emma pointed to Raphael's loafers.

Raphael nodded. "I like good-looking shoes." He stretched out his foot and moved it around, so the cordovan leather caught the overhead light.

"When Stacey saw you in the Quarter the day she was reading tarot cards, she said you told her people were asking about her. Who was that?"

"Mariana and Gabriela. They both worked at the temple, and now they're both at The Wiz."

"Stacey thought you were either threatening or warning her."

"Nah. There wasn't any of that." Raphael swung his foot. "We were all worried about Stacey. She always kept to herself. Maybe because she felt bad about recruiting the girls to work for James. But none of us thought Stacey killed James."

"You just said you did what you could to help. What was that?"

"Before James was killed, I helped a few of them escape the temple. The girls interviewed for other jobs on their days off, and if they got an offer, we'd plan their escape. I'm sure I could have done more, but I feel good about what I was able to do."

"Do you remember about how long Mariana and Gabriela stayed at the temple?"

"Not that long, really. This would be a guess, but I'd be surprised if either one of them were there longer than six months."

"Six months? I guess there was a lot of turnover."

Raphael nodded. "Yes, there was. Stacey stayed busy dredging up new spa workers in the Quarter. There was no shortage of young girls in need of shelter either."

"Didn't James or Cecelia figure out you were the one helping the girls escape?"

"We always planned the getaway on a night the girl was scheduled to work at ETC. That way, it appeared they ran away from the smoke shop unassisted. But I hid their suitcases in the trunk of the car, then dropped them off at the shop. After Mira checked out for the night, I'd come back and drop them off at their new workplace, usually The Wiz. A girl who works there has a big apartment with several bedrooms she rents out, and Mariana and a few of the girls who left the temple have rented rooms from her. So it's all worked out pretty well so far."

"Is that the place where you're crashing now?"

"It is."

Emma inhaled deeply, detecting a smoky odor. Perhaps Raphael was a smoker. She hadn't noticed before.

"It's just temporary until I can find a place of my own." Raphael smiled.

Emma's eyes began to sting. Now she was positive. She could smell smoke.

"Do you smell something burning?"

"Maybe. Yes. That could be a problem. We should probably go." He stood up and headed toward the back door.

Emma grabbed her purse and turned out the light as Raphael tried, unsuccessfully, to open the door.

"What's the matter? Is the door stuck? Swollen from the rain or something?"

"I don't know. It seems to be locked from the other side." Raphael shook the door. "When I shake it, it moves a little, but I can't seem to bust through. I'd guess someone attached another padlock. And it's not budging. See?" Raphael shook the door again.

"That had to have been done on purpose," Emma could feel her heartbeat quicken.

"It doesn't matter right now. We just gotta get out of here."

"I've got an idea." Emma scrambled to the bottom of her purse, searching for her metal fingernail file. Several seconds later, she tried to shove the pointed end of the file through the crack in the door in an attempt to reach the padlock, but it was futile. The file wasn't long enough. "I can't reach it." She peered through the crack. "We don't have time to mess with this." Emma looked around the room. "I don't see any smoke yet. Maybe we should try to remove those burglar bars, unless you think you can take the hinges off the door."

"The hinges look pretty rusted. They're in that door pretty good, too. Let's see if we can remove the bars, and don't forget to yell." Raphael raised the blinds, then picked up one of the chairs and smashed it against the back window. "Help! We're locked in!" he yelled as glass broke and scattered along the inside and outside of the building.

Emma ran over to the side window to inspect the construction of the burglar bars.

She took off her shoe and banged it against the ancient glass from the window until it broke, and screamed for help from the open window. The burglar bars were coated with rust and screwed onto the outside window frame. She shoved her arm through the bars and tried to insert the curved end of the fingernail file into the slot of the screw. But the screw was welded onto the casement with rust. It didn't budge. Then she inserted the file under the screw in an attempt to loosen it. It still didn't move.

Emma felt increased heat behind her and turned. Smoke and flames were pouring from the vent along the ceiling at the back of the room. They didn't have much time.

"Do you have a cell phone?"

"No. You don't either?"

"No. I've been putting off getting one." Emma hesitated. "Think we can take the chair and make any kind of a dent in the bars? Enough of a dent for me to get through the window?"

"You're not very big, but I doubt it."

"I'll try to unscrew one of the bars while you bang away at the other one. One of us has to make a difference. The smoke will take over soon."

Emma continued working on unscrewing the burglar bars in the side window frame while Raphael worked on opening the space between the bars on the window that faced the back alley. The room was beginning to fill with smoke.

Emma turned around to check on the source of the fire. Paint was beginning to bubble along the back wall, especially close to the light switches. The fire had to be located in between the walls. Suddenly an outlet burst into flames, and Emma and Raphael began to cough. The plaster walls seemed more resistant to the fire than the beadboard wainscoting, which was starting to smoke.

Raphael wedged a metal chair between one of the bars and his shoulder and pushed, pressing against the side of the wall for leverage. The rust which strengthened the screws and hinges seemed to have weakened the bars, which began to move. Raphael turned and began pushing against the opposite bar, forming a space large enough for a small child to crawl through. Emma was afraid she wouldn't fit. Smoke drifted from the open window. She hoped a passerby would notice and report it to the fire department.

"You gotta try, Emma."

She nodded, struggling to breathe. She pulled a chair over to the window and hanging onto the bars, put one foot, then the other through the opening. She tried to push her body through the opening, but it was no use.

"I can't get through."

Raphael pulled her back through the window.

"Let me try again," Raphael said. He shoved the chair against the metal bars, pushing against them with all his force. He was able to get them to move a fraction of an inch.

"Try it again."

By this time, the flames had crawled up the wall from the outlets and were encroaching on the back wall. Plaster was beginning to crumble where the paint had bubbled. The ceiling tiles were blackening. Black smoke was pouring from the ductwork.

Emma climbed back onto the chair and grabbed the bars on the window again. Raphael supported her back as she began to ease herself out through the window. This time, her hips seemed to be a better fit for the space, although jagged edges of glass ripped the skin along her back as she dropped to the ground.

As soon as Emma's feet touched the alley, she ran around to the door to open it, but, as Raphael suspected, another padlock had been placed on the door. She grabbed the door handle and screamed as she shook it. "Shit!"

"What's wrong?" Raphael yelled from the other side.

"You were right! Someone put another padlock on the door! I'll go get help!"

Emma turned the corner of the building and ran as fast as she could down the alley to the ETC shop front door. She tried to pull it open, but it was locked. A sign on the door said, Will Return In Thirty Minutes. Emma ran to the souvenir shop next door.

"Please call the fire department! The back of the building next door is on fire, and someone is still inside! Do you have something we can use to remove the door or cut the padlock? A screwdriver or a hammer? Cutters? Anything?"

One of the employees of the souvenir shop grabbed a hammer and a screwdriver and handed them over to Emma while another employee scrambled to call 911. Emma dashed back to the alley, peered into the room, hoping she wasn't too late. Raphael had collapsed underneath the window, but he raised his hand when she shouted his name. Flames were lapping out of the ductwork, and black smoke was pouring out the window. She ran around to the back door and began hammering the screwdriver into the padlock. It wouldn't budge.

Emma ran up to the entranceway to the alley to check on the fire truck. She ran back to the shop's window every few minutes to check on Raphael, yelling to see if he was okay. The last time she ran back to check on him, he didn't respond. She was frantic.

The New Orleans Fire Department, known for its swift response time, had honed its skills in a city where the structures were often connected by common walls or were so close together that fire easily skipped from building to building. And the buildings were so old they served as kindling, making the fires spread quickly and fiercely. Within four minutes of the shopkeeper's phone call, Emma finally heard sirens wailing down the narrow French Quarter streets, finessing the turn onto Bourbon. Emma marveled at the driver's skills as he drove his huge vehicle down the slender street, barely avoiding parked vehicles as he slid by like a ship coming to moor, brakes hissing, coming to a stop in front of the shop. Another truck followed closely behind.

Emma waved to let the first responders know where the fire was located, although by now, it was obvious. Smoke and flames leapt from the back of the building. She feared for Raphael's life.

"It's back here, down this alley! There's a man inside!" Emma waved her arm and coughed.

The fire department personnel flew into work, hooking up their hoses from a nearby five-inch hydrant to the pumper trucks. One man entered the front of the shop, pushing back the fire with the force of water from his hose. Another ran down the alley and began spraying other buildings. A woman took an axe and broke into the building through the back door. Several other firefighters followed her into the building with a hose. A few minutes later, they emerged with Raphael and laid him on the ground in the back alley. His head rolled backwards, his arms and legs limp and lifeless. Emma couldn't tell if he was breathing, but he didn't seem to be. His hands and face were charred in places, badly burned, perhaps by falling debris. She feared he'd inhaled too much smoke and, based on the age of the building, some of it had to have been toxic.

EMTs began working on him, applying chest compressions for several minutes. Then they brought out the defibrillator. Soon they were shaking their heads. They put the defibrillator aside. It was too late.

Emma sat on the sidewalk in front of the shop, her arms wrapped around her legs, her head pressed against her knees. She was devastated. Tears streamed down her face. She couldn't believe Raphael was dead. And it was her fault. Raphael's body lay, covered, on the side alley. Someone said they were waiting for the coroner. She didn't want to look at his body, and she didn't want to see him leave in the coroner's wagon. It was a horrific end to a horrific day.

She was breathing heavily and had a difficult time catching her breath. She didn't know if she was crying, if the smoke was making her eyes water, or both. Her body felt heavy. She didn't want to move, but she stood up and approached one of the firefighters who was winding a hose.

She blotted her face with the back of her sleeve. "Could you guys tell me what caused the fire?"

"From the looks of things, it seems to have started in the ductwork. We found evidence of oil-covered rags up there. But there will be an inquiry based on what we've seen, an investigation, and an official report."

Emma nodded. "That's pretty crazy, but thanks for letting me know." She shook her head. "Can you tell me," she hesitated. "Do you know whether my friend who died in the fire suffered?"

The firefighter shook his head. "We don't really know what happened here without an autopsy. But for the first minute, he probably coughed, and those coughs might have been painful, but after that, he very likely lost consciousness. There was a lot of black smoke in the room. Sometimes loss of consciousness and death can happen really fast, depending on the intensity of the heat, like, within thirty seconds. But I think it took a little longer in this fire. You've got to get out of a fire fast, and looks like you guys were trapped. There was a padlock on the back door. A police officer should be here soon to speak to you. I'm sorry for the loss of your friend."

Emma, her eyes tearing, started to move toward Raphael's body.

An EMT moved toward her with a clipboard. "Ma'am, you need to sit back down. We need to check your vitals, your airways, and some of your abrasions. We've called an ambulance. You've been in a serious fire. They'll probably want to do chest x-rays at the hospital, at the very least. I've already heard you demonstrate a couple of symptoms associated with smoke inhalation…cough, and hoarseness. Do you have shortness of breath?"

Emma nodded.

"Headache?"

Emma shook her head. "No."

He walked over and peered at her. "Tilt your head back."

Emma obliged.

"Well, you've got soot in your airway passages. So stay put until the ambulance gets here. Smoke inhalation can be serious. It can inflame your lungs, cause them to swell, and block oxygen intake. It isn't something to be taken lightly."

She nodded toward the smoldering rubble. Somewhere in the debris, she had a purse.

"I need to go get my purse."

A firefighter standing nearby shook his head. "Nope. You need to stay away from that area."

The police had already begun to mark off the site with yellow tape. "But my purse has my car keys in it."

She saw the man's shoulders slump. He walked toward her.

"You can't go get your purse now, if there's even anything left of it. The fire marshal has to inspect everything here first. But you can tell me what it looks like."

Emma described the purse, and the firefighter began walking toward a police officer who was standing nearby.

Emma called out. "One more thing?" She coughed.

The firefighter stopped, turned around, and walked back.

"Yes, ma'am?"

"The door was padlocked from the outside by somebody else, locking us inside. It had to have been deliberate. Is there any way to preserve what's left of the door and the padlock?"

"Yep. The officer will be here soon to speak to you. He'll make sure everything is properly preserved and gets to the correct authority. Make sure you tell him everything. And everything on the site, the door, the padlock, everything will stay where it is through the inspection. So don't worry. It's too hot for anyone to disturb it now anyway.

"I'll write down your statement too. I'll complete my notes today and get them out to the fire investigator."

Emma thanked him. Her face was itchy. She wiped her face with her hands, shocked to see that they were covered with black soot.

Chapter Twenty

Emma was shaky. So shaky, she didn't think she could have stepped up into the ambulance if she'd had to. But she didn't. One of the EMTs strapped her onto a gurney and loaded her into the ambulance. She didn't want to go to the hospital, but since she was coughing and had some difficulty breathing, she wasn't given a choice. She just wanted to go home. She wanted no part of cold emergency rooms, wasted hours waiting for a doctor, or chest x-rays.

She didn't know how she could have let Raphael die. For a moment, she started shaking uncontrollably. Then she closed her eyes and started deep breathing, an exercise which usually calmed her. But this time, it only aggravated her cough. The EMT sitting next to her in the ambulance gave her some oxygen, and she felt better immediately.

She kept her eyes closed for a moment, listening to the EMT's chat.

"She's lucky. Her friend got trapped in the place. Died from smoke inhalation. They said it was deliberate. They'd stuffed old rags in the ductwork and lit 'em up."

Emma felt like she was in a bad dream. But she needed to wake up and think things through. Moonstone and Mira were the only people with keys to the shop. But why did Moonstone step out of the store at the exact time of the fire? It couldn't have been for lunch. She'd already eaten a late lunch with Raphael. The fire must have started when she left the building unless Moonstone had started it herself. Who would have wanted to kill Raphael? And did anyone want her dead?

Emma didn't think Raphael was the one who set up Stacey for James' murder, especially since he had been working so hard to help the other girls at the temple. She wished she could go back now and redo the entire afternoon. She should never have gone into that horrible room behind the shop.

The ambulance pulled into the hospital's emergency driveway and parked. The EMTs opened the vehicle's back door, pulled out the gurney, and rolled Emma into the hospital. Once inside, she was left in the hallway until triage could assess her condition thirty minutes later.

Two hours after that, Emma was taking the bumpy ride home in Ren's truck.

* * *

"I'm glad they let you go. But you need to listen to what they said. You have to take it easy for the next few days. Inflamed lungs are serious. It could get worse if you're not careful."

Emma nodded. All she could think about was getting back to her apartment and a tub full of hot water. She felt her body begin to relax as they pulled into her parking space. Ren scurried around, trying to hold her elbow as she climbed up the stairs. She smiled. It was unnecessary, but so nice. She knew that having him in her life on this difficult day made a difference; being cared for made a difference. She squeezed his arm as she walked up the stairs.

Lulu and Maddie greeted her at the door, sniffing her madly until she made her way to her bedroom. The first thing she wanted to do was to take off her clothes. She'd probably have to throw them away; they'd never smell the same again. Even though she wanted to take a bath, she had to wash off all the soot, so she hopped into the shower. Then she fell into bed and didn't wake for an hour when she heard the twins slamming the door downstairs.

"Mom! We're home!"

"I'm back here, guys."

Ren's steps from the living room to the front door echoed down the hallway to her bedroom. He spoke to the twins in hushed tones.

Billy and Bobby walked back into Emma's darkened bedroom, their eyes widened. "You sick?" Bobby whispered.

"Nah. Just taking a little rest. I do that sometimes. How about we order in dinner for tonight?"

They nodded, their faces more solemn than usual.

Emma didn't want the boys to worry about her. "Any homework over the weekend?"

"A little. Not much." Bobby shrugged.

"Yeah. Me too," Billy said.

"You two can grab a snack now, and then we'll order something later. Let me know when you're hungry."

The boys moved into the kitchen. Emma heard the rattle of glass bottles as the refrigerator door opened.

She heard footsteps in the living room, then the kitchen, and knew Ren was making his way in to see her. She sat up in bed.

"How's the most gorgeous woman in the world?"

"If that's me, I'm better." Emma got out of bed, crammed her feet in her slippers, and grabbed a robe.

Ren sat down on the bed. "Come back here and tell me what happened, please." Emma crawled back into bed. He bent over, planted a kiss on Emma's forehead, and gave her a gentle hug.

She took a deep breath, reached out to touch Ren's hand, and told him everything that had happened that afternoon.

"I heard some EMTs say he was overcome with smoke, and I couldn't do anything. I tried. I failed at everything." She blew her nose and moved over so she could rest her head on Ren's shoulder.

"That was the fire in the Quarter I heard about. The one on Bourbon Street," he shook his head, "I can't believe you were there. You're so lucky to be alive." He held her close.

She sat up. "Yes. But Raphael was a great guy. It was my fault that he died. It was my idea to go back there. It was my idea to interview him. And I should have saved him." She put her head in her hands.

"Smoke inhalation can be a swift death."

153

She nodded. "It was so awful." She wiped her eyes and nose with the tissue.

"Do they know the cause of the fire?"

She looked up again. "They think it might have been arson. That could mean that Raphael's death could have been manslaughter, or maybe even murder. Someone may have even wanted to kill both of us."

"Can you think of anything that you've uncovered in Stacey's case that could have exposed you to this kind of danger?"

Emma nodded. "Maybe. I've got a couple of ideas. Her case is getting complicated."

"That's what I was afraid of. You've got to be more careful. You were minutes, maybe even seconds away from death. And, I hate to say it, especially now, but you've got to stop going into situations unprotected, without backup." He stood up and began pacing. "You should always let me or someone know your plans. You can be reckless." He paused. "I'm sorry. I don't mean to make you feel bad. But I'm upset too. I don't want to think about how close you were to dying today." He sat back down on the bed and reached out to her. "And I think it might be a good idea for you to see a counselor about the fire. It's tough to cope with a death like that, especially if you're the only survivor."

Emma shook her head. "I couldn't have anticipated a fire, so I never would have called you in advance of this. I don't see how I was reckless. And I'm okay. I was thinking of seeing a forensic psychiatrist about the case. Dean Munoz had given me the name of one earlier."

"It wouldn't hurt for you to talk to someone about your feelings too."

She sighed. "I think I'm fine. But you might be right, at least about one thing. I do feel guilty about Raphael. I'll try to come to some resolution about that. If I can't, I'll talk to someone. I promise." She leaned over and kissed Ren.

That night, when she tried to sleep, Emma couldn't get the image of Raphael lying in the alley out of her mind, and his shoes, his beautiful shoes, emerging from the blanket.

Chapter Twenty-One

Emma drove to a small uptown townhouse, entered the waiting room of Dr. Susan Vaidya's office, and sat down on an overly stuffed settee. Dr. Vaidya, a forensic psychologist, had come highly recommended by Dean Georges Munoz, Emma's former mentor from law school and current boss. Dr. Vaidya had helped the dean out on one of his cases years ago.

Emma was early and didn't want to admit it, but she was anxious about the meeting. She wasn't sure why. Her stomach was in knots.

The tiny waiting room was comfortable enough. Decorated in shades of beige, everything in the space was measured, reserved, and more than slightly boring, designed to put everyone who entered at ease, or to hide every nuance of Dr. Vaidya's personality. Emma found herself growing numb. She glanced at the stairs leading to the second floor and wondered if Dr. Vaidya lived in the rooms above.

After a few minutes, the door at the back of the room opened, and an attractive woman with long dark hair entered. Following brief introductions, Dr. Vaidya led Emma to her office, where on a small table, Emma noticed a tiny Ganesha, the Hindu elephant god, the god of beginnings and remover of obstacles. Emma smiled.

Dr. Vaidya gestured for Emma to have a seat on the couch. "Dean Munoz said you needed a little help on a case."

Emma thanked the doctor for agreeing to take the case on a pro bono basis, and summarized the events and issues.

"I heard about the murder of the leader of the temple. I know you must

155

have been shocked when you learned of Stacey's charges."

"I was. I don't believe Stacey killed James Crosby, and I don't believe the evidence will bear that out. But it's only been twelve days since the murder, and I don't have the supplemental reports yet. I hope to have them soon. I'll run everything by a pathologist to see what he thinks once they're in. But," she paused. "I'm here because I feel a little over my head in this case."

"There's a lot going on, isn't there? I'm happy to help a friend of the dean's."

"Thank you." Emma breathed in deeply, then exhaled, coughing. "I'm sorry. I've got an inflammation issue from smoke damage. I was caught in the French Quarter fire yesterday." She cleared her throat. "Dean Munoz tells me you have expertise in religious sects and cults. Of course, from what I can tell, the Japaprajnas don't consider themselves a cult."

"Expertise is an exaggeration. I have experience with cults. I have testified about them and have worked with several clients who were members of cults to help them detach from the group. I was born in India, where there are a number of active cults, but I moved here when I was young. So I'm more familiar with the cults in this country. And I'm still learning. Each group is different."

Emma nodded. "I'm sort of familiar with a couple of them too, and that's why I'm concerned." She told Dr. Vaidya about the confirmation that James was using his knowledge of the girls' secrets to coerce them into sexual activity with him and to manipulate Stacey into staying at the temple.

"Was there drug use there as well?"

"It looks that way, but, like I said, this is something I'm just now piecing together. I don't have a complete list of names of the girls who worked there or of the followers."

"You need a few names at least. See if anyone is willing to talk. The name of the organization is interesting. Japaprajna means, literally, 'chanting wisdom.' So when they put this group together, someone had something good in mind."

"I think so. And that would have been the founder, J.R. Crosby, James Crosby's father."

"There are four elements to a cult that are nearly always present. The first thing is a charismatic leader. Looks like James Crosby may have had a talent for drawing people in, and I would bet he also had a talent for bringing in money. Cults always have a transcendent belief system. And J.R. Crosby seems to have established that with his philosophies.

"Cults also have systems of control and influence. It looks like James Crosby may have used the information he gathered to control his followers."

Emma nodded. "He was a manipulative guy."

Dr. Vaidya paused and pulled a book down from her shelf. "Cults don't always fit into a neat category, but, from what you've told me, the Japaprajnas could fit into one fairly well. See what you think." She flipped through the book and found the chapter she was looking for. "This is it. The psychotherapy/human potential/ mass transformational cult[2]." Dr. Vaidya began to read, "This type of cult is motivated by personal transformation. The leader is self-proclaimed, and is sort of a super life coach. Their practices usually include encounter sessions, like James,'" she looked up from the book, 'which involve probing into personal life and thoughts. They use drugs, shame, and intimidation, verbal abuse, or humiliation in private or group settings to motivate followers.' Much like James did." She pointed out the paragraph to Stacey.

Emma nodded. She felt relieved. Validated. And so grateful someone could understand the dangerous dynamics of the group Stacey once belonged to. "Yes, from what I understand, James used all those tactics."

"Does that help you think about the way you want to approach the Japaprajnas and the case?"

Emma nodded. "It gives me a little more confidence that my suspicions are correct about the group. It is a cult."

"What you've described certainly sounds like the group had the dynamics of one. But you'll want to learn more. I've discovered that cults can be hard to unravel because the people in them don't want to face the fact that they're even in one. So, you should speak to a few followers. You'll probably be surprised by what you find. I'm guessing they'll be far more educated than you think. Most people who join cults are interested in self-improvement or the betterment of mankind. They want to live a more fulfilling life. Cult leaders tend to prey on good people. They're vulnerable because they're people who want to change for the better. They're often in the middle of a period of transition, a divorce, or a spouse has died. They can be manipulated. Many followers in cults are manipulated for money or contributions. Of course, you also need to speak to some of the employees at the temple. They're in a different category, and it sounds like they may have been controlled in a different way."

Emma raised her eyebrows. "I guess anyone can be manipulated."

"Some more than others. People who want to change are especially vulnerable. If you can find someone to talk to, see if you can get them to tell you what it was like when they first joined, and have them compare it to how it is now. I'm sure it changed. It would be best, actually, if you could speak to someone who left the group. It would be good to know if they were pressured to make a financial commitment or recruit other members."

"I haven't been able to get the name of any of the followers except for one man who passed out in the spa. I could contact him. It sounds like he was a follower."

"That's a good idea. See what his experiences were with the Japaprajnas. You said he passed out?"

Emma nodded. "He was probably drugged. But I'm pretty sure Crosby exploited the situation, insinuating that he brought the man, Mr. Zubowitz, back to life. Crosby's followers increased substantially after that."

"Have you spoken to any of the temple employees?"

"I've spoken to several. One girl, Angelina Diaz, was killed shortly after we spoke. Cecelia Crosby, the leader's wife, was there when I spoke to Angelina. She prevented me from asking most of the questions I'd prepared that day."

"One of the girls you spoke to was killed?"

Emma nodded. "Yes."

Dr. Vaidya shook her head. "Have you seen anything that might alert you that the group is a cover for other illegal activities?"

Emma nodded. "Yes. There seem to be shady labor practices going on, probably illegal. I think James was abusing his position for sex, but I don't think he was prostituting the girls, or making money from the girls for sex.

At least I haven't seen any evidence of that. And like I said, there may have been illegal drug activity. But I haven't figured it all out yet."

"You should try to speak to at least one additional young woman privately. But, if you don't mind my asking, where are you going with all of this? Are you looking for another motive for murder? Something you could use at trial to show reasonable doubt? Are you trying to find others who had motive to kill Mr. Crosby?"

Emma nodded. "I think my client was set up. But that's just a theory; I have no proof. And I also think several others had their own reason to kill James. All I have to do is raise a reasonable doubt at trial, but the evidence they have against Stacey so far seems compelling. I'm hoping we'll have some concrete facts we can rely on to prove Stacey's innocence once the supplemental reports are in. And I also need to figure out why Stacey was treated differently from the other workers at the spa.

"The best thing I can do right now is to develop a full understanding about what's going on at the temple, see who would have benefitted from James' death, and if and how drugs played a part in what happened. I've learned that defenses almost always develop from the facts surrounding a crime. So, the deeper my understanding of the case, the more I should be able to help Stacey."

Dr. Vaiyda nodded. "That makes sense."

"But another reason I'm here is to ask you to meet with Stacey. I didn't mention that she ran away right after she was released on bail. She finally found her way back, but I'm worried she might run away again. And so much depends on her following the rules the judge has laid out for her," Emma raised her hands, palms up. "I'm worried about her. I don't know what she's going to do next, and I don't know if I can trust her."

"That's reasonable."

"Don't get me wrong. I think Stacey has the mental capacity to understand the charges against her, and to help prepare her defense. But what sort of kid runs away? Is there a hidden trauma she won't talk about? Is she too impulsive to stand trial? Would she hold up to cross-examination? I need to figure out these issues too." Emma sighed.

" '*What sort of person runs away?*' is a pretty broad question. But I'd be happy to meet with Stacey and do an evaluation. Kids have a hard time expressing emotions. She's nineteen years old now, but I suspect she hasn't matured much over the age of sixteen, the age she was when she ran away from home, especially since that was how old she was when she joined the Japaprajnas.

"The brain isn't fully matured at age nineteen. And when kids have a hard time expressing their thoughts and emotions they feel powerless. They often feel the need to break away from the chains of authority, so, sometimes, they run away from home. At some point, someone will need to identify her trigger for running away when she was sixteen, because whatever it was, it's still affecting her. It's still influencing her decisions."

"I've tried to get her to open up, but nothing's worked so far. And there's been so much turmoil in her life."

"I'm sure it would be tough to get very much from her."

"I spoke to Stacey about coming in to meet with you, and she's okay with it. She's free all week. Do you have any time available?"

"I'll try to squeeze her in this week. Let's try Thursday at ten o'clock.

"Sounds good." Emma paused. "In joining a cult, Stacey was seeking another family, wasn't she?"

"I think she must have been. But it looks like she traded an unhappy one for something much worse."

Chapter Twenty-Two

Several days had passed since the fire, and Emma was anxious to speak to Moonstone. It was noon, and she didn't have an afternoon class, so she decided to take the chance that the shop was open. She hopped in her car and headed to Bourbon Street.

She was pleased to see the door propped open when she neared the store. The frame was cracked from where the firefighters had kicked it in on the day of the fire. Yellow crime scene tape had been broken and was fluttering in the breeze. But other than that, the front of the building seemed unharmed. Moonstone was sweeping the floor.

"Hello, Moonstone."

"Oh. Hi!" She ran to give Emma a hug. "Are you okay? I'm so sorry you were involved in that awful fire. And Raphael! How awful!"

Emma stepped back, surprised by Moonstone's warmth. Emma's eyes filled with tears at the mention of Raphael's name. She shook her head. "It was devastating." Her voice sounded much shakier than she'd anticipated. "I came here because I wanted to ask you a few questions about what happened that day."

Moonstone invited her in with a wave of the hand. Emma looked up toward the ceiling and noticed that the area around the air vents was blackened with soot. The back door of the room, which was usually closed, had been kicked open by the firefighters, as well as the locked door at the end of the short hallway. She would see all the way through to the back room.

"I'm surprised you're open."

"The fire inspector said the front section of the building was sound, so it was okay. They don't build them like this anymore."

Emma blinked. Her eyes welling. "Did you know that I was able to escape from the fire because Raphael managed to bend the burglar bars so I could squeeze through? I owe my life to him. But he couldn't escape." She blotted the tears from under her eyes. "After I got out of the room, I ran around to the front of the building. You were gone, and everything had been locked up. Where were you?"

"I'm so sorry. I feel awful." She wrung her hands. "Right after you left, I called Mira because I was low on some inventory. I mentioned seeing you and Raphael since she always likes to know who comes in the shop. Right after that, I got another call from Natalia, one of the girls who works at the spa. She said Mira wanted me to go pick up a package down at the post office on Loyola, and that the package contained the materials that I was missing. She gave me a package number so I could identify it. It was a pretty day, so I decided to walk."

Emma could feel her senses awaken. Natalia's immediate call back with an errand was suspicious. "How long is that walk?"

"Thirty minutes, round trip. But I spent a few minutes at the post office, too. So I was probably gone forty minutes, total. I thought if it was a big package, I could take a cab back. But when I got to the post office, they didn't have anything with the code number she gave me, not a package or an envelope. They didn't have anything addressed to Mira or the shop either. So I just walked back. When I got back to the shop, fire trucks were there, but the fire had already been put out. The police had put up the yellow tape, and the inspectors had begun their investigation. I wasn't even allowed back into the building to get my things. You were gone too. I had to leave my purse and keys and other stuff in the shop for the next couple of days. Things aren't exactly back to normal yet. It still smells like smoke in here. That's why I left the door open."

Emma frowned. "What happened here was a nightmare. And it was deliberate. Someone shoved rags in the ductwork and set them on fire." Emma pointed to the vents along the ceiling. "That's why the smoke is

162

blacker from the vents. The murderer would have entered the building from the shop to do that."

Moonstone sat down in the chair behind the counter. She put her head in her hand. "The fire inspectors questioned me the day it happened. I knew they suspected arson."

"Did you get the sense they suspected you?"

"They told me I'm one of the suspects and told me not to leave Orleans Parish. But I should be able to prove I was at the post office at the time of the fire."

"That doesn't really clear you. You could have planted the rags, lit them, and then walked to the post office. That sounds like something an arsonist would do."

Moonstone sat up and looked at Emma. "Well, I didn't."

"Did you tell them about the mix-up at the post office? That there was no package under your boss's name?"

She nodded. "I didn't want to, but I had to. But I don't think Mira is capable of killing anyone."

"What makes you so sure of that?"

"She struggles to do the right thing all the time."

"Like sell drugs?"

Moonstone sighed. "I realize it looks bad. But Mira isn't a bad person."

"You're correct. It looks like Mira would do just about anything to protect her territory, her sales, her business. Raphael must have threatened that in some way. It looks like she got you out of the way so she could come back here and light up the back of the building to rid herself of a couple of problems, namely, Raphael and me."

"I don't think so. But I don't have any proof. I really like Mira, even though she has problems. Big problems. She struggles to raise her son, and function on a daily basis. She's trying to overcome them. Except for Raphael's death, which is devastating, the fact that the back room burned is one of the best things that could have happened to her."

"Why? Because it destroyed her drug business?"

"It slowed it down anyway."

"Are you saying she has a drug problem?"

Moonstone nodded.

"I've heard that from one other person. And I suspected James did too."

"James? That's my understanding. I didn't know him as well. Mira introduced him to her connections out at the racetrack, and some of them dealt in animal tranquilizers. Mira seemed to be able to ignore James but not the drug."

"How does Mira's drug problem affect her?"

"She's changed since I met her. She was always such a good mother. And now, she's more forgetful, even a little irresponsible. She miscounts cash. She doesn't have the energy she used to and even slurs her words sometimes."

"I see. Well, someone set the fire. My bet is still on Mira. But if she didn't, who would want to kill Raphael - and me?"

"I really don't have a clue. I don't know why anyone would want Raphael dead. You might have just been an unlucky bystander."

"I'm guessing since the yellow tape has been broken, the investigators don't consider the building an active crime scene."

"That's my understanding. They said they're done with the criminal inspection."

"This is going to be tough for me, but I'd like to take a look in the back. Maybe there's something there that I haven't noticed before."

"Sure. Since the firefighters broke through the hallway door at the back of the shop, the one that was always locked, we could go straight through to the back room now. But you'd have to watch your step." She pointed the way through the rubble.

"If you don't mind, I'd like to see it from the back entrance, the same way Raphael and I entered the room on the day of the fire. I think I'll have a better sense of everything that happened that way."

Moonstone locked up the front of the shop and walked down the alley with Emma.

Emma was shocked by the devastation. Charred wood stood where a room had been earlier. Since the fire started in the ductwork, and dropped down into the walls, the sections of the back wall that were still standing were charred. Plaster on the remaining walls was blackened, and crumbling, exposing scorched beams.

"There must be a room or rooms separating the front of the shop from that back room. Otherwise, the back wall of the shop would have gone up in flames too."

"Right. The bathroom and the storage closet sit in between the shop and this back room. I guess they acted as a buffer for the shop."

"Could I see those two rooms?"

"Mira doesn't allow that, normally. But I don't see the harm. Let's go around to the front again. Now that we're here, I don't think it's a good idea to walk through all of the debris from the fire."

Moonstone unlocked the front door, then opened the door to the small hallway at the back of the shop a little wider. The back door of the short hallway had also been kicked in by the firemen. At either side of the hallway were doors that led to a small storage room and a bathroom. Moonstone unlocked the storage room, and Emma stepped inside, glancing up at the empty shelves. The wall of the room which faced the alley was blackened and crumbling.

"Do you know if the fire inspector looked in these two rooms?"

"They did. And they removed some stuff."

"Did you see what they took?"

"Maybe a plastic container of something."

"Do you recall what it looked like?"

"It was a blue plastic container with a label. That's all I know."

Chapter Twenty-Three

Craig Zubowitz wasn't hard to find. He owned a chain of pizza parlors in the city by the name of "Zubowitz's." Emma had combed the phonebook for his name and found five pizza restaurants. One was close to Pirates Alley in Jackson Square. She wasn't familiar with the chain and had never visited any of the stores. But she knew the connection between the man who fainted in the spa and the pizza place off Pirate's Alley would have to be an interesting one.

She dropped Stacey off at Dr. Vaidya's office for her evaluation and drove down to Jackson Square the following Thursday for lunch, thinking she'd give Zubowitz's hand-tossed crust a try. It was Halloween, and things were starting to get crazy in the Quarter, but she was able to find a spot on the street and fed the meter a few quarters. She checked the address she had scribbled on a sticky note.

The restaurant blended in with the other eighteenth-century French Quarter shops and buildings on the block. The storefront was quaint and charming, with a wide bay window framed by a red and white checkered curtain. The window box was overflowing with herbs and tiny flowers. A duplicate of the restaurant could easily have been found anywhere in Europe.

Emma walked into the compact eatery, delighted to find the walls covered from floor to ceiling with paintings and photos of Italian beauties: Sophia Lauren, Gina Lollobrigida, Claudia Cardinale, even the Mona Lisa, and Botticelli's *The Birth of Venus*. The room was filled with spindly tables covered with red-and-white checked cloths. The two chandeliers, which

166

had to be original to the building, cast a hazy glow about the space, making it even more appealing. She couldn't help but notice the stack of empty pizza boxes lining the wall along the back counter. From what she could see, they were identical to the boxes she'd seen at the back of the ETC shop. She sat down at a round-topped table for two and was immediately greeted by an eager waiter.

"Can I get you something else to drink?" He asked as he placed a glass of water down on the table with a flourish.

Emma shook her head. "No, this is good. And I think I'm ready to order. But I have a question."

"Sure, shoot."

"Would it be possible to speak to the owner, Mr. Zubowitz?" She paused, glancing up at the young man.

"Sure thing. I'll put your order in and let Mr. Zubowitz know. What would you like?"

"A Margherita pizza, hand-tossed." She paused. "He's here?"

"He just walked in." The waiter scribbled down her order in his notepad, turned on his heel, like he was on parade duty for the Marine Corps, and marched into the kitchen.

Emma sipped her water, enjoying the portraits surrounding the room. She was wondering how much they'd paid for Andy Warhol's print of Sophia Loren when a lumbering man pushed through the swinging doors from the kitchen. He approached her table.

"Hi, I'm Craig Zubowitz. What can I do for you?" He grasped the back of the empty chair at her table, puffing from the exertion of his short walk.

Emma smiled and invited him to sit down next to her. Mr. Zubowitz plopped down, exhaling loudly. Emma couldn't tell if sitting was a relief or painful for him.

Craig Zubowitz wasn't what Emma was expecting. Middle-aged, paunchy, pale, and graying, he was everyone's tired uncle. The sort of guy who worked hard and didn't take care of himself, he was the nice man people worried about as they watched him eat too much and fail to exercise. Even though he returned Emma's smile, his eyes were melancholy.

Emma introduced herself and explained who she represented.

"Nice to meet you. I remember Stacey. I hope everything is going to be okay with her."

"We're working up her case now, and I'd like to speak to you about a few things. But first I'd like to compliment you on your restaurant. Such great atmosphere. How long have you been here?"

"About ten years. Ever since I moved to the city. I always wanted to open a pizza place. I'm half Italian, on my mother's side. Her parents were from a little town by the name of Ferrazzano." He smiled. "She made the best pizza in the world, and that's no exaggeration. She gave me the recipe for the crust and the sauce. Plus, my dad ran a restaurant in New York City for a while, so I guess it's in my blood." He raised his hands. "My wife is responsible for the décor. Not me. She had a touch."

"I agree." Emma smiled. "The main reason I came by was to speak to you about your experiences with the Japaprajnas. I know you had a health episode at the spa once, too. I'm doing this in preparation for Stacy's trial, but if you're uncomfortable about anything I'm asking, just let me know, and I'll stop."

"Okay." He paused. "I don't mind talking to you. I've been thinking about the group lately, especially since James died. I was a member. My wife died several years ago, and I felt the need for something more in my life. I was at an all-time low then and needed to belong to something. Or maybe I just needed something besides the restaurant to occupy my time. And I wasn't ready to see anyone else. I'm still not.

"Anyway, I drove by their place one day and decided to go in. I liked the color of the building. It reminded me of Judy, my wife. Magenta was her favorite color." His eyes had a wistful, faraway look.

"So I started going there regularly. Once a week at first. Then more. I liked the candles, the incense, and their rituals. I found it comforting." He leaned back in his chair. "James had sessions where he talked about how to love yourself and find meaning in your life, even if you were alone. I started going to more and more meetings because they were making me feel better. Of course, you paid for the sessions, but that was okay by me. They were like lessons."

"I'm so sorry about the loss of your wife. But you enjoyed going to the temple?"

"At first. One of the other things he insisted on was this cleansing thing. You had to confess all of the bad things you'd done in your life, and he recorded them. He said that was the only way to become whole. To recognize everything you'd done wrong, and to atone for them.

"Before I knew it, James made me a commander in the temple and said I had to invest. I sent monthly checks. He said recruiting people was important too. Soon I'd approached almost everyone I knew. My manager here at this store, Lenny, joined."

Lenny. The name sounded familiar. Then Emma remembered. Ren had told her about him. He was the pizza restaurant manager who had identified Angelina Diaz the night she was murdered. "How old is Lenny?"

"He's a young guy. I'm pretty sure he's still in his twenties. I can verify that. Is it important?"

"We can get back to Lenny later. I'd like to talk about the day you passed out at the spa. Do you have any recollection of what happened?"

He nodded. "Yeah. I remember that day. I was there for one of my personal sessions. James had been working with me about loneliness. How to deal with the loss of my wife. He thought a massage would help me. I agreed to it because I was missing human touch. I mean, I still do. I'd never had anything like a massage before. So I was nervous. He put a powder in his hand and asked me if I wanted a little dust to calm me down, and allow me to enjoy the massage. But once the massage started, I passed out. I think my heart stopped beating for a couple of seconds."

"What made you think that? Were you told you had a heart attack?"

Mr. Zubowitz shook his head. "No. My doctors ran an ECG. Everything was fine. They said I had an episode of something called syncope. I just passed out for a few seconds."

"Do you know what that powder was?"

He shook his head. "I don't. But it looked like cocaine."

"You didn't ask?"

"No. Now I can see that was pretty stupid."

"How much did James put in his hand?"

"Just a little. He gave me a little tube, and I inhaled it real quick."

"How did the powder make you feel?"

"For a moment, I felt utter bliss and happiness. Then I got dizzy, and then I saw some strange colors and things. Then I guess I passed out. I don't have any memory of anything after that until I woke up."

"Had they started the massage, or don't you remember?"

"Yeah, they started."

Emma hesitated and glanced up at Mr. Zubowitz. "Was the massage sexual in nature?"

"No. It wasn't anything like that." Mr. Zubowitz's face turned red. "I wouldn't feel right doing something like that."

"How long ago did that happen?"

"That was a couple of years ago, I'd guess."

"Did you ever hear anyone say that James brought you back to life?"

"I knew others said that, and he didn't discourage it. I think he probably used it to get people to come to the temple. And it was probably one of the reasons I decided to leave."

"When did Lenny join the group?"

"Right about then. About two years ago."

"So you're not a member any longer?"

He shook his head. "No."

"Because James took credit for healing you?"

"That was one thing. But he also started pressuring me for money. I was already giving five thousand dollars a month, and he wanted more. What he really wanted was the deed to at least one of my restaurants." He shook his head.

"What did you do?"

"I stopped going so often, at first. But he kept pressuring me, and I told him to back off. That I was going to quit going altogether."

Emma jotted down a few notes. Apparently, James pressured, bullied, and blackmailed more than just the girls who worked at the spa. "What did

CHAPTER TWENTY-THREE

James do about that?"

"He said he had my tapes, and he'd make them public. That no one would go to my pizza places at all if he did that."

"What was on your tapes, if you don't mind saying."

"I told him things I did when I was younger. Things I'm not proud of. I hung out with some guys I shouldn't have. Got involved in a few minor robberies, just petty theft stuff. But there was never violence or anything like that. I never got caught. James threatened to go to the newspapers, even the local TV stations, with what I told him so I'd look bad in the community. I guess he thought it might hurt my business. But he was really trying to force me to keep making those payments."

"What did you do?"

"I kept making them for a while. Then I realized he was just a bully, and I told him I'd file charges against him for extortion if he kept up his threats. So he backed off."

"How long ago was this?"

"Probably about a year ago."

"Way before James was killed."

He nodded. "That's right. Most of the members of the temple are women. Mostly well-educated. They drive nice cars, wear nice clothes. I'm sure James has exploited a few of them too. I joined at one of those times in my life when I was really down. And then, after a while, I woke up. I could see what James was up to. But I don't think a lot of people who are still there see it at all. It's like an addiction."

"Do you know anyone who is still at the temple?"

He shook his head. "No, except Lenny. I never really got to know any of the other members, except for him."

"Is Lenny still a member?"

"I think he might be."

"Does he pay thousands a month for his membership?"

"I'm pretty sure he doesn't have thousands a month to pay."

"I'd like to speak to Lenny before I leave today, if you don't mind."

He nodded. "Sure."

"This is a change of subject, but do you have a delivery service for your pizzas?"

He pointed to the back of the restaurant. "Here, in house. We have a truck, and we also have a guy who delivers pizzas on a bicycle sometimes, if they're really short trips."

"Who do you use for your deliveries?"

"Sometimes Lenny, on both truck and bicycle, and sometimes we use other guys who work here. It just depends."

"Lenny, the manager, delivers?"

"He likes to get out of the shop sometimes. So he asked me if he could make deliveries. If he's caught up, I have no problem with that."

"Could I speak to Lenny now?"

"He might have gone out on a delivery. I'll check." Mr. Zubowitz turned around in his chair and motioned to one of the busboys, who was cleaning the table next to them. The busboy stopped what he was doing and walked over. "Check on Lenny. If he's here, have him come out here and join us for a minute." He faced Emma. "They're checking."

Emma nodded. "How long has Lenny worked for you?"

"He's been with me about three years. He was a kid when he started on deliveries only. Then he moved up to waiting tables, and then I let him try his hand at hiring waiters and managing the schedule. He seems pretty good at all of that. Better at that than waiting tables. We all have our talents." He paused. "Here he comes."

A slim young man in a black t-shirt entered the room. His limp blonde hair, parted down the side, hung in his eyes, and his face looked clammy even though it was cool inside the restaurant. There were noticeably dark circles under his eyes. He looked like he needed a shower and a good night's sleep.

He nodded toward Emma and sat down at the table.

"I represent Stacey Roberts, who you might know has been charged in the murder of James Crosby. Do you know Stacey?"

"I know who she is."

"How is that?"

"I'd see her at the temple sometimes. And she asked me if she could leave her table and chairs behind the shop a few weeks ago when she read tarot cards in Jackson Square." Lenny looked down at his hands and began fidgeting with a ring on his little finger.

"Do you know Mira Godfrey from the temple too?"

He shrugged. "I know who she is, too."

"Has she ever asked you to do any work for her at the ETC shop?"

He stared at Emma.

Mr. Zubowitz leaned over the table. "Can't you answer that question?"

"Did James ever ask you to do anything for him either at the shop, or anywhere else?"

Lenny crossed his arms. "I don't have to answer any of these questions. I know my rights. And you're not a cop."

"You're absolutely right. You don't have to answer any of my questions. But I'd like to know the answer in case you are subpoenaed for trial, and the DA asks you the same question." Emma flipped a page in her notepad. "Just a few nights after Stacey had gotten out on bail Angelina Diaz was killed. And only a few days ago, Raphael, the driver from the temple was killed in a suspicious fire. I have a feeling you might have information to share about one or both of these murders."

Lenny looked up at Emma, sneering. "I don't know what you're talking about."

"Why can't you just answer her question, Lenny?" Mr. Zubowitz was beginning to turn a darker shade of red.

"Okay. No. Mira and James never asked me to work for them."

"Can you tell me why someone your size and who fits your description was picking up pizza boxes behind the ETC shop the night Angelina Diaz was killed? The description of the boxes matches those in the back of the room here. Do you know anything about that?"

Lenny raised the palm of his right hand. "Just because the guy was my size doesn't mean it was me."

Mr. Zubowitz stared at Emma. "Wait a minute. Why were my pizza boxes in the back of another shop? I had those boxes designed for my shop. No one else has permission to use them." He looked at Lenny. "What's going on here?"

Mr. Zubowitz stood up and strode to the back of the restaurant, quicker than Emma thought a man of his size and age could ever have moved. He crashed through the swinging doors. Emma followed him as he ran through the kitchen and out of the back door to the delivery truck in the back alley. Lenny lagged behind, keeping an eye on his boss.

When he reached the truck, Mr. Zubowitz unlocked it and checked the back of the covered bed. It was empty. Just then, the delivery boy wheeled around the back of the alley, a few pizza boxes strapped on the back of his bicycle.

Mr. Zubowitz gestured for the delivery boy to approach him.

"Let me see what's inside those boxes."

The boy hopped off the bicycle, unstrapped the boxes from behind the back seat, and handed the boxes over to Mr. Zubowitz, who immediately opened one of the lids.

"What's this?"

He showed the contents to Emma. The box contained plastic bags of white powder.

"I suspect, if you get it tested, you'll discover it's ketamine."

Emma glanced up in time to see Lenny walking swiftly down the back alley. Mr. Zubowitz looked up at the same time.

"Lenny. Get your ass back here!" he said loud enough to be heard a block away.

Lenny started running.

"Go any farther, and I'm calling the police," Mr. Zubowitz yelled across the parking lot.

Lenny stopped, turned around, and walked back to his boss.

"You have some explaining to do."

Chapter Twenty-Four

"It might be a good idea for both of you to call your attorneys and get some advice on what to do next," Emma said.

"First, let's go up to my office, away from my other employees and customers. I need to understand what's going on. Ms. Thornton, I'd appreciate it if you'd come, too." Mr. Zubowitz's face was contorted with rage.

Mr. Zubowitz marched the small group up a flight of stairs, each step causing the stairway to quake. He grabbed his keys from his back pocket and shoved one in the lock. The door swung open before he turned the key.

None of the attention and care poured into the restaurant had been given to the upstairs office. Stains from the leaky roof covered the ceiling, and water had dripped down the walls, discoloring the plaster and causing it to crumble in several places. Mr. Zubowitz pulled up a couple of chairs in front of his desk and gestured for Emma and Lenny to sit down. He glowered at Lenny, his face purple.

"This situation isn't a good one for Zubowitz's, or you." His voice was low and his hands were shaking. "So, start from the beginning. How did you get involved with drug runs in pizza boxes, and where did you get the drugs in the first place?"

Lenny pressed his lips together and shook his head. "I'm not going to answer any of your questions. Everything's just going to blow up in my face if I do, especially with her sitting here." He pointed his thumb at Emma.

Emma turned toward Lenny. "I'll leave. I'm sure you and Mr. Zubowitz can handle the issues about the pizza boxes and the drugs. My main concern is what you saw the night Angelina was killed. And I'd like to know if you saw who left Angelina's body in the alley behind the restaurant. I know you identified Angelina to the police."

Lenny flushed.

"If you can't identify the person, can you at least identify the car?" Emma said.

The veins in Mr. Zubowitz's neck were starting to protrude. He glared at Lenny. "What body? Why was a body dropped off here? My entire business is on the line because you decided to carry on a little side drug business, and now there's a dead body?" He turned to Emma. "And Ms. Thornton, I appreciate your help, but I really don't want to call a lawyer who'll just charge me an arm and a leg. This is between Lenny, me, and the cops." Mr. Zubowitz's face grew a deeper shade of purple as he punched his finger into his desk. "And Lenny, you're up to your ears in it. For all I know, you've been operating your little side business out of my other restaurants, too. I need to check with the delivery boy about deliveries from those shops." Mr. Zubowitz reached for a notepad. "What's his name?"

"George. The delivery guy is George." Lenny crossed his arms.

"Mr. Zubowitz, there are ways to handle this, and I can't really give you advice. Of course, Lenny could go to the police himself. But something needs to be done. If Lenny reports what's been going on himself, it could work in his favor."

"So if I talk to the cops, they'll let me off?"

"No. I'm not saying that, Lenny. What I'm trying to explain is that so far, three people from the Japaprajna temple have died, and it seems that at least two of them have some connection to the drug activity you've been involved in. It's only a matter of time before the police discover it for themselves, and if you come forward now and help them unravel everything that's been going on, you might be able to cut a deal for yourself. But I can't promise anything, especially since the DA is the only one who can cut deals."

Mr. Zubowitz frowned. "I don't feel like messing around any longer with this. I'm just going to call the cops now and be done with this and him. I have nothing to gain by delaying. But I do need to know if there are any more drugs on my property. If there are, I need to find them and get rid of them."

Emma shook her head. "That wouldn't be a good idea, Mr. Zubowitz. That would be tampering with evidence."

Lenny shook his head. "No. That's it. There aren't any more drugs, right now anyway. There was a fire at our usual pick-up place the other day behind the shop, and we haven't figured out another spot to meet."

"I guess I'll just hold on to it for now." Mr. Zubowitz gestured toward the pizza box on his desk.

"I can just flush it." Lenny extended his hand.

Emma frowned. "Nope. You can't do that, Lenny."

"That's okay. I'll take care of it." Mr. Zubowitz glared at Lenny, closed the lid of the box, and put it on his desk. He grabbed his keys.

"Okay. Let's go, Lenny. I'll drive you to the station, and I'll bring the pizza box with me. If you want to tag along, Ms. Thornton, you're welcome."

"Hey, um," Lenny nodded at Emma. "I saw the car that night. But that's it. I saw it drive up, and Angelina was pushed out."

"You didn't see the driver?"

"No. It just happened so fast."

"What did the car look like?"

"It was big and black, and I think it only had two doors."

* * *

Emma followed Mr. Zubowitz and Lenny into the police station but motioned for them to have a seat in the waiting area while she asked if the detective in charge of the Angelina Diaz case was available to speak to them.

A few minutes later, Ren walked down the hall into the waiting area. He smiled when he saw Emma.

"Well, this is a surprise. What brings you here?"

Emma made introductions to Mr. Zubowitz and Lenny and gave a brief overview of why they were there. Ren signaled to a uniformed cop to show the men to a couple of conference rooms in the back, then turned to Emma.

"Why don't you step back here with me for a minute?"

"Sounds good." Emma was nearly screaming inside. Lenny's statement about the black car should prove to Ren that Stacey had nothing to do with Angelina's murder, at least.

He led her down a corridor and into a room with a two-way mirror. Lenny was waiting in a small room.

"I wasn't sure what was up, but I thought it was probably best to speak to Mr. Zubowitz and Lenny separately."

"I think that's a good idea too."

"So, lady, what's this all about?"

"From what I can tell, drugs, ketamine, and how to cleverly sell them without being detected, in broad daylight, in pizza boxes. And to top it all off, Lenny said he witnessed the killer dumping Angelina's body behind the pizza restaurant." Emma raised her eyebrows.

"Whoa! He saw the dump!" He nodded. "I wondered about that when he told me he knew the girl that night. So I will need to talk to him, and I'll need to get Narcotics involved in this, too."

"Yes, and I told the guy, Lenny, that the DA might be interested in cutting a deal with him if he talked."

"Oh, great, Emma."

"Well, couldn't you ask the DA if he was interested at least? He might be. Depending on what information he gives you, of course."

"You brought his employer, Mr. Zubowitz, too? Was he involved in the drug sales?"

"Doesn't look like it."

"He found out about the drugs in his pizza boxes and was going to the cops?"

"That's about what we were looking at."

"So, Lenny would have been arrested one way or the other. I'm not sure what he has to bargain with."

Emma shook her head. "I don't know either. You'll just have to talk to him. He could know a lot more. The important thing for me, since you think my client is a person of interest in the Angelina Diaz case, is that he saw Angelina being thrown out of a car. And since Stacey doesn't have access to a car, that takes her out as a suspect from that case, anyway."

"I'm not sure about that yet. But, I agree, it could help. I'll set this up and see what they both have to say. It'll take a minute, and since you brought them in, and don't have any interests that are adverse to Lenny, I'm going to let you watch. But you'll have to go through regular channels if you need to use any of this information at trial."

* * *

Emma sat in the small dark room, watching as Ren and two detectives dressed in street clothes walked into the adjoining room where Lenny had been waiting for about fifteen minutes. He was biting his fingernails, and his knee was jumping up and down like a piston.

Ren cleared his throat. "Before we begin, even though you're here voluntarily, you still have the right to an attorney at any time. You still have the right to remain silent. Anything you say can and will be used against you in a court of law. If you decide to proceed at this time and change your mind, you can stop the questioning and request an attorney. If you cannot afford an attorney, one will be appointed for you. Would you still like to proceed?"

Lenny nodded.

The detective identified himself and started the recording.

"So Lenny, Mr. Zubowitz tells us that approximately ten bags of this product was found in one of his pizza boxes today. Let the record reflect that I've picked up a small, clear plastic bag containing approximately 10ccs of white powder. Do you know anything about what's in this bag?" One of the detectives pulled the bag of drugs from the pizza box and dangled it in the air.

Lenny pursed his lips like he was about to answer but paused. "Can we work out a deal first, before I talk?"

"No. That's not how it works. Talk first, then we'll speak to the DA to see if he might be interested in what you have to say. Your deal, if you get one, depends on how good your information is. And if we discover your information isn't true, then the deal is dead." He paused. "So what's in the bag?"

"It's ketamine."

"Where did this ketamine come from?"

"I picked it from some suppliers at the Fairgrounds. Then the stuff is packaged up by some girls at the back of the ETC shop, and I'd pick it up there again for delivery around the French Quarter."

"How long have you been making these runs?" The officer adjusted his seat so that it was closer to Lenny.

Lenny hesitated. "Maybe a couple of years."

"Who supplied the ketamine?"

Lenny looked down at his folded hands.

The officer stood up, looming over Lenny, and leaned over the table. "You're not going to get anywhere with the DA or any of us here if you play little games with us and waste our time." He sat back in his chair. "You're the one that's supposed to be talking. And, you're the one that wanted the deal. I don't care about a deal. We have enough information to arrest you today and go home. I don't care what happens to you." He pointed in the direction of Central Lockup. "But you're going to end up on the other side of those bars over there if you don't start talking soon."

Lenny glanced at the other officers in the room and cleared his throat.

"Bradley Adcock and Theodore Cook."

"Were you the head of this operation?"

"No, that would have been James Crosby, I guess. He's the guy who was killed about two weeks ago."

"Did you work for James Crosby?"

Lenny cocked his head to the side. "I guess you could call it that. About two years ago, when I was at the temple one day, James and Mira Godfrey called me up to their office and asked me if I wanted to make some extra money. Mira is his assistant. They said they needed someone to move some medicine, tranquilizers, to places around the Quarter. Most of the places were clubs. A lot of strip clubs and some bars. They said they'd need me to go to the Fairgrounds sometime and pick up the medicine, and then they'd package it up for delivery. We deliver it on bicycle mostly."

"In pizza boxes?" Ren asked.

"Yeah."

"Where did you get the boxes?"

Lenny hesitated, glancing up at Ren. "I stole them from the restaurant I work at. I'd bring in a few boxes at a time to the shop, maybe about ten. They worked real good. And bicycling was the best way to get around because the boxes weren't that big, and we could weave in and out of traffic really easy. Parking wasn't a problem either," Lenny said.

"Who did the packaging?"

"The girls who worked at the temple. They'd work at the back of the shop and package the stuff up in the boxes. I'd pick up the boxes in the truck, and George, the delivery guy at Zubowitz's, or I would make the deliveries."

"Did George realize he was delivering drugs?"

"I never told him he was. He may have figured it out." He shrugged.

"Did you see Angelina Diaz the night she was killed?" Ren asked.

Lenny hesitated. "Yeah."

"That means she was preparing the pizza boxes right before she was murdered."

"That's right." He nodded.

"Do you remember anything unusual about that night?" Ren said.

"No. I just picked up the boxes and left. I wasn't there that long."

"What about the fact that I saw you later on that night, around midnight, when Angelina's body was found behind the pizza restaurant?"

Lenny's mouth dropped open. "Oh yeah. That's who you are. I knew you looked familiar. I remember now." He nodded. "Yeah. I guess you could say that was unusual."

"Tell me everything that happened that night."

"I got back with the stuff and was moving it into a refrigerator in the back of the restaurant that has a lock on it. I was afraid to leave the stuff in the truck overnight because the camper top lock doesn't work too good. So I was locking stuff up in the refrigerator when I heard a car pulling in the back alley real fast on that gravel and a car door opening, and then a kind of soft thud. I went running out to see what it was and saw a car pulling out and Angelina on the ground."

"What did you do next?"

"I checked on Angelina. She didn't look too good, so I called 911, I didn't know what else to do."

"Did you get a look at the car?"

"Yeah, it was a big, black two-door car."

"What about Angelina?"

"She wasn't breathing. I think she was already dead."

"Were you able to see anyone in the car?"

"They were peeling out by the time I got there."

"No other questions," Ren said.

"Have you ever used ketamine?" A detective asked.

Lenny shook his head.

"No one tried to give it to you at the temple?"

"Once, but I wouldn't take it. They didn't tell me what it was, but I knew. I didn't know why they were offering it to me. I thought it was weird."

"Have you ever given this drug to anyone else?"

He shook his head. "Nah. That sort of stuff ain't for me."

"Write down a list of everyone you delivered the drug to." He handed a notepad and pen to Lenny.

Lenny wrote down a list of names and handed the list back to the officer.

"The main guy we delivered to was Robert Henderson, a bouncer at The Wiz."

"Did you ever contact any dealers or sources outside of the country for the drug?"

"Nah. I only dealt with James or Mira, and those girls who packaged everything up for them. Never anyone else, except of course, the guys at the Fairgrounds and the guys at the clubs. You know, the sellers and the buyers."

"We're going to process this information, Lenny. We need to run a screening on the contents of the package that was in the pizza box. We're going to hold you while we investigate. I take it you don't have an attorney?"

Lenny shook his head. "That's right. Do I need one?"

"That's up to you."

Emma glanced at her notes. The name Lenny mentioned, Robert Henderson, was the bouncer at The Wiz, the club where Mariana Hernandez worked. The same club where Raphael used to work. It was right around the corner.

Chapter Twenty-Five

Emma left the police station and walked down Chartres, something rare for her, especially in the middle of a work week. It was even more unusual to be there in the middle of the day. The Quarter looked dirtier and seedier in the afternoon than at night, particularly when it was less crowded. It was easier to see the debris which had collected in the street gutters and the cracks along the sidewalks with fewer pedestrians crowding the walkways. But she still loved it. She loved the shops and swooned over the antiques and avant-garde clothing in the windows as she passed. Since it was Halloween day, shopkeepers were dressed in a variety of creative costumes. Store front windows exploded with black and orange ghoulish creativity. Sometimes she couldn't help but walk in to gush over something stunning. But she couldn't stop this afternoon. This afternoon was about meeting Mariana Hernandez.

It had been obvious that James and Mira were behind the ketamine sales, but Emma was glad to finally have it confirmed. Ketamine was an unusual specialty in the drug trade, but Mira's connections at the track and its current popularity made it less remarkable. Still, Emma was surprised the police hadn't caught them before now. ETC's merchandise should have been a red flag for the cops, warning them to keep an eye out for drugs.

The Wiz was on Bourbon Street, just a few blocks away. It was one of the nicer clubs, but they were all about the glitz and glam, lights and action, and didn't fare well during daylight hours.

Emma arrived at the club in the middle of the afternoon only to discover that she was too early to see bouncer Robert Henderson. His work shift began at five o'clock. She pushed through the black velvet curtains covering the front door. Blasted by frigid air conditioning and the rancid odor of spoiled fruit juice and whiskey, Emma considered turning around and walking back outside. But she thought better of it.

She moved into a dark space dominated by a bar that stretched the entire length of the room. Mirrors, bright neon lights, and a giant wine glass filled with last year's Mardi Gras beads decorated the back wall, along with a choice selection of whiskeys, liquors, and liqueurs. A handful of people were sitting on stools drinking Appletinis and Cosmopolitans. House music played overhead.

An exhausted-looking woman with purple bags under her eyes stuffed a dirty rag in the back pocket of her pants. Her spiky hair, double nose piercings, and neck tattoo signaled a warning. She was not one to mess with.

"What would you like?" She pulled the rag out of her pocket and cleaned the counter in front of Emma with the dirty scrap. Her voice was warm and friendly, in sharp contrast to her appearance.

"I'd like to see Mariana Hernandez, if she's here."

"Mariana!" The woman threw a dirty glass in a sink filled with hot soapy water. "She's here somewhere. But she doesn't come on until later tonight."

"What does Mariana do here?"

"She's a dancer. And she's real good. Some of the girls just get up there and move around, but Mariana really dances. She's got talent."

Emma watched a slender young woman with long black hair approach the bar.

"Did you call me, Frances?"

"Yeah, this lady wants to speak to you." She nodded toward Emma.

Emma stepped forward and introduced herself to Mariana.

"I'd like to ask you a few questions when you're free."

"I have some time right now. Want to go sit down in the club section? It's more private than the bar."

They walked into the club and sat down at a small table in front of the stage area. Black velvet curtains surrounded the large room, and bright fluorescent lights shone brightly. Since it was empty, and the air conditioning was still set for a large crowd, the room was freezing. The floor was covered with a shiny laminate, but it hadn't been cleaned from the night before. The tiny tabletop was sticky; Emma avoided touching the surface.

"I'd like to start at the beginning and ask you where you were at the time of James' murder?"

"I was right here. The police already checked me out. I had been working here several months at the time James was killed. I'm sure you can see my schedule for that day or speak to my boss, if you'd like."

"Thanks. I'll check it on the way out." Emma pulled out her notebook and reviewed what she'd been told about Mariana's circumstances when she began working at the temple. "So, you weren't a runaway like Stacey?"

"No. About a year ago, my parents had to go back to Mexico to bring money to our family there, and they left me at our apartment. I was seventeen. Old enough to be left alone. They didn't know the city was going to shut down the place. There was a problem with the plumbing, a sanitation thing. Everyone who was living there had to go find somewhere else to live, and I didn't have the money to do that. So, when it was time to leave, I found a bench in the French Quarter and started sleeping there. Stacey found me after I'd been there for about a week. She told me about the temple and said that I could stay there with free room and board if I worked in the back, giving massages. That sounded pretty good to me. I went with her and met James and Cecelia."

"And you worked there about six months?"

"That's right." Marianna reached into her purse and pulled out a pack of cigarettes. She pulled out one and lit it. "Everyone smokes here." She smiled. "Would you like one?"

Emma shook her head. "No. Gave them up years ago, but I still love the smell." She took a deep breath and smiled. "Can you tell me why you left?"

"I thought it was going to be a regular job. Instead, it was a trap. There was no salary. Cecelia had a million rules, and James was always around, trying to get one of us into a session, or his bed."

"Did you ever attend any of James' sessions?"

Mariana nodded. "I did."

"Did he ever offer a white powder substance to you during any of your sessions?"

"He tried. He put some white powder in the palm of his hands and gave me a little straw to inhale it with. But I didn't do it."

"Why not?"

"Because I didn't trust him and because I didn't know what it was. He said it was something to relax me. I didn't need to be relaxed."

Emma paused. "Did James ever try to have sex with you?"

Mariana sighed. "Yes. Several times. He asked me to go to that little cottage in the back courtyard with him. He even threatened to have my parents deported if I didn't have sex with him, but they were still in Mexico then. He was always using some threat to get girls to do what he wanted. If they snorted that powder of his, they were in trouble. That was key. I heard the powder knocked you out. Otherwise, it was easy to keep him at arm's length."

" Was James the main reason you left?"

She nodded. "I think so, although like I said, there was a lot wrong with the place. But James made life miserable. He was a monster. I had to get out of there."

"And Raphael helped you escape?"

"Yes, me and several other girls, too."

Emma paused. "Have you heard about the fire at the shop?"

"Yes. And I know that Raphael died in the fire." Mariana bit her bottom lip. "One of the girls from the temple told me. I still can't believe it." Her eyes welled with tears.

"I was there that day. He saved my life." Emma was doing all she could not to cry.

Marianna reached out and touched Emma's clenched hands. "Raphael was a blessing to us, and it looks like he was one for you too. He loved doing for others. So do you, or you wouldn't be helping Stacey. I'm sure you did your best that day. We are working to find his sister so we can finalize plans to have him cremated and have a memorial service for him. Give me your information before you leave, and I'll let you know the details."

"Thank you. I want to contribute something toward the costs. Get flowers. Anything I can do." Emma looked down at her hands for a moment, then glanced back up. "Do you know of anyone, any of the other massage girls, any of the followers, or anyone else who may have had a reason to kill James Crosby?"

"Just about anyone who lived at the temple might have wanted him dead. He took advantage of everyone, and treated the people who worked there like he owned them. That included his wife and Mira. He didn't have respect for anyone."

"What can you tell me about his relationship with his wife?"

"Not much, really, but it was obvious to anyone who hung around the temple for any time at all that James was trying to seduce every girl who worked there. That must have been humiliating. Cecelia never seemed to notice or mind, though."

"What about Mira?"

"Mira was nothing more than another worker to him. And was probably the only one he didn't try to have sex with. Except I guess she'd had sex with him at least once. She called herself his partner, but he ordered her around as if she was his gofer. She kept the company books and seemed to know more about the business than he did, but he treated her like his personal servant. And he never gave her any credit for any of her ideas or her work."

"Sounds like he didn't like women."

"It was more than that. He seemed to enjoy humiliating them." She turned her head, quickly exhaling a cloud of smoke.

"Are things better for you since you left?"

"The job I have isn't great, but I'm saving money, and I'm free to take classes at a community college. I'm going to get my degree. So, I'm not going to be stuck here."

"Can you tell me anything else about the use of drugs at the temple?"

"I think James may have used the same stuff he was giving everyone else. That's just my opinion. He was irritable. Forgetful. He was always tired, and sometimes his speech was slurry. His face would get very red. He used to teach karate but stopped because I think his coordination nosedived. He reminded me of my uncle who drank too much. I think James was an addict."

"Do you know anyone who took ketamine, other than James?"

"Mira, and one of the girls who worked at the spa who's gone now. She said it makes you feel so happy, like it's the best day of your life. And then you pass out. I think the happy feeling she felt is why people want to take more. She said she lost control of her body the second time she took it, then passed out. It scared her. I've watched people in my family who have drug problems. It's always the same. It's a terrible trap."

"Have you ever seen Robert Henderson, the bouncer, selling ketamine here at The Wiz?"

"I haven't, but I don't pay much attention to what Robert does. If Frances caught him selling it, she'd be on him like crazy. She doesn't put up with that sort of stuff."

Emma nodded. "That's good."

"Yeah. She's tough."

"Did you ever see drug sales at the ETC shop?"

"Not sales. Drugs, I guess it was ketamine, were packaged up for sales there. But nothing was sold from that place - that I know of. I don't know the name of the guy who picked up the drugs, but he was a skinny kid who worked at a pizza place off of Pirate's Alley."

"Is there anything you'd like to add?"

"Yeah. Um." She looked around the room. "I told you I was taking courses at the Community College?"

Emma nodded.

"Well, one course was Business Law. We were required to do a research project, just to show the professor that we knew what a statute was."

"Okay."

"So, I did my project on a few labor law statutes in Louisiana."

"Really? And what did you learn?"

"That James and Cecelia are violating state labor laws by not paying the massage girls at least minimum wage, and by not paying their social security. They have them trapped there. They're kind of like indentured servants, and that's illegal. And I think there are some other laws that they need to worry about too. I mean, I know Natalia isn't in the country legally. They made sure she couldn't get her visitor's visa renewed."

"I think you're right about that."

"So I called the INS, and the Louisiana Department of Labor, and made anonymous complaints. I'm not sure what's going to become of that. Maybe nothing, but at least I've been able to sleep better at night. These people shouldn't be able to get away with what they're doing."

* * *

Emma picked up Stacey from her meeting with Dr. Vaidya and dropped her off at the carriage house. It was late. She was exhausted and couldn't wait to get home. She didn't feel like talking, but before Stacey got out of the car, Emma thought it was important to tell her about Lenny.

"We got some good news today, and I learned a little more about Lenny, the guy who came to pick up the pizza boxes behind the shop the night Angelina was killed. He told me that you kept your table and chairs behind the pizza restaurant when you read tarot cards in Jackson Square."

Stacey stared straight ahead.

"I wish you'd told me you knew him. But today, Lenny told the police that he saw Angelina's body being dumped behind the pizza shop. He said she was thrown out of a large black car. His statement should change the focus of their investigation. I don't think you will be considered a person of interest in Angelina Diaz's murder much longer." She paused and glanced at Stacey.

"This is very good news for you, Stacey, but I was disappointed that you didn't let me know that you recognized him the night Angelina was killed. You should have been able to clearly see his face. The window was large. The light was bright."

Stacey's face flushed.

190

"It's difficult to represent you if you're hiding things from me. I feel blindsided. Is there a reason you didn't tell me about him?"

Stacey stared at her hands. "I didn't want to get him in trouble."

"That was nice, but you've been arrested for murder. You can't afford to worry about anyone else now. We've got to protect you, and I have to know the truth about everything if I'm going to do that. Are you protecting anyone else?"

She shook her head. "No."

"Did you ever see Lenny speak to James?"

"I don't think so. I mean, of course, he did during sessions. But otherwise, no."

"What about Mira?"

"No. I don't think so."

"If you remember anything, please let me know. I hope you feel good about Lenny's statement anyway."

Stacey got out of the car and slammed the door.

* * *

Happy to see a light burning on the second floor of their building, Emma parked and walked up the stairs to her apartment. Ren was home, standing in the kitchen, peering into the refrigerator. She could hear the boys upstairs. They'd be getting ready to go to a Halloween party soon. Friends were picking them up. No costumes this year. They were far too cool.

Lulu and Maddie greeted her, tails wagging.

Suddenly, all of the memories of the week's events flooded in. Emma ran up to Ren, threw her arms around his waist, leaned her head against his chest, and cried until she had to come up for air. Ren walked with her to the living room and eased Emma and himself onto the couch.

"They're going to cremate him," she sobbed.

"I'm so sorry, sweetheart." Ren rubbed her back.

They stayed on the couch, with Emma crying and Ren holding her for the next hour, Lulu and Maddie at their feet.

Chapter Twenty-Six

E mma gazed out of her office window the next day, watching students walk by. The wind was blowing the branches in the trees, and many of the kids were wearing sweaters. It was the first day of November, and a brisk snap of cooler air had hit the city. The sky always seemed bluer and the air clearer in the fall.

She was startled by the ringing phone.

"Hello. This is Dr. Susan Vaidya."

"Hi, Dr. Vaidya. I wasn't expecting to hear from you so soon. Stacey said your meeting yesterday was a good one."

"Yes. I believe I got some decent results. Stacey made a good effort. I don't believe she was malingering, not that I suspected she would. Her answers were consistent, and she remained attentive and eager to respond throughout the entire session. Since she's been charged with murder, I also did a risk assessment for violence along with my usual assessment."

"I don't think Stacey is a violent person."

"But murder is a violent act. So I thought the assessment was important. I interviewed her about her current feelings or fantasies, if she has any, for violence. Just to put your mind at ease, she has none. She may even have been offended by the question."

"I'm not surprised."

"She reported that she has no history of violent behavior, and I don't doubt that. But I'd like to speak to her mother. I suspect they have a difficult history. Stacey doesn't have a police record, with the exception of her arrest for sleeping on the street down in the French Quarter and now, of course, this arrest for murder."

Emma nodded. "I don't know of any prior acts of violence. But she lived in New Mexico most of her life. I'll need to check those state records before trial, just to make certain."

"Another big issue is whether she considers herself a victim. And that's where it gets a little gray."

"What do you mean?"

"She clearly does, but I'm not sure why. She grew up in an affluent neighborhood in Albuquerque, New Mexico. Her parents were strict, especially her mother. But beyond that, she doesn't have many complaints. Her mother seems to have been rigid. A rule maker, you know? Sometimes teens rebel against that. It could have been a factor in her running away, sort of an effort of Stacey's to assert her own control, or a method of manipulating her parents. A "let me just show you" sort of thing. But there were no complaints of sexual abuse or extreme physical abuse."

"What about emotional abuse, shaming, or bullying?"

"Yes. That's a possibility. She has anxiety issues, which could have been brought about by a difficult childhood, and exhibits signs of an anxiety disorder. She finds her anxiety difficult to control. She complains of some sleep disturbance and irritability. She's fatigued and restless. She has difficulty concentrating and says she has some muscle tension."

"That sounds like just about everyone I know, including me."

"Not really. True anxiety is excessive. It breaks into your daily life, your thought processes, and takes over. You're functioning pretty well, as far as I can tell. I'm not sure Stacey does. For instance, she's a smart girl. She should be in school, getting her education, deciding what she wants to do with her life. Instead, she was on the streets and then was working for the leader of a cult. Now she's preparing for a murder trial. Something's amiss."

"I see."

"She has no psychological process which would make the trial a problem. But you knew that already. She doesn't have any other impulsive behavior disorder. But you never know what could provoke someone to commit a crime."

"I've always wondered why she ran away. Did you come closer to figuring that out?"

"Stacey's hiding something. She has always found her mom disapproving, judgmental, and that's why she ran away, but she doesn't say what her mom disapproved of. She could be gay, or maybe she had an earlier pregnancy and couldn't live with her parents' disapproval. Whatever it was, she wasn't ready to tell me. She has some trust issues. And she also has feelings of shame around the fact she brought so many girls into the temple before she figured out what James was doing. She's very upset with herself about that."

Emma concluded her phone call with Dr. Vaidya, wondering what Stacey could be hiding. Whatever it was, it was big, and it left a scar.

* * *

The final reports were ready in James Crosby's case. Although Emma had seen the preliminary police reports earlier, she'd never seen the full report, or the affidavits from any of the witnesses, or even the autopsy report. The DA's office was late in responding to her request for supplemental discovery, and even though they'd said they'd mail all of the documents to Emma, she knew better than to wait around for that. Emma's classes were over by one o'clock, which freed her up to run downtown to the DA's office to pick up the reports there.

Emma's initial thrill at not having to stand in line was short-lived. She stood for at least five minutes in front of the clerk's little round window, waiting for a nod, a frown. Something. Finally, the clerk glanced at Emma, her eyebrows arched over her glasses, wisps of her blonde hair flying upwards on the top of her head where her glasses had sat only moments before.

Emma showed the clerk the order the judge had signed, granting her the right to copies of all supplemental reports, autopsies, witness statements, and affidavits in the Crosby case. Fifteen minutes later, Emma ran out of the DA's office and headed home, copies in hand.

* * *

Emma settled in at home. She glanced at the report on the syringe found in Stacey's nightstand and confirmed that Stacey's fingerprints were found on the barrel. She checked the date of the autopsy, relieved it had taken place on the evening of the murder, at seven thirty-five p.m. She pulled out Crosby's supplemental autopsy report next. She had a couple of hours to read and absorb the information before the boys got home.

Her eyes flew to the bottom of the page. The probable cause of death was listed as 'impalement by rod from iron fence.' From what she could understand from the pathologist's description of the wound, the fence prong pierced Crosby's lower left abdomen and tore through his body on an upper pathway, fracturing the left tenth and eleventh ribs. The spleen was lacerated, leaving substantial bruising, and perisplenic fluid in his abdomen. The diaphragm was also lacerated where it attached to the eleventh and twelfth ribs, and the fifth and sixth ribs were fractured along the middle axillary line.

She winced. The impalement had killed him. She wasn't surprised. That would do it. But the physical examination of Crosby also included a finding of an injection site at his neck and the evaluation of post-mortem ketamine concentrations in the heart and femoral blood samples. The medical examiner noted:

A 43-year-old man who was the head of a local temple was found dead at his residence after falling from a second-floor balcony. The fall was initially thought to be an accident.

His body was draped across an iron fence; a fence rail had penetrated the torso. He was declared deceased at the site.

On examination, an injection mark was found at the left sternocleidomastoid muscle. External examination of the body revealed a hematoma below the puncture site.

Ketamine and its major metabolite, norketamine, as well as an additive, fentanyl, were identified in heart and femoral blood samples by a general drug screening procedure capable of detecting numerous chemically based drugs. The identification of ketamine, norketamine, and fentanyl was based on retention times relative to internal standard and confirmation was by gas chromatography-mass spectrometry.

The report also included that Crosby had received a fatal dose of 10 ccs of ketamine before he fell. The fentanyl concentrations were much lower, but the pathologist noted that fentanyl is highly lethal, and that two milligrams had been known to cause death. He concluded that, since fentanyl has a 7.9 hour half-life, "…it can be safely assumed that the decedent received a fatal dose of fentanyl as well as ketamine, and that the two drugs acted in concert to render the victim, Mr. Crosby, unable to defend himself when pushed out of the window."

The medical examiner also found bruising on the back, indicating Crosby was pushed. Emma read further, tracing the language of the report, until she got to the last paragraph.

The bruising, in conjunction with the forced injection of the drugs at the neck, indicate that the death was not an accident. The victim's lips were blue. Ketamine's and fentanyl's toxicities, which included depression of the respiratory center of the brain, immediate drowsiness, sedation, difficulty breathing, and cardiac toxicity, contributed to the fifteen-foot fall from the balcony and the impalement on the fence below. The death was found to be a homicide.

Emma had looked up the statistics. Humans could withstand a fifteen-foot fall, although likely not without injury. But James' window was positioned within a few feet of the wrought iron fence that surrounded the courtyard, which was also a few feet from the garconniere. A fall from James' balcony all but insured impalement. And, thanks to the drugs that were in his body, he was nearly helpless at the time he was shoved. Plus, he wouldn't have survived the lethal dose of ketamine or fentanyl even if he'd survived the fall. The murder had to have been planned, premeditated.

Emma sifted through the documents and found one more lab report. The lab had completed a two-step testing process on the residue inside the syringe found in Stacey's room. Using gas chromatography to separate the components, mass spectrometry was used to identify each compound by comparing its chemical signature against the reference materials. The lab found the compound in the syringe to be ninety-eight percent ketamine and two percent norketamine. No traces of fentanyl were found in the syringe.

Emma was stunned. The syringe the DA was relying on as evidence against Stacey, the syringe with Stacey's fingerprints, the alleged murder weapon found in Stacey's bedroom, wrapped up in her t-shirt, couldn't have been used to kill James. It didn't contain fentanyl. If she could get a forensic scientist, or a pathologist to sign an affidavit verifying that the syringe with Stacey's fingerprints couldn't have been used to kill James Crosby, she should be able to get the case dismissed on that evidence alone.

Emma looked for Cecelia's affidavit next. Emma was surprised by her square, firm handwriting. Her statement was substantially different from what she'd told Emma on the day of her interview. Cecelia wrote:

Raphael was not at the temple on the day James was killed. I am sure of it. He was out that day and didn't return until 5:00, which was about the time I returned from shopping.

Emma flipped through her notes. They were detailed and clear.

Cecelia said there were a couple of people at the temple on the day of the murder.

Raphael was at the temple before Cecelia got home. He came running down from his upstairs room when he heard Cecelia scream. Cecelia said that afterward the police spoke to Mira, Angelina, Raphael, and her.

Why would Cecelia change her story in her affidavit? Even Raphael admitted he was at the temple before Cecelia got home from shopping.

Emma flipped through her notes until she reached the section where she had interviewed Raphael. She wrote:

Raphael was in his room until early afternoon, which is when he went to the Quarter. He returned to the temple that afternoon and took a nap. He didn't know whether he returned before or after the murder, or if he was at the temple at the time James was killed. He didn't see or hear anything. When I asked him if he would have heard the sound of James' body hitting the roof of the garconniere from his bedroom, he agreed he probably would have if he'd been there, unless he was taking a nap at the time.

A little before 5:00 he heard Cecelia scream and came running down the stairs to see what was going on. He saw Cecelia and then saw James' body on the fence.

The police spoke to him briefly at the temple following James's death.

Then Emma found Angelina's affidavit.

I was there all day. I remember when Stacey went out for her usual walk. She returned in the afternoon around 4:00, maybe 4:15. I saw her when I walked out of the kitchen after I grabbed an afternoon snack. She was walking up the stairs to her room with something in her hands. I'm sure it was a syringe.

I saw Cecelia that afternoon too. She was walking down the hallway, next to the stairs and the closet that is there. I think it was around 4:30.

So Angelina's affidavit was the one that incriminated Stacey. Emma spread the police file across her desk. She found the affidavits of Cecelia, Mira, Angelina Diaz, Raphael Evans, and Moonstone Carville.

Emma skimmed Raphael's affidavit again and compared it to her notes. Even though Raphael told her Cecelia was standing close to James's body after she found him, in his affidavit, Raphael stated Cecelia was standing in front of a closet door next to the staircase. Emma didn't remember a door in that area. Why hadn't Raphael mentioned this detail to her if it was important enough to be included in his affidavit?

Emma sat back and glanced over her notes and the papers scattered in front of her. The most important discovery that day was the discrepancy in the chemical compounds found in the syringe and those found in James Crosby's body. The empty syringe was the only hard evidence the police had against Stacey, with the exception of Angelina's affidavit. Emma was nearly certain she could exclude the affidavit from trial. It was hearsay. Emma never got a chance to question Angelina about the affidavit, and she'd never have a chance to cross-examine her about it.

Emma didn't believe Angelina saw Stacey walking up the stairs with a syringe in her hands. Emma still believed Stacey was set up, and that the person responsible for framing Stacey managed to persuade Angelina to write that affidavit. Emma suspected that this same person murdered Angelina before she had a chance to say anything more.

Chapter Twenty-Seven

Emma drove down Esplanade to Stacey's carriage house, hoping to catch her at home. She hadn't called first and probably should have. But she needed an excuse to get out and think a little. It was a beautiful day. The drive through City Park and Bayou St. John always put her in a good mood, especially when the weather was nice.

She pulled into Binh's driveway and parked in front of the garage. Tea roses covered the latticework surrounding the structure with a network of lush vines. Emma could hear bees buzzing in the deep red blooms as she dashed up the stairs to the second floor. She rapped on the door.

"Come on in!" Stacey shouted.

Stacey's studio apartment was unchanged with the exception of a few apples in a bowl on the table. She was a neat housekeeper. The bed was made. Everything was in its place. Sun streamed through clean window panes. The odor of lemons filled the air.

"I needed to talk to you. And, since I'm here, I thought I'd also run by the temple and check out a few things there."

Stacey gestured for her to sit down on the sofa.

"What do you think if we take a walk down the bayou, or down Esplanade? I'd like to get a little exercise while we chat. Breathe in the fall air. How many perfect days do you get in New Orleans?"

"Okay. Let me change shoes." Stacey grabbed some tennis shoes from her closet and sat down to put them on. "I think I'd like to walk down to Taconi's. I need a couple of things for dinner."

They headed toward Esplanade.

"You must be becoming quite the cook!"

"Not really. But I've progressed beyond the sandwich." Stacey smiled.

It was a gorgeous autumn day. The sky was a clear, cerulean blue. Emma loved the shaded boulevard with its huge overhanging oaks. The lumpy tree roots upended the sidewalks so badly, they were forced to keep their eyes cast downward to avoid tripping. But it was impossible not to glance up at the magnificent display of Queen Anne and Victorian architecture as they walked down the street.

"Dr. Vaidya was pleased with your meeting the other day." Emma avoided a large root and stepped behind Stacey. "She said you made a good effort to answer every question. That's important, especially since we're faced with a trial in less than four months." She paused. "I want you to know that I'm going to file a motion to dismiss, but we still have to be prepared to go forward. I found something in the documents the DA produced that made me question some of the evidence they think they have against you. Frankly, I don't know why the DA's office hasn't caught it." Emma hesitated. Stacey turned and look at her curiously. "Don't get your hopes up. I have to run this by a forensics person, but it looks like the chemical compound found in James' body, and that found in the syringe with your fingerprints was different."

Stacey's eyebrows shot up. "You've got to be kidding! That's great!"

"It's not conclusive yet. Plus, the DA also has Angelina's statement, which they'll try to use against you, but I hope to get that excluded, too. She's the witness who said she saw you going up the stairs with a syringe in your hand."

"Well, that's just a lie."

"I'll file both motions, and we'll see what happens. I have them ready now, and as soon as I speak to the expert and get an affidavit from him, I'll be ready to go. But like I said, we need to continue to prepare for trial." She glanced at Stacey. "There is something else I'd like to talk to you about, too."

"Okay." Stacey kept her head down.

"Dr. Vaidya was concerned with your anxiety issues. But I would think that anxiety issues might go along with a pending murder charge and an upcoming trial. That would make anyone feel stressed. Did your anxiety develop recently?"

"I don't know. I don't think so. I've always had some anxiety. Sleep problems too." She shoved the hair off her forehead with both hands as she walked.

"Dr. Vaidya looked at your relationship with your mom and thought there was tension there. Is that what led you to run away when you were sixteen?"

Stacey hesitated, then nodded. "Yeah. We've always had issues. I couldn't take it anymore and left."

"Care to talk about it?"

"Not really."

Emma wasn't surprised. "Is that what James used against you to keep you at the temple?"

Stacey nodded. "That was part of it. James was a creep."

"Dr. Vaidya would like to have your mom come into her office for a chat."

Stacey shook her head. "No. I don't want her to do that."

"Okay. I'll tell her no. But, why not?"

"Because I don't want my mom representing anything on my behalf. I'm nineteen. She doesn't get a say in anything I do any longer. Dr. Vaidya doesn't have my permission to speak to my mom."

"I can understand that. But why do you feel so strongly about it?"

"Because she doesn't have my best interests at heart."

"What do you mean?"

"She thinks a person has to be just like her or they're not okay. She doesn't believe in freedom of expression. She never allowed me the freedom to be who I am. And if anyone, especially me, failed to live up to her expectations, she could be hurtful, even cruel." Stacey crammed her hands in her pockets.

Emma was afraid she'd hit a raw nerve, but at the same time, she needed to know what could trigger Stacey. If they went to trial, they couldn't afford for Stacey to fall apart.

"What happened?"

"I just never measured up to her expectations. I didn't want to wear the type of clothes she wanted me to wear. I didn't want to do my hair like she wanted me to. I didn't have the friends she wanted me to have. I didn't go out for cheerleading. I didn't want to do the debutante thing. I just didn't do anything she wanted me to do. Finally, she asked me why I wasn't dating anyone. I mean, really. Was that any of her business?"

"I understand. I really do. My mom never approved of anything I did either. I think she loved me, although I didn't always like the way she showed it. And sometimes, she didn't really show it. I'm sure your mom loves you too. It's just hard to see it sometimes." She shrugged. "Well, maybe all the time."

"She kept pushing me on the dating thing. Then she started pushing me with my friends. 'Who are your friends? Why don't you hang out with this girl, and that girl?' I finally had it. I told her I was gay." Stacey stopped walking. Her face was red. Emma thought she was going to cry. "She slapped me. She told me I was a mistake, that my dad wasn't my real dad, and that she wished she'd never had me. So I left. That was it." She thrust her hands in her pocket and started walking down the sidewalk.

"I'm so sorry." Emma struggled to keep up with Stacey.

"I mean, I've never even had a girlfriend, but I've known I was attracted to girls since I was in elementary school. I didn't know how to tell my mom then, and from the way she reacted when I finally told her, it looks like I never should have. It was a terrible mistake." She continued to walk, keeping her eyes on the sidewalk.

"I don't think it was a mistake, Stacey." Emma was a step behind.

"I was so scared when I left. I didn't know what to do. I was alone, really alone for the first time in my life. I had enough money for a bus ticket, so I got one to New Orleans. Traveling across the country was awful. The bus smelled. One guy kept staring at me.

"My mom didn't try to find me, but my dad started looking for me. Then he had a heart attack and died, and she blamed me for that, too." Stacey brushed a tear from her face. "So she really hates me now."

"I don't think so."

Stacey looked at Emma and rolled her eyes. But she slowed her pace.

"She wouldn't have bailed you out of jail twice if she hated you. And she calls just about every other day wanting to talk to you." Emma was breathing heavily.

"She just doesn't want a kid of hers in jail."

"I'm sorry there are so many years of pain between you two."

Stacey shrugged.

"Why do you think she's here in New Orleans if she doesn't care about you?"

"I don't know. Maybe she hired a hit man to do James in. I wouldn't put anything past her."

"Interesting theory, Stacey. But your mom got here after James was killed. Did she ever tell you who your biological dad is?"

"I was wondering if you were going to ask that question." She hesitated and took a breath. "Yes, she did."

"Who's your biological dad?"

Stacey stopped on the sidewalk and turned so she could face Emma. "James. James Crosby was my real dad. Seems like my mom and James got together once or twice when my mom visited the Japaprajnas in Idaho years ago. Almost twenty years ago, apparently. Back when the original leader, J. R., was in charge. It was a little fling." Stacey rocked back on her heels. "They were both very young. I'm the only result. I wanted to find him. That's why I traveled to New Orleans. But my mom never really wanted to find me after I left. She had to have guessed where I was going. And she knew how to find me."

"Oh my God! I never would have expected that! I am stunned!" Emma stood, riveted on the sidewalk. Her eyes opened wide. "I was trying to figure out why you were treated differently, and it was right under my nose! You traveled to New Orleans, found your dad, and went to work for him. Except for your massage job, the work he gave you set you apart from the other girls. Why didn't I see that?"

"You're right. And I wanted to believe in him. I wanted to believe what he was saying and that he had good intentions. I didn't want to see what was right in front of me. I don't know if I ignored what was obvious, or if I didn't want to see it. I guess it doesn't matter, but I finally woke up. I saw who he was and what he was doing. And still, after all of that, I couldn't quite get it together to leave. Then he was killed."

"That's a lot to deal with. Why didn't you tell Dr. Vaidya about this?"

"I didn't want anyone to know he was my father. I told James as my secret confession at the session one night. I think he told Cecelia, but as far as I know, no one else knew. And that's how I wanted it. When I threatened to stop recruiting, he said he'd call my mom, tell her where I was, and tell everyone I was his illegitimate daughter, too. So I kept signing up new girls for a while. And then I thought I'd call his bluff. I didn't want my mom to know where I was, but she'd probably known I was in New Orleans with the Japaprajnas all along. And, once I realized that, nothing else really mattered." She shook her head. "But you're the first person I've told, except for James."

"I'm so glad you've included me." She reached out and squeezed Stacey's arm.

Stacey nodded. "It was hard to tell you."

"I'm sure. And I'm proud of you. Did you and James ever get along?"

"It was weird. He never treated me like a daughter. But now I can see that he also protected me from things. He didn't want me working at the smoking shop like the other girls. And he kind of left me alone, and that was a good thing."

"I have another question about an entirely different issue." Emma paused and glanced at Stacey. She didn't know if Stacey was ready to discuss the facts of the case after this break-through.

"Okay." They started walking again.

"Raphael and Angelina both described a door in their affidavits. Raphael said it was a closet door next to the staircase. I've never noticed it. Do you know which door I'm talking about?"

"Yeah, it could be the broom closet next to the stairs. It's a pretty small door. The closet only held a couple of brooms and a mop."

They arrived at Taconi's. Stacey went inside to shop. Emma followed, charmed by the original furnishings and fascinated with the array of cheeses. Stacey bought some fresh tomatoes, fresh buffalo mozzarella, fresh basil, and eggs for an omelet.

"Impressive purchases for a novice chef, Stacey."

Stacey's cheeks flushed when she smiled.

They headed back down Esplanade, walking on the lakeside[3] of the street.

"Did you ever see anyone go inside the broom closet and not come back out?"

"No, I don't think so. Why?"

"Let's cross over."

There was no crosswalk in the area and no traffic light. They were alert to the danger, especially since New Orleans drivers were notoriously impatient with pedestrians. They walked over to the neutral ground and were nearly home free, stepping into the street to cross over to the riverside[3].

Charging out from a secondary street, a large, two-door black sedan accelerated from the opposite direction and aimed its wide grill at the two women, barely missing them. Emma hopped backward onto the median and grabbed Stacey's arm. Both women fell into the grassy neutral zone. Emma twisted her ankle.

"Are you okay? That hurt!" Emma rubbed her ankle. "Did you get the license plate number?" She looked down the street, unable to find the car.

"No! I didn't get a thing." Stacey stood up. "Except for the windows in the back. They were tiny oval-shaped ones. Just like the windows in the car that Angelina was killed in. It was a black two-door, and I saw the words *Town Car* written on the side window."

"That had to have been deliberate." Emma continued rubbing her ankle.

"Yeah, it was aimed right at us. Plus, a car like that has been following me around."

"What? Why haven't you told me?" Emma sighed. "Let's get you home." Emma tried to take a step and stopped. "I think we should tell Binh and Harry what happened, just so they know. And we need to report this to the police. When we do that, we need to tell them what you saw the night Angelina was killed, and that she may have been murdered in the same car that's been following you. We've been putting that off, but it's clear that your life is in danger. We can't wait any longer."

Emma tried another step. "I need to move extra slowly. It's going to be a long hobble to your place."

Chapter Twenty-Eight

Emma's ankle was swollen, but she could drive. And she'd be fine after a hot bath. It hurt, but she managed to get out of the car and walk around the corner to the front of the building. And there, waiting, resplendent in his many layers of clothing was Raymond Collier, the self-appointed leader of the New Orleans homeless community.

"It's good to see you, Raymond. We found Stacey! I've been meaning to run by to let you know." She limped toward Raymond. "What can I do for you?"

"That's good, Mrs. Thornton. I wanted to come by to tell you about something else."

"Would you like me to get you something to eat or drink?"

"Nah, that's okay. I just wanted you to know that a couple of days ago, a guy came by and said that he saw Stacey a couple of weeks back. He knew we were looking for her, but it just took him a while to get by and let me know. The guy's name is Jerome. He'd been sleepin' in an alley off of Bourbon Street behind some garbage cans. He said a big black car came down the alley and woke him up. He said a girl was watchin' all of this around the side of the building, and he thinks that it might have been the girl we were lookin' for, Stacey. Another girl who'd been working inside the shop got in the car. But that girl, the girl from the shop, got killed. He saw someone shoot something in her neck when she had her head turned. Said she dropped over right away. That girl, Stacey, just stood there, watchin' the whole thing. He thinks maybe she was seen by the killer because the killer pointed at her as he was leavin.'"

"Did Jerome go to the police?"

"Nah. He didn't want to have anything to do with the police."

"He saw the girl in the car getting killed?"

"I guess it was real fast. He didn't think he could have done anything."

"Did he see who did it?"

"He said he thought it might be a woman, but I don't think he got a real good look."

"Can I talk to this guy?"

"He doesn't want anyone to know who he is."

"But I really need to talk to him. He has evidence no one else has."

"I can ask him again."

"Tell him I will need to know what the driver looked like. It's very important. And I'd like to arrange a time to meet him."

Raymond nodded. "I know it was dark, and I don't know how much he can really help. I'll see what I can do. I'm not making any promises, though."

* * *

Emma eased herself into her bathtub filled with water as hot as she could stand. She didn't care that doctors and physical therapists recommended ice packs for injuries. She preferred a hot tub of water for nearly everything: sprained ankles, bad backs, cricks in the neck, headaches, whatever ailed her. She filled it as high as she dared and immersed herself, forgetting all of her cares. Everyone knew to leave her alone if she was taking a bath. No one would dare invade her sanctuary. The boys were upstairs pretending to do homework, which meant they would be quiet for an hour or so.

She breathed deeply, something she forgot to do almost any other time, and drifted off to sleep, then awoke to doors slamming. Twice. First a car, then the front door. Ren was home. She was going to have to tell him something about the car incident.

She heard the bathroom door open, then saw Ren's face. He had dark circles under his eyes, and his skin had a gray haggard tone.

"How was your day?" Ren clomped in and kissed the top of her head.

"Sort of iffy. I sprained my ankle. But how are you? You look tired."

"Oh no, babe! How did that happen?" He sat down on the toilet seat next to her. "And I'm fine."

"A car tried to run Stacey and me down."

"What? What's going on? First the fire, now this! What's going on?" Ren frowned as he leaned closer to Emma.

"Stacey said a car had been following her for a while. She didn't take it seriously until today. I noticed one in front of the apartment about a week ago that looked a lot like it too. Today it seemed to bear down on us, and I tripped, trying to get back up onto the neutral ground. That's when I sprained my ankle."

"Bear down? You mean the car was running you down? You could have been killed! Did you get the license plate number?"

"No. I didn't even look up until the car was gone."

"How long has this been going on?"

"Since Angelina was killed. She was killed on October 24, so,"...Emma paused to count on her fingers..."that's about nine days."

"Why didn't you bring her down before now, especially if there was a problem?"

"I didn't know a car had been stalking her, for one thing. And for another, she was a person of interest in Angelina's murder. I didn't think it was a good idea to bring her to the station until that was figured out. Now it's got to be clear that Stacey couldn't be a suspect. And she has a statement to give about the night of Angelina's murder."

"Can't you tell me what that is all about?" He grabbed her towel.

"I shouldn't. You know that. But she was in the area of the ETC shop the night Angelina was killed. She witnessed it. The killer may have seen her." She leaned over to let the water out of the tub. "I'm assuming what I said is correct? After Lenny's statement, Stacey's no longer a person of interest in the Angelina Diaz murder?"

"I'd like to take a look at everything on Monday once I see what Stacey has to say."

"Okay. By the way, aren't two-door sedans kind of rare?"

"Depends on the make of the car. And a two-door sedan is called a coupe." Ren smiled.

"I think the car that tried to run us over today was a Lincoln. My dad had one once. It had a hood ornament, and this one did too. And it had a small oval side window. The oval was horizontal. I'm guessing it's about six inches wide." Emma indicated the width of the window with her hands. "And Stacey said she saw the words *Town Car* written on the back side window."

"If that's the case, then yeah. Most Lincolns are four-door vehicles. I can do a run with the DMV and if there are any two-door Lincolns registered to anyone in New Orleans. I've got a Blue Book too. I'll see what that tells me about Lincoln coupes. I don't think they're that common. And those little windows are called opera windows." He picked up her towel and wrapped it around her as she stood up. "Let's see that ankle."

Emma sat down on the edge of the tub and propped her foot in his lap so he could get a good look at her sprain. Her ankle and foot were all red and puffy from the hot bath. A slight bluish tinge had started to emerge right above the ankle bone.

"Well, you look like you've been parboiled. Maybe we'll let you cool off a bit while I tend to that sprain." He turned to grab the first aid kit on the shelf behind him.

Emma tried to wiggle her toes, wincing. "No broken bones, at least." She hesitated and glanced up at Ren. "I've been thinking. Have you compared the drugs you all found at the back of the shop to those found in Angelina Diaz on autopsy?"

Ren squinted at Emma. "Do you know something you're not telling me?"

Emma pursed her lips. "Just food for thought."

Chapter Twenty-Nine

Emma and Stacey climbed the steps to the Eighth District Police Station and walked through the double glass doors to the desk clerk's station. Emma showed the clerk her bar card.

"I have a potential witness in the Angelina Diaz case. I'd like to speak to the officer in charge."

The clerk nodded, and soon, Emma and Stacey were escorted to a small conference room. Soon they heard steps in the corridor, and Emma wasn't surprised to see Ren walking into the room.

"Hello, ladies. It's good to see you two again. Hope you're having a better day than you had on Saturday." Ren said.

"So far, it's better. Let's hope it stays that way. We're here today because Stacey has a statement she'd like to make in the Angelina Diaz case. Stacey, I'll let you proceed."

"First, I'd like to record this, if I have your permission." Ren slid an authorization form to Stacey for her review.

Emma stood up and read the form over Stacey's shoulder. She could tell Stacey was nervous. "This form authorizes the police department to record your statement. The prosecution can't use your recorded statement at trial." Emma glanced at Ren. "I assume you'll also ask for a written statement today?"

"Yes, I'd planned on it. That's standard procedure."

"And the written statement will be notarized?"

"Yes."

"Wait a minute. I don't understand what I'm about to write," Stacey's eyes widened in panic.

"It's okay. It's simple, really. You're going to give an oral statement about several things that you witnessed, and then, after that, you'll put what you said in writing. After you sign it and it's notarized, that will be your sworn statement. Sometimes it's called an affidavit. The prosecution can't use the affidavit in lieu of live testimony at Angelina's trial unless your live testimony contradicts your affidavit. I'll explain that later. But we don't need to worry about that now. Just tell the truth today, and we won't have any worries." She sat back down in her chair, then noticed that Stacey's eyes seemed even wider than they were before. "You'll be fine. I promise." Emma smiled, hoping that would help her feel more at ease.

Stacey signed the permission form.

"I need to record a brief statement before Stacey starts, " Ren said and hit the record button.

"This is the statement of Stacey Roberts recorded on November 4, 1996. The interview commenced at 0900. Present are Detective Ren Taylor, City of New Orleans Police Department, and Emma Thornton, Attorney for Ms. Roberts."

"Okay, Stacey. When you want to talk, just press the button."

Stacey moved closer to the microphone. She rubbed her hands together and swallowed. "I just wanted to say that I think I saw Angelina Diaz being killed. She was killed inside a black car. It's similar to the one that tried to run over Emma and me yesterday."

Ren nodded and smiled at Stacey. "This is Detective Ren Taylor of the City of New Orleans Police Department. I have a few follow-up questions, Ms. Roberts."

Stacey answered Ren's questions, giving him the same details she'd given Emma the morning after Angelina was killed.

Ren cleared his throat. "Thanks, Stacey. Can you tell me why you decided to go by the smoke shop that night?"

"I'd been living in a chapel at St. Roch's cemetery in the Bywater. I was looking for a safer place to sleep at night."

"So you decided to break into the back of the ETC shop?" Ren raised his eyebrows.

"Objection. Please don't suggest motivations for my client's actions."
Emma frowned.

"No. I thought I could work something out with Angelina so I could pay
her a little cash and get her to leave the back door of the shop open for me so
I could stay there at night. I was going to leave early in the morning before
anyone got there." Stacey shook her head. "But I never got a chance to talk
to her."

"Why not?"

"There was just so much going on. She locked up right after Lenny left.
And then, right after that, the black car came by to pick her up. She was
attacked before I do anything."

"About how long did Angelina struggle in the car before the driver pulled
off?"

"Not long. She fell back against the car seat and then fell forward. And
then she struggled for a little against the passenger door with her back facing
me, and then I didn't see her after that." Stacey put her hand up to her mouth.
Her hand was shaking.

"Are you okay, Stacey? Do you need a break?"

"I can go on. It's awful to see someone attacked and probably killed right
in front of you. At first, I froze. Ever since that happened, I've felt I should
have done something more to help her, and I didn't. I was frozen like a big
ice cube. Then when I finally moved out a little and stepped toward the car
to help her, the driver pointed at me, you know, like I was next. I've never
been so scared in my life."

"I'm sorry, Stacey. Do you remember anything else about the driver or
the driver's clothes that you haven't told us about?"

"I already told Emma about the hoodie. I saw that. But I think it had some
writing on it. Maybe a school name. Small letters. It was printed about
where a pocket would be. "

"Do you recall the color of the writing?"

"I think it was yellow."

"What did you do after the driver left?"

"I ran and hid out in the French Quarter for the night. In the morning, I headed out to find Emma's house."

"And, you are referring to Ms. Thornton, your attorney?" Ren glanced at Emma.

"Yes."

"Is there anything else you'd like to add, Stacey?"

She shook her head. "No."

"Interview terminated at 0916." Ren turned off the recorder.

"Okay, see if you can write all of this down in as much detail as possible. We have a recording, but, as I said earlier, I'd still like it in writing." Ren handed Stacey an affidavit form for her to complete and sign.

Ren looked over at Emma as Stacey was writing. "Care to join me in the hallway for a minute?"

Emma followed Ren into the dimly lit corridor. "Yes?"

"So you still think your girl Stacey is stable after her testimony about sleeping in a cemetery?"

Emma frowned. "That's not very nice."

"Okay." He paused and looked at his shoes for a moment and cleared his throat. "Just so you know, I agree with you, that after our chat with Lenny and after listening to Stacey today, we no longer consider her a person of interest in Angelina Diaz's murder."

"That's a relief. Especially since I brought her down here today, into the lion's den."

Ren cocked his head. "Really, Emma? You know I'm fair."

"I know. But I was a little nervous." She grimaced.

"Just so you know, I'm glad you brought her. Her statement about that night is important. It corroborates everything Lenny said, too. I don't know how the DA will want to use it. I still think she comes across as a little unstable, and I'm not sure if she'd be a good witness. But, I'm glad she admitted she was at the scene the night Angelina was murdered. Some of her fingerprints showed up on the outside of the building, around the window frame. But that's consistent with everything she said today. So I believe her."

Emma nodded. "All we really care about is making sure you understand what happened that night, and now that you do, and Stacey is no longer a person of interest, we're good."

He reached out and squeezed Emma's elbow. "I have some more good news. I heard back from the DMV this morning about the Lincoln two-door coupe. And I also looked up Lincoln coupes in my Blue Book. If it's the Town Car, they made two doors for one year, and that was from 1980 through 1981."

"That makes the Lincoln fifteen, sixteen years old; pretty old for a car."

"Right. But Lincolns could hang around that long if they are well taken care of. I asked the DMV to pull any two-door Lincolns registered in the state. They sent the list over a few minutes ago. Guess how many there were?"

"One?"

"Two. I was surprised there were that many. But only one of them is in New Orleans."

"Can you tell who it's registered to?"

"Yes. The Temple of the Japaprajna People."

"Wow." She paused. She wouldn't have thought anyone from the temple would have brazenly chased Stacey and her down in a car as distinct as that Lincoln in the middle of the day. "That was some pretty good detective work." She smiled. "Were you able to take a look at the chemical breakdown of the compound found behind the ETC shop?"

"I did. Ketamine and norketamine, something that acts to metabolize ketamine. That's it."

"What about the distribution of drugs found in Angelina Diaz's body on autopsy?"

"There was a small amount of fentanyl there. So, the batch used to kill Angelina was different from the batch found at James' shop."

"Yep. Have you had an opportunity to read the reports in James' case yet?"

"Not yet, why?"

"The syringe with Staccy's fingerprints didn't contain a drop of fentanyl, but James' autopsy showed that fentanyl, as well as ketamine, contributed to his death."

"You're kidding."

"I would think that means that it's very likely the same person killed both James and Angelina. And that person wasn't Stacey."

Ren nodded. "I think you could be right. The chemical breakdown is a good clue."

"It's more than a good clue. Someone else is murdering these people. Not Stacey."

Ren nodded. "Maybe Stacey was set up after all."

* * *

Emma and Stacey left the Eighth District Station, driving down Royal Street, which was lined with some of the most expensive antique and jewelry shops in the city. They continued their drive through the city, passing pawn shops and tattoo parlors to North Claiborne, the location of the largest homeless encampment in the city, and Raymond Collier's home base.

"Did you ever meet Raymond Collier when you were on the streets?" Emma turned her car toward the I-10 overpass, near Claiborne.

"I think I may have heard the name, but no. I've never met him." Stacey glanced out the window. "Are we headed to the camp at the overpass?"

"Yep. You never stayed there, did you?"

"No. I always stayed in the French Quarter. It just seemed safer to me."

Emma raised her eyebrows. "Well, that was questionable."

"It seemed safer because tourists were always there."

"Which is why you got arrested."

Stacey laughed. "Right."

"Anyway, Raymond keeps his finger on the pulse of most homeless issues and knows when there's trouble. I asked him to keep an eye out for you when you were missing." She glanced at Stacey.

Stacey pursed her lips. "Okay."

"He came by my house yesterday to tell me that another guy, a man named Jerome, was sleeping in the alley the night Angelina was killed. Something woke him up, and he saw the whole thing. He even said he thought the killer might have been a woman. I don't know if he can identify her or not, but I need Raymond to speak to him about it. Since we're out this way, I thought I'd run by and remind Raymond. I don't want Jerome to feel intimidated, but I'd like to see if Raymond could talk him into speaking to the police."

"But you don't know if Raymond's there or not."

"No, but I suspect he is. Raymond stays right under the overpass most days. If he wanders a little, he's always back there at night. I'm guessing that's where he was when he spoke to this witness too."

Emma parked across the street from the homeless encampment in the lot of an abandoned church. Most of the businesses had vacated the area because of the encampment. The bedding, backpacks, tents, piles of clothing, food products, garbage, and waste of the homeless had encouraged rodents and other vermin to set up housing. The rats had invaded the businesses, creating a public health hazard. But even though the city acknowledged the hazard, and even though the police made occasional sweeps to clean up the mess or arrest the homeless, there was no city or governmental solution to the problem. Only religious or private interests offered to help.

Emma and Stacey made their way across the street to search for Raymond, headed toward the area Emma had found him thirteen days ago. Sure enough, there he was, his backpack propped up against the outside wall of his red tent, reading a well-worn book—*A Prayer For Owen Meany.*

"Hi, Raymond. I've brought Stacey with me today. I don't think you two have met."

Raymond sat up. "I've heard a lot about you. Glad you're okay." He put his book down.

"We were hoping Jerome, the man who saw the murder in the alley, is here at the encampment today. Have you seen him?"

"It's been a couple of days." Raymond stood up. He peered out over the crowd of people in the encampment. "It's impossible to find him this way. The last time I spoke to him, he was camped out over by that piling." He pointed to a bridge span close to Claiborne and Franklin Avenue. "Let's walk over there and see if we can spot him. If he's not there, I don't think we'll have much luck finding him anywhere else. It's just so crowded right now."

They followed Raymond, walking across an entire city block of the encampment, passing makeshift tents, cots, grocery carts, wheelchairs, any number of devices used for shelter, and makeshift furniture. Emma, concerned she was violating the campers' privacy, kept her eyes down as she walked but could feel their stares as she passed by.

They finally reached the area by the span, stopped, and looked around.

"There's Jerome. You guys stay here for a minute. He's shy," Raymond said and walked over to a mound of clothes, blankets, shoes, and broken-down cardboard boxes draped over a grocery cart. Raymond bent over the mound, and a man emerged. He stood to speak to Raymond. Shortly, Raymond walked back to Emma and Stacey.

"What did he say?" Emma asked.

"Not much. He said he saw someone with long hair that night. He couldn't tell the color. It could have been a man or a woman. And that's all."

"Okay. Did you ask him if he'd be willing to talk to the police ?"

"I already know he doesn't want any part of the police."

"We'd appreciate it if he'd reconsider. Maybe tell him that it's important to Stacey and her case. I don't know. Whatever you can do."

"I'll tell him I'd do it if I were him. Maybe that would help."

Chapter Thirty

The water sparkled along Bayou St. John when Emma dropped Stacey off at the carriage house, but the sun had already fallen on the horizon. She took a right on Esplanade toward the temple. She had two goals that afternoon: one was to find the old Lincoln somewhere on the Japaprajna's property, and she also wanted to locate the broom closet in the house and get a look inside. She had a strong hunch about that broom closet.

When she rapped on the front door to the temple, no one answered. She knocked again, and the door creaked open ever so slightly. She pushed the door wide enough to step in.

"Hello! Is anyone here? It's Emma Thornton!" She could hear music from the spa in the back of the building.

She called out again. "Hello!"

No one answered. She walked down the corridor. The door to the spa was ajar. Emma knocked and poked her head in. Natalia was tidying up the waiting room, her blonde hair tied up in a scarf.

"Hi. Nice to see you again. I'm looking for Cecelia or Mira. Are either of them here today?"

Natalia started. "I didn't know you were there!" Her Russian accent was only faintly discernable. She put the lid on the furniture polish and set it on the table. "No. They aren't here right now."

Emma opened the door a little wider. "Could I come in for a few minutes to chat?"

"I don't know. I shouldn't be talking to you, but I suspect you know that."

Natalia set her cloth on a small table in the corner of the room.

"I just have a couple of questions. I won't be long."

Emma walked in, still limping from her sprain, and sat down on a chair.

"Cecelia will do her usual inspection of the spa around four-fifty, so you'll need to leave before that. It wouldn't be good for her to catch you here."

"Do you have any patrons here right now?"

She nodded. "Yes, we have one man who's finishing up. He should be out in fifteen minutes. And a woman, a regular customer, has an appointment at four on Wednesdays, every week."

"Are these clients also followers of the temple? People who attend sessions consistently?"

"Yeah, a lot of the spa clientele are. James would recruit the people who came to the spa for the temple sessions, and then he'd recruit the people who came to the temple to try the spa. He was very good at making money."

"Have you ever seen, or have you given anyone a white powder during a spa session?"

"I've never given my clients anything like that. But I know James has." Natalia crossed her arms across her chest.

Natalia's posture was defensive, but she was telling Emma what she needed to know. Emma sensed Natalia didn't feel particularly loyal to James or the Japaprajnas.

"But I didn't think James gave massages."

Natalia nodded. "That's right. But sometimes, he'd offer that to his followers right before their massages. I think he wanted to get people to like it so they'd take it more and more."

"Do you know the name of the drug?"

"No, I don't."

"Did you ever take it?"

"No."

"Why not?"

"It can knock you out, for one thing. And I could see what James was up to. A few of us could tell. It was easy if you watched."

"Did you ever see James take the white powder?"

Natalia nodded. "Yes, I did. A few times."

"How did you happen to see James do this?"

"I help with the house cleaning. So, one day I knocked on his office door to see if I could come in to clean. He didn't say anything so I didn't think he was in, and I opened the door. That's when I saw him sniffing something that looked like a white powdery line on his desk. I guess he didn't hear me when I knocked."

"What did he do when you came in?"

"He just finished what he was doing, sniffing the stuff up like I wasn't even there."

"Did you ever see him doing this any other time?"

She nodded. "I think one of his favorite places to do this was the altar room. He'd put a long line there and try to snort it up, but he never got it all. He left a little bit every time. There was powder all over the place in that room."

Emma heard footsteps and paused to listen. The footsteps faded, and she continued. "Do you know anything unusual about the broom closet in the hallway?"

Natalia wrinkled up her face. "I don't know what you mean."

"This is a weird question, but have you ever noticed someone going in but not coming out?"

"Funny you asked about that. I did notice it once, and it stuck with me. It was Mira. She went into the closet and shut the door. And that was it. She didn't come back out. I thought it was strange. I went upstairs to see what was going on, and I found Mira at her desk in that office she shared with James."

"And you never figured out how she got there?"

"I have some ideas. But I can't find the time to explore by myself. Cecelia is almost always around. But not today."

Emma smiled. "Did you ever see Cecelia enter that closet?"

She shook her head. "No. I haven't."

"Do you plan to stay on at the temple and continue to work in the spa?"

"I want to leave, but I don't have any other place to go. I have a place to sleep here, I eat all of my meals here, and that's about all I can hope for right now."

"How old are you, Natalia?"

"I'm seventeen. I'll be eighteen in a couple of months."

"You told me the first time I met you that you're from Russia. But are you a naturalized citizen of the United States?"

She shook her head. "No. I came over here on a thirty-day visitor's visa. I was going to take a summer school course in English literature at City College, but it didn't work out. Then I overstayed my time here. I can't get another job because I don't have a visa or a Green Card. And none of us gets a real salary here. So I'm stuck. And Cecelia knows it."

"Your English is impressive."

She nodded once. "I took English at school since I was a little girl. It's required."

"Do you recall ever seeing an old Lincoln Town Car, a black one here? It's a large, square-looking car with a hood ornament."

"These are like the cars of governmental officials, maybe? No. I don't think so."

"Is there an alley behind the house?" Emma pointed to where she imagined the alley might be.

"There's a very narrow road back there. It's been taken over by banana trees."

"Banana trees?"

"Yeah. I never go back there. It's a jungle. I've never needed to anyway. The banana trees don't even grow bananas."

"Do you remember the day that Raphael died?"

Natalia nodded. "Yes. It was very upsetting. He was a very nice man."

"Do you remember placing a call to Moonstone at the ETC shop that day?" Emma readied her pen.

"Yes. I did that."

"Do you remember what you said to her?"

"I think it had something to do with picking up a package for Mira."

"Who asked you to do that?"

"I'm sure it was Mira. She said to call Moonstone and have her go pick up a package at the post office. And she gave me the package number." Natalia clasped her hands together in her lap.

Emma wrote down Natalia's answer as quickly as she could.

"Did she tell you anything else?"

"No. Not that I can remember."

Emma closed her notebook. "Natalia, do you have the time to show me where that broom closet is?"

"It's right down the hallway."

Emma took a deep breath. "I think there might be a hidden passageway in this house. A few minutes ago, you seemed curious about it too. If there is one, I think it's there in that closet. You said Mira entered the closet, and then you found her in her office. There has to be something, a corridor, or a secret staircase, that leads from that broom closet to the upstairs rooms. I'd like to try to find it, and I'd appreciate it if you'd go with me."

"Go with you? You mean to the broom closet? Why?"

"You're in charge of the temple today, right? I need to make sure that I have your permission."

Natalia nodded. "Cecelia said I was in charge, yes. So why are you doing this?"

"It's important to find that passageway. It's important for Stacey's case. If you're okay with that, let's go!"

Natalia walked out of the spa with Emma, craning her neck down the hallway toward the door. "This is crazy, but I've always been curious. We don't have long. Cecelia will be back soon."

Natalia opened the narrow door of the closet, and they both stepped in.

Once inside, they left the door ajar so they'd have some light. Emma moved the brooms and mop to the side and began pushing against the walls and feeling the floorboards, searching for a secret door or a latch, something that would indicate the closet was more than it appeared. Just as she was about to give up, she found something. A small lever at the right side of the closet, about four feet up from the floor. She pulled it. As soon as she did, the back wall opened ever so slightly. Natalia shut the closet door as Emma pushed against the wall, opening it so they could fit through.

Emma and Natalia stepped onto a hidden landing and walked up the stairs, which opened to a back corridor. There were three doorways to the left and three doorways to the right. Emma opened the first door on the left, which led her directly into James and Mira's shared office space, the room where James was murdered.

Emma stepped into the office. Natalia stood at the doorway. Papers were stacked on both desks. Merchandise samples teetered on the shelves. The afternoon sun caught an object in a bowl on Mira's desk, flashing briefly into Emma's eyes. She blinked, bent down to get a better look, and saw a set of keys in the bowl. They were square with the Lincoln compass emblem embossed on the head. Did Mira try to run down Stacey and her that day on Esplanade? Was Mira the murderer?

She tiptoed out and closed the door behind her. She looked at her watch. They still had twenty minutes before Cecelia was expected. They walked the few steps to Cecelia's office. Emma moved toward the desk and looked out over the courtyard. If Cecelia had been sitting here the day of the murder, she would have had a prime seat to James's plunge to the fence below.

Several stacks of envelopes were neatly arranged on top of the desk. One letter was unfolded, opened, and laid flat, held down by a paperweight. Emma picked up the letter, stunned to discover it was a notice of foreclosure from the temple's mortgage company.

Emma skimmed the notice. The Japaprajnas had not made their last three mortgage payments. Unless they could make the full payment of $10,525 within the month, the house would be foreclosed. She'd assumed that the temple, ETC sales, together with James' drug sales, brought in a great deal of money. She didn't understand why the mortgage wasn't being paid.

The Japaprajnas seemed to be in some financial trouble.

She put the notice back under the paperweight as she'd found it and walked back to the secret passageway. She and Natalia slipped back down the stairs to the broom closet and listened at the door. They heard the front door slam.

"Natalia!" Cecelia sounded angry.

Emma could hear footsteps down the hallway. Then the spa door opening and closing.

They opened the closet door and eased out. Natalia headed toward the spa, and Emma, still limping, tiptoed down the hall to the front door. She managed to slip out of the house undetected.

* * *

Emma hobbled to her car on Esplanade, still in pain from her sprain. She couldn't see the alley from her position across the street from the temple, but knew there was access to that back street from someplace other than the courtyard. It made no sense to have a passageway behind the house unless it connected to an adjoining street. The Lincoln had to be back there somewhere. But it didn't seem like this was a good day to snoop around, especially since Cecelia was in such a foul mood. She'd come back another day.

Chapter Thirty-One

Back at home, Emma sat down on the couch to hug Maddie and Lulu. She broke one of her rules and let them both on the couch at the same time. They calmed down after a few seconds, and she could stroke their heads. It helped her think. It had been a long day. She needed to make some plans in Stacey's case. She'd already risked a lot and couldn't afford to make a mistake.

Ren walked in the front door.

"Hey! How was the rest of your day?"

"It was okay. Stacey and I drove out to Claiborne Avenue to the homeless encampment. How about yours?"

"Not much happened after you left. So I want to hear all about yours." He threw his coat on a chair and sat down at the end of the couch. He picked up her feet and tenderly pressed on her sprained ankle. "Still swollen, huh?"

"Some. But it's a lot better." She leaned over and gave Ren a kiss. "What I didn't tell you earlier today was that Raymond Collier told me that one of the guys he knows from the encampment on Claiborne was asleep in the alley next to the ETC shop the night Angelina Diaz was killed. He said he saw everything. But he doesn't want to speak to the police about it. I was hoping Raymond could talk him into coming down to the station. So far, we've gotten nowhere. I thought maybe he'd be able to pick out the suspect from photographs." She shrugged. "Raymond's going to talk to him again."

"Do you have any thoughts about who may have killed Angelina?" Ren adjusted a pillow behind his back.

"Maybe. Since it's got to be the same person who also killed James, I'm thinking about a couple of people. I'd prefer not telling you right now, because I could be wrong, and I don't think you even know about one of the people I'm considering." She hesitated. "By the way, I've filed the motion to dismiss the case against Stacey. I don't have a hearing date yet, but I'm going to call the DA and talk to him about dropping the charges as soon as I'm able to speak to my forensics expert. If he won't drop the charges, I'll attach the affidavit and get a hearing date." She paused.

"How about you? Who do you consider a suspect in Angelina's murder now that you've dropped my client from your list?"

He shrugged. "I'm thinking about a couple of people who could be suspects, too. But I don't have enough information or evidence to arrest anyone right now." He hesitated. "All I have is speculation. And just so you know, I'm coordinating my investigation of Angelina's murder with the detective who is investigating James' case."

Emma nodded. "That's good to know. What do you think about having a sketch artist go out to the encampment and get a rendering made of the person the guy saw? If the artist gets a good likeness, and someone can be identified, then you'd have your probable cause for arrest."

Ren nodded. "I like that. And we've got a great sketch artist. She works miracles."

"It will be interesting to see if we can recognize anyone from his description."

"Right. There were a few more suspects, but they weren't at the temple at the time of James's death, so they were immediately eliminated. I think that was one of the reasons Stacey was arrested as quickly as she was."

"That may not be true."

Ren raised his eyebrows. "What's not true? I'm not sure I'm following you."

"After I dropped Stacey off today, I went by the temple and snooped around a little. I had reason to believe there was a hidden room or passage in that house. I searched inside a broom closet and found what I was looking for. A hidden staircase."

"I hate to ask, but why were you looking in a broom closet?"

"Raphael mentioned a closet in his affidavit. I thought it could be important, and I had a hunch because so many Pre-Civil War houses had them."

"I'm just a little surprised you were nosing around in private quarters."

"I told the girl in charge for the day, Natalia, what I was doing, and asked her to join me, which she did. Natalia was in the spa, which was open to the public when I talked to her about it. The door to the temple was open to the public, too. She'd always been curious about that broom closet. So she came with me."

"What was your thinking? A hidden passageway would allow someone to commit the murder and escape, sight unseen?"

Emma nodded. "That's exactly what I was thinking." She leaned back on the couch pillows. "After I discovered it, Natalia and I climbed up the secret stairs to the second-floor rooms. When I was in Mira's office, I found a set of keys to a Lincoln. They were in a bowl on her desk, but I just left them there. I also found a notice of foreclosure on Cecelia's desk."

"What? That's a shocker. What's the date?"

"The end of the month."

"How much do they owe?"

"A little over ten thousand dollars. Not that much if they were getting such big monthly stipends from followers. I wonder what's going on with all the money they were making?"

"Good question. They probably had a lot of debt with all the repairs they made to that house."

"That's what you get for having a huge old place on Esplanade."

"Do you know if the NOPD is interested in questioning Mira about the drug operation going on at ETC? "

He ran his fingers through his hair. "Emma, it's time for you to let the cops take over this part of the case. You've found the information you need to get Stacey off. Let us handle it from here."

Emma nodded. "Okay."

"I'll need to get a search warrant for the temple and the car. Even though you found some interesting stuff there, I'd rather use a sketch from the homeless guy to support my affidavit if we can get one. I'm not going to use your testimony about the closet.

"Number one, you're my fiancé. That complicates things. The DMV identification of the car doesn't help with Angelina's case either. I'd prefer to be able to search the car for evidence related to Angelina Diaz's murder.

"So, the best thing would be to get the homeless guy to cooperate with a sketch artist. If he does, and the sketch reveals someone recognizable in the car the night of Angelina's murder, I'll have the probable cause I need for the search. So, I'll start there. Still, the hidden staircase was a great find."

"I think it's the key to solving the case. It had to have been used by the killer. The only other escape from James' office was down the front staircase or the window, which would have been obvious to anyone in the house. Natalia can testify that she's seen the secret passageway. And anyone lurking around the broom closet that day is suspicious. But none of that puts someone in the secret staircase or James' room on the day of his murder. It's still more theory than fact. But it's getting close."

"I can see where you were going. But it's still just a theory."

"I tried to find something today I could use either to prove Stacey's innocence or to show the court that someone else was the murderer. I took a risk, and I guess don't have that much to show for it. The Lincoln key on Mira's desk doesn't really get you anywhere either." She slumped back on the couch.

"You might be right about that, but it sounds like you've made a lot of progress on the case. Still, you need to stop sleuthing like you did today. Please? I know you hate it when I preach, but you're not a detective, and what you did was dangerous. It doesn't matter that you had the permission of that girl who was in charge today. Cecelia wouldn't have been happy to have you snooping around in her closet. It could have turned out badly for you. There could be, and likely is, a murderer living at the temple, and maybe more than one. You were taking a huge risk."

Emma nodded. She understood why Ren was upset. But she wasn't as certain as he was that James' and Angelina's murderer lived at the temple.

* * *

The next morning, after Emma got the boys off to school, she set up an appointment with Binh to speak with him in person.

Emma pulled into Binh's driveway and ran up the steps, dodging flower pots overflowing with begonias, to his massive front door. Music was playing inside the house. Elton John. *Mona Lisas and Mad Hatters.*

Binh opened the door, his face glowing with cheerfulness. "Come in, Professor. It's so good to see you! How are things?" The light from the sparkling bayou reflected on the ceiling of the living room, giving the illusion that the place was under water.

"Things are okay. But I need some help figuring a couple of them out."

Binh offered Emma one of the turquoise club chairs and curled up on the jade velvet sofa. Emma smelled onions, garlic, basil, oregano, and perhaps a dash of thyme sauteing in the kitchen.

"That's the lunch Harry is cooking up. I don't know what it is yet, but it sure smells good, doesn't it?"

"It does! Maybe I should hang out here a little longer." She laughed. "But, like I said, I have something to ask. And I'd like you to keep what I'm about to tell you confidential. I'd especially like you to keep this from Mira, if you don't mind. Do you have a problem with that?"

"If it's about the temple, I don't, and I understand. Mira has been deeply involved in its organization, and I don't think she ever completely understood what sort of man James Crosby was. He was the father of her child, so I think she always wanted to see whatever good there was in him."

"You might be right." Emma paused. "I saw something the other day I shouldn't have. I won't go into what it was, but it was obvious that they are having serious financial problems at the temple. I found that surprising."

He raised his eyebrows. "It is."

"I'm not sure what any of that means for Mira or anyone else, but I was surprised because I thought the temple took in so much cash on a monthly basis from followers."

"I don't know anything about that."

230

"I understand, but I wondered if you could help me with something. Following the money, in this case, has always made sense to me, especially since drugs may have played a role in James' life and in his death. I'd like to find out the street value of ketamine, per dose, without having to hire an expert. They're expensive, especially retired FBI or drug enforcement agents. I'd like to cut down my expenses as much as possible by doing some of my own leg work."

"I understand, but I can assure you, Professor Thornton, I have no clue."

"Would it be possible for you to make an introduction for me? I'd like to speak to the guys down at the racetrack that you mentioned before, Bradley Adcock, and Theodore Cook. They're trainers, right? I'd like to ask them a few questions."

Binh shook his head. "No, I'm sorry. I don't think that would work very well. But I might have a better idea. Adcock and Cook could still be actively involved in some illegal sales, if you follow me. They might have even have sold product directly to James. They're not going to talk to you.

"But I can put you in touch with another couple of guys who sold ketamine and animal tranquilizers years ago. They were trainers too. That's how I know them. They're okay, but trainers are a different sort of breed. These two made a lot of money in drug sales, but got out of the business because the police were starting to crack down. I think they'll talk to you, but I also think they'll insist on being anonymous. So don't expect a formal introduction.

"Sometimes old drug dealers don't mind talking about old times if the statute of limitations has run on their crime. If I can convince them you're not with the federal government, and I'm sure I can, I think they'll talk to you. How does that sound?"

"Perfect! It sounds perfect!"

* * *

Emma and Binh pulled around to the back of the Fairgrounds lot, toward the green stables with their green and white overhanging awnings, tack sheds, and training tracks. It had been raining, and the rutted, dirt road in front of the stables was full of puddles.

"The guys said they'd meet us in front, over there." He pointed.

Two men were standing under an awning. The smell of horse manure permeated the air. Trainers were walking a couple of horses on leads. They clopped by, each horse more magnificent than the other, their muscles rippling with each move.

"I'm not even going to get their first names?"

"Nope. They're being cautious, and I don't blame them."

As they picked their way through the puddles to the horse barn, Emma could see that both men were middle-aged, tanned, wiry. They squinted at Emma. Binh greeted each man and shook hands, then introduced Emma.

"Emma, my friend here, is trying to figure out a few things for a case she's involved in. Like I told you earlier, she's not a law enforcement officer. She's not with the IRS or the DEA. And you can trust her. She just needs some information."

"Nice to meet you, ma'am." The tall one spoke. The shorter one nodded.

"Thanks for talking to me today. Like Binh told you earlier, I need some information on ketamine. I'd like to know about how much it costs if you were to buy it on the street. I found some ketamine infusion clinics which offered doctor supervised doses of the drug which ran anywhere from four hundred to two thousand dollars a dose. But I'm sure that sort of pricing is different from what you'd find on the streets," Emma said.

The taller of the two shook his head. His partner laughed. "It's nowhere near that on the street. Just so you know, we're out of the business, and we've been out for years, so long now that we don't have to worry about law enforcement or anything like that. If we did, we wouldn't be talking to you. But we keep up with things, if you understand what I'm saying, and like to know what things cost. The price of ketamine hasn't changed that much through the years.

"Most Special K is stolen out of Mexican pharmacies or from Mexican pharmaceutical suppliers. From what you've said, it's a lot cheaper than what's offered in medical clinics, although I don't know much about that. But on the streets, the price is usually a hundred forty dollars per ten-milliliter vial, and powdered ketamine is typically around a hundred dollars per gram."

"Wow. That is a big difference. How much is one dose, usually?"

He shrugged. "That varies. Most people take an injection of forty to sixty milligrams or snort about sixty to a hundred milligrams. People who take up to a hundred milligrams can get sick or have a convulsion if they're not used to it. But you can build up a tolerance to it, like anything. Some people get hooked, and end up taking it every day. A few people around here got hooked on the stuff. No one could meet the demand for the drug if they took their supply from the surplus that's around the tracks."

"What do you mean by surplus?"

The shorter of the two men chimed in. "Sometimes a horse will get a pulled muscle or something like that, and a vet will prescribe ketamine for pain management, but maybe the horse responded better to hydrotherapy, or the horse got better before the medicine ran out. So there's left-over ketamine. Sometimes that surplus gets misplaced, and is sold to someone, usually someone who works at the tracks. But, like I said, there isn't enough of that sort of surplus to sell in high volume. That's why we found suppliers out of Mexico."

"So everyone who uses it doesn't get addicted?"

"It just depends on the amount they take and how often they take it. There are some who only use it recreationally, you know, just every once in a while. If you only take it a couple of times a year, of course, you're not going to have a problem with it. But if you build up a tolerance to the stuff, you need to take more and more to feel the buzz.

"I heard about that guy who was murdered recently. He ran that church down on Esplanade. He had a two hundred milligram dose a day habit. Now he was addicted. His habit cost him forty dollars a day, which isn't bad. But he got it for everyone at that church he ran, too," the shorter man said.

"Sounds like you're talking about James Crosby. That's two-eighty a week, or a little over a thousand dollars a month. Do you know how much he got for the members of his temple or church?" Emma realized these men knew Crosby's supplier. They had to.

He nodded. "I think that's the name. Crosby. Mira worked with him, right?" He looked at Binh.

Binh nodded.

"That's why I remember him. I heard he bought a hundred-milligram dose for about a hundred people every month. His dealer was always excited when he ordered."

"That set him back about two thousand dollars, right? And that was just for his church."

The shorter man nodded.

"So, the purchase of ketamine for Crosby and for the temple was about three thousand dollars a month."

"Yeah. That's right. And then he'd double that for sales to bars and clubs."

"Then, all together, Crosby was out six thousand dollars a month, or about seventy-two thousand dollars a year."

"Yeah," the taller man said.

"I have a question about some ketamine that's been found with fentanyl in it. Would the suppliers that Crosby used also sell ketamine laced with fentanyl?"

The two men looked at each other. The taller of the two men shook his head. "That's really unlikely. I don't think anyone from the tracks would be adding fentanyl to anything. Everything coming out of here's going to local suppliers. It's not that big of an enterprise."

"Do you know any dealer who might be adding fentanyl to his supply of ketamine?"

The taller of the two men shook his head. "I can't say for sure, but as far as I know, it doesn't come that way from Mexico. Fentanyl has to be added, either by the dealer or by someone else. Fentanyl's real cheap, and it can knock you out quicker than ketamine. Just a few grains of the stuff, the equivalent of a pinch of salt, can kill. You have to be real careful with it."

"You said you weren't sure about which dealers might be adding fentanyl. Can you tell me anything about this practice?"

The shorter partner shuffled his feet in the dirt and sighed. "I've been hearing more about it lately because it's cheap, like we said, and it makes the drug go farther. And it's a good high. But only people who don't care sell that stuff. People who have protection, if you understand what I'm saying. People who can't be traced."

Emma was surprised that the former dealers knew so much about James, his habits, his drug operation, and his suppliers. She wondered if they'd actually sold ketamine to him at some point. Of course, they knew Binh and Mira as well. Mira, who came to know everyone at the race track as a child. She wondered how involved Mira was in the back side of the race track.

* * *

Emma and Ren sat on the balcony as the boys put the dishes in the dishwasher. It was nice to have them do a few chores every once in a while. It was good for their soul and hers too. But they made so much noise banging the dishes, silverware, and glasses about, that Emma wondered if she'd have anything left when they finished.

"I found out today that James Crosby spent almost seventy-five thousand a year on ketamine, and at least a third of that went up his own nose."

"Good God. That's a lot. And it's at least part of the answer to the financial crisis."

"Yes. You can build up a tolerance to that stuff. And it's a tranquilizer. He'd have been drooling otherwise, " Emma shuddered.

Ren shook his head. "How crazy is that? I can't imagine spending that much money on drugs. But I added up my coffee expenses the other day, and that was pretty scary too.

"By the way, I got a sketch artist scheduled for the Diaz case. I'd like to go out to Claiborne Avenue tomorrow. Want to go with me? You can introduce me to Raymond, and then maybe Raymond can talk that other guy, the witness, into working with the sketch artist."

Emma was relieved Ren had scheduled the artist's meeting, but at the same time, she was anxious that after all this planning Jerome, the homeless man, wouldn't cooperate.

"Yes. I'll go."

235

Chapter Thirty-Two

T he next morning Ren and Emma grabbed their coffees to go, with three extra, one for Raymond, one for Jerome, and one for the sketch artist, and pastries for the five of them. They headed out to the I-10 overpass at Claiborne. They were meeting Brenda, the artist, there.

Ren and Emma pulled into the abandoned church's parking lot across from the camp. Brenda, who had already arrived, slid out of her car when she saw them and began unloading her equipment. She was a petite redhead who wore her hair pulled back in a ponytail so tight the skin on her face was taut. She'd brought a briefcase with her that was half her size, and a collapsible stool.

Emma searched for Raymond's red tent. Since he rarely moved locations, she spied it quickly in the same spot as before. Raymond was leaning against his backpack, probably sleeping.

Ren grabbed Brenda's briefcase, Emma grabbed the coffee and pastries and pointed the way toward Raymond. Brenda picked up her stool, and they started across Claiborne, headed for the encampment. The inhabitants of the camp were stirring about, rolling their blankets, lighting cigarettes. Some were making coffee. Others were still sleeping. Emma noticed that breakfast was being made on a few makeshift burners and camping stoves.

"Camping stoves are illegal. All of this will be shut down and cleaned out at some point, you know." Ren said.

"I doubt it. City Council keeps making those noises, but it never happens. Any governmental funding the city gets in for the homeless goes to pay the administrative salaries for various agencies. Nothing is ever done to help this group. Families can grill in Audubon Park, can't they? I know there are safety challenges under the highway that don't exist in a park, but, these people need a break. They don't have a home, and they need to eat. Things are stacked against the very poor." Emma stomped through the debris.

The camp inhabitants eyed the three of them with suspicion as they made their way to Raymond.

"We should have brought enough for everyone." Emma glanced at a young girl who couldn't have been over eighteen.

"How could we have done that?" Ren asked.

"We could have bought a bunch of donuts."

"There are at least two hundred people here. Maybe more." Ren paused. "It's okay, Emma. We don't have to feed everyone. Feeding Raymond and Jerome are good enough for today."

They reached Raymond's campsite. He was sitting up, a sleepy haze still settled on his face.

"Good morning, Raymond. Hope we're not too early. We brought you coffee and some pastries," Emma said.

"You're good. I was just waking up. This smells delicious." He stood up, grabbed the coffee, and took a sip. Then he chose a pastry and put it inside his tent. "Thanks for breakfast. What can I do for you?"

"This is Ren, a detective with the police department, and this is Brenda, a sketch artist. We were all hoping Jerome is still here somewhere. If he is, we'd like to have him speak to Brenda so he can describe what he saw the night Angelina Diaz was murdered. Can you speak to Jerome and explain that to him? We brought breakfast for him too."

"I saw Jerome yesterday. He should still be over there somewhere. I'll go check. Why don't you stay here?" Raymond grabbed Jerome's breakfast.

Raymond walked over to Jerome's grocery cart mound. From a distance, Emma watched Jerome stand up and take the coffee. He and Raymond spoke for a while. Raymond turned and motioned for them to come forward.

Brenda picked up her portable stool and briefcase and made her way toward Jerome. Emma and Ren followed a short distance behind. Jerome had parked his grocery cart in a small clearing. The cart, which was filled with blankets, cardboard, and even a broken baby buggy, had almost become too big to move.

Brenda approached Jerome. "I'd like to talk to you about what you saw in the alley behind the shop off of Bourbon Street the other night."

Jerome nodded. He was a young man. Emma, who never remembered names but never forgot a face, remembered Jerome from her clinic. He'd come in about a year before to ask her about veterans' benefits. He'd seen combat in 1991in the Gulf War, and still proudly wore the shirt from his Army uniform. All of his Veteran ID cards, money, papers, everything was in his pocket, wrapped with rubber bands. He'd showed it to her. He'd probably shown that bundle of cards and money to anyone who had taken the time to speak to him. He needed help, but he didn't want to wait around at the VA or anywhere else to fill out the paperwork for his benefits.

"Let's get comfortable. This will take a while. Do you have something to sit on?" Brenda asked.

Jerome turned and walked to his grocery cart, pulling up several layers. At the bottom, he found a small canvas stool.

"I got this."

"Great! That's perfect! Let's get started."

They sat, and Brenda pulled a notebook out from her briefcase, opened it, and turned it around so Jerome could see its contents.

"I have a notebook full of cutouts of various foreheads, eyes, noses, lips, and chins. I don't want you to think any more about that night. I want you to feel what happened. Then I want you to pick the drawing of the face part that feels right to you. When you find one, we'll place it over this blank outline of a face until we've completely constructed who you remember seeing that night.

"Which of these cutouts feels like the right forehead? Don't worry about hair and skin tones. We'll get that later."

Jerome looked at all of the cutouts of foreheads, finally choosing one.

"Here are the cutouts of chins. Which of these feels like the correct chin?"

Jerome pointed to a chin.

Brenda had him complete the same exercise with eyes, a nose, and lips.

She placed all of the face parts on the outline of the face. Emma stretched her neck to get a good look at the configuration. She thought it looked vaguely familiar, Frankenstein-ish, but familiar.

"We need to choose the hair now." She flipped toward the back and showed the hairstyles and colors to Jerome.

He flipped through the hair samples.

"I ain't sure about hair color. Most of the hair was shoved in a hoodie."

"Okay. Just do your best," Brenda said.

He chose a gray-tone hair that had been pulled back.

"And skin tone?"

"I think it was light, like this. But I'm not sure."

"Okay. I'll take this composite to the police station and make a drawing from it. Then I'll bring it by for you to look at. You'll get a chance to approve the sketch."

Ren stepped toward Brenda and glanced at the patched-together work. "How long will this take?" Ren asked.

"I'll have the sketch completed by the end of the day, probably around three or four."

* * *

Ren dropped Emma off at home so she could pick up her car and get to work. But Emma didn't have class right away and had set up a telephonic meeting with Dr. Vincent Holloway, a forensic pathologist at a local medical school. She'd faxed him the autopsy and other reports so she could ask him about the finding of fentanyl in James Crosby's autopsy, and about the report on the syringe found in Stacey's closet.

"Dr. Holloway? This is Emma Thornton. Thanks for reserving this time for me. I have a few questions about the reports I sent you."

"I always like your questions, Emma. Fire away."

"The autopsy said that Crosby was pushed off of a balcony and impaled on a fence about fifteen feet below. The impalement was found to be the cause of death. But before that, Crosby had also been given an intramuscular injection in his neck." She paused. "When they performed the autopsy, they found ketamine as well as fentanyl in his blood. The fentanyl level was at one point nine milligrams. Then there's also a separate report on the syringe found in my client's bedroom. The syringe had her fingerprints on it, and as far as I can tell, this evidence was the main reason she was detained and later arrested and charged with Crosby's murder. But this syringe only contained ketamine residue. No traces of fentanyl were found.

"Could you conclude that the syringe found in my client's bedroom was not the syringe which was used to kill, or which contributed to the death of James Crosby?"

"Yes. If that was the syringe used to kill James Crosby, traces of fentanyl should still be there along with the ketamine. There's only one puncture wound. So he wasn't shot up once with ketamine and once with fentanyl. That was a good catch. I'd bet they didn't mean to release that report yet. Ketamine is a slower-acting drug. Fentanyl begins working instantly. It's used as a painkiller, and it starts to relieve pain right away. People who are given this in the hospital report instant relief. It reaches its peak effect in five to ten minutes, and it'll last two to four hours.

"But as a street drug, it's dangerous. And when it's used with ketamine, it's effect is immediate and strong. A dose of only two milligrams is considered lethal. And that's a tiny amount. And its half-life is short. About eight hours. He still had a substantial amount of fentanyl in his body at autopsy. I think he had to have been given a lethal dose of fentanyl too. So if the syringe they found in Stacey's room didn't contain fentanyl, it wasn't the murder weapon.

"One other thing. One of the signs that help police or EMTs identify fentanyl on the street is blue lips. And Crosby had blue-tinged lips. Fentanyl was a significant factor here. I'll sign the affidavit you've prepared."

* * *

Excited about her conversation with Dr. Holloway, Emma called the DA's office as soon as she hung up, asking to be connected to the Assistant DA in charge of the Crosby case. ADA Deborah Davis picked up the call.

"How can I help you, Ms. Thornton?"

"Have you received the Motion to Dismiss the Crosby case I filed last week?"

"I did, but haven't been able to look at it closely yet. It says something about dismissing the case against your client because of the difference in the chemical compounds found in Crosby's body and the syringe they found in Ms. Robert's room? Do I have the gist of it?"

"You do. And this week, I'll file a supplement to the motion attaching an affidavit from Dr. Vincent Holloway verifying that the syringe you found in Stacey's room couldn't have been used to kill Crosby. I was calling to see if you'd consider dropping the charges against Stacey. It's clear she didn't kill James and that you don't have a case against her."

"I don't think we can do that, Ms. Thornton. We have a witness, Angelina Diaz, who clearly stated she saw your client walking up the stairs with a syringe in her hands. So, no. There are many unanswered questions here."

"That witness is dead. I didn't have an opportunity to question her about her affidavit and will never have the opportunity to cross-examine her. And I've also filed a motion to exclude the affidavit."

"All of this is interesting, Ms. Thornton. Especially since I understand you actually did speak to Ms. Diaz at the temple. That was a few days after Crosby's murder, I believe. But whatever happened, we will not agree to dismiss your client."

"I'll see you at the hearing, then." Emma placed her phone down.

Crap. The ADA was right about her conversation with Angelina. But that was before she knew about the affidavit, of course. Not that the DA would care about that.

It was clear the DA's office didn't care about the truth. They just wanted a win.

* * *

Emma paced the living room floor. She had no choice but to proceed with her plans. File the motions and continue with trial preparation. The DA had the burden of proof which was always more difficult. But she had to admit there were a couple of accountability issues in Stacey's story.

Stacey came back to the temple at four o'clock on the day of the murder to put her clothes in the dryer, a task that couldn't have taken more than fifteen minutes. She then returned to the coffee house across the street. She didn't walk back over to the temple until the police responded to the 911 call about James' fall from the balcony, which was after five o'clock. But she didn't buy a coffee. Instead, she sat outside at the coffee house and didn't see anyone there or at the temple that afternoon. No one would be able to verify the timeframe of her presence at either place. This would be a strike against Stacey at trial, especially since, if Angelina's affidavit got in as evidence, an argument could be made that she was in the house at the time James was killed.

But, she wasn't. Cecelia, and Mira were at the temple within the timeframe of the murder and used the side door to enter the building, even though Cecelia denied it. Mira didn't arrive until five-fifteen and stated she heard Cecelia scream after she'd been home long enough to get settled in her office. So the death occurred between the time Stacey finished putting her clothes in the dryer, which would have been about four fifteen, and five fifteen, which was the time of the scream. Stacey was sitting outside at the coffee house during that time. She didn't come back to the temple until the police showed up. But she couldn't prove it.

It was clearer than ever to Emma that Stacey had been set up. Someone, perhaps the killer, found ketamine from another source for the murders, not realizing there would be a difference in the chemical composition of the drug sold through ETC and the drug used to kill James. Then the killer set Stacey up with a used syringe found in James' office.

But who? Who found the supplier for the ketamine laced with fentanyl? There were so many possibilities. If she could figure that out, she might also be able to figure out who the killer was.

Emma ruled out the massage girls immediately. They were all young and naïve. She'd be surprised if any of them had ever been exposed to the drug world beyond their experience at the ETC shop. Only one person stood out as a person who might have something to hide. It was a guess, but she was willing to bet on it. Emma got in her car and headed toward the French Quarter.

* * *

Emma halfway hoped Moonstone wasn't in. She liked her and considered her straightforward and honest. She wasn't looking forward to this confrontation.

She pushed open the door to the shop and listened to the tinkling of the overhead bells.

"Hi there! What brings you to this part of the city? I hope everything's okay." Moonstone was dressed in a simple black dress which emphasized the paleness of her skin and eyes. She was straightening items on the top shelf of the glass counter.

"Things are moving along. I do have a couple of questions for you, though. You never told me what James was able to get you to confess to him. Did you write it down, or did he record it?"

"Why do you need to know? And why now?"

"Things like that are important in a murder investigation."

"I wrote it down. But I don't see the need in telling you what it was about."

"Did James keep your confession?"

"Apparently."

"And he blackmailed you with it?"

Moonstone hesitated. "Where are you going with this?"

"I have the feeling you might be hiding your identity. Your hair is obviously dyed black, and your tattoos might be part of a disguise too."

Moonstone was silent.

"It's obvious now that I think about it. You have prior convictions? No one else would hire you but Mira, and then you confessed everything to James? What was your crime? Were you a dealer? Do you still have connections to that world? Did those connections help you with your position here?"

Moonstone crossed her arms across her chest.

"James was given a lethal dose of fentanyl as well as ketamine. And I believe we'll find out that Angelina was given a dose from the same batch. The drug they were given came from different batches than the stuff that James sold, and we think it came from a different dealer. The killer could have had connections to the drug world, but if not, someone else did. Someone connected the killer to this new dealer and helped make the sale. Do you know anything about that?"

"I don't know what you're talking about."

"I think you do. And I think either you're the killer or you know who it is."

Moonstone sighed. "All I received was a note. One of the girls from the temple walked over with it. It said to furnish the ketamine, in four ten cc syringes, or they'd tell the police I was dealing again, and that I was the one running the drugs from the shop. That could have ended badly for me. So, I got it."

"You're still on probation?"

"Yes."

"Why were you asked to get this when there was so much ketamine already available there at the shop?"

"James was generous with the stuff, and a bit messy, but he still watched his stash. He always knew how much he had on hand, and watched it like a hawk. He and Mira never let any of it out of their sight. Either they had it in their possession, or the girls had it, counting it, and packaging it. They would have known if anything was missing, and there would have been hell to pay."

"Who was the dealer you contacted?"

"A guy out of Slidell. I didn't want to go local. It felt safer."

"Did you question the girl who brought you the note? Did you ask her who instructed her to speak to you?"

"Yes. But they've been trained pretty well. She didn't even change her facial expression. She had nothing to say."

Emma sighed. "This is important to Stacey's case. Would you be willing to testify in a court of law that someone from the temple asked you to obtain the ketamine, and then right after that, James was killed?"

"No. I can't do that. I may as well get a megaphone and shout out that I'm in violation of my probation. Plus, I think there's a chance I wouldn't live a lot longer after giving that sort of testimony."

"Would you be willing to complete an affidavit explaining what happened?"

Moonstone nodded. "Maybe. Could I get immunity from prosecution for getting the drugs? If I can, I'll do it."

"I can't promise that. That's something the DA would have to grant. And the DA's office probably wouldn't be willing to give you immunity since your testimony would help Stacey's case. But let's see what happens. I'd like to find a way to protect you and use your testimony."

Chapter Thirty-Three

The next day Emma went in search of that banana-tree-lined alley behind the temple. All of the homes on the block, including the building the temple was in, were built very close together. Most of the residents had enclosed their courtyards with fences that left a narrow, shell-covered passageway behind each of their houses. Emma stepped into that path, relieved to see banana trees ahead.

The alley behind the houses was wide enough for a car, but not much more. Several neighbors kept their garbage cans there, but she knew the temple trash cans were kept closer to the house.

She walked toward the clump of banana trees. The tires of a dark-colored vehicle were visible through the leafy green trunks. If you looked hard, it was easy enough to see, especially if you were trying to find it like she was. As she neared the vehicle, she could see that it was an old two-door Lincoln. Black. With tiny opera windows in the back. It was once quite fancy and had obviously been well taken care of. She walked up to the dashboard, pulled out a pen, and began writing down the VIN number so she could verify the car's owner.

She heard a creak and then a snapping sound. She turned around, but saw nothing. She continued copying down the VIN number.

"Can I help you, Ms. Thornton?"

Emma started, then pivoted to face Mira, who stood three feet away, next to the clump of banana trees.

Emma exhaled. "Oh, hello, Mira! Interesting to find this car in the alley. I was just writing down some information." She smiled, though her heart began beating more rapidly. She shoved her pen and notebook back in her purse and began moving toward the alley entrance.

"What about?" Mira took another step toward Emma.

"I needed some of the vehicle identification information."

"None of that's any of your business. You're trespassing."

"No, I'm not. Alleys are public in New Orleans unless you have a restriction in your deed making it private." Emma waited a moment for a response. "Plus, I'm not even touching the car."

"It doesn't matter. You need to leave."

"Look, a car that looked a lot like this one tried to run down my client and me the other day. I need to know who owns the car."

"I don't care what you're doing. You need to go, now."

"I'm going." She stepped away from Mira, then turned around. "But before I leave, I thought I'd let you know that Moonstone and I spoke recently. She said Natalia called her the day Raphael was killed and asked her to go pick up a package at the Post Office. But when Moonstone arrived, nothing with the parcel number she'd been given was there. And Natalia said you were the one who told her to give Moonstone the message. Do you know why there was no package?"

"I don't know what you're talking about."

"Did you send Moonstone on a wild goose chase?"

"Of course not." Mira took another step toward Emma.

Emma stepped back, preparing to run back down the alley, when the iron gate squeaked again. She turned to see Cecelia walking toward her.

"Well, hello, Ms. Thornton. Mira told me you were here. And thanks to Mira's suggestion of the security camera out back, this wasn't such a surprise."

"I was just asking Mira about the day Raphael died." Emma continued to inch backwards, toward the alley's entrance.

Cecelia shook her head. "Such a tragedy."

"I've also been talking to Mira about this car. A car just like this one almost ran my client and me down a few days ago. I don't imagine you'd know anything about that? I believe it's registered to the Japaprajnas."

"I'm sorry you're having so many problems, Ms. Thornton. But I don't have any information that can help you." Cecelia smiled. One hand was in her jacket pocket.

"I didn't think so." Emma put her purse on her shoulder and turned to leave when she heard swift steps approaching from behind. She turned around. Cecelia was running toward her. Emma started to run, but Cecelia's strides were longer than Emma's. Cecelia reached Emma and grabbed her jacket, yanking her closer, then wrapped her left forearm around Emma's neck. She gripped her left hand with her right and squeezed Emma's neck in a choke hold, cutting off her air supply.

"You weren't expecting this, Professor?" Cecelia pulled a syringe out of her jacket pocket and began priming it.

Emma gasped as Cecelia's arm tightened around her throat. She tried to pull Cecelia's arm away from her neck, gulping for air. Then she lowered her chin, grabbed a couple of Cecelia's fingers, and bent them backwards as far as she could. Cecelia yelped in pain as Emma began to wriggle free. Emma turned to her side and spun around, smashing her knee into Cecelia's stomach. Cecelia released her grasp.

As Emma scrambled away, Mira grabbed Emma's arm, and flung her backward. Cecelia sprang forward, seized Emma's other arm, jerked her to the side, and forced her to the ground, smashing Emma's face into the shell alleyway. Before she fell, Emma had a full view of the syringe Cecelia held in her hand.

Emma struggled up and kicked Cecelia in the shin. Mira tackled Emma and held her torso down. Aiming for the syringe, Emma kicked again but missed.

Cecelia began pushing fluid down the chamber of the syringe as Emma swung at her wildly. Emma hesitated for a moment, interrupted by a glimpse of Natalia creeping out of the courtyard carrying the large antique brass candelabrum that usually sat on the altar.

"The police are on to you. You're not going to get away with this," Emma said, hoping to distract Cecelia from Natalia, who was sneaking toward them.

Natalia tiptoed out of the gate, lifting the heavy candelabrum as high as she could, and smashed it down on Cecelia's head. Cecelia fell to the ground. Emma leaped up, kicked the syringe out of Cecelia's reach, and ran to grab her purse, neatly binding Cecelia's wrists together with its straps.

Mira wrestled the candelabrum from Natalia. But Natalia, who was at least six inches taller than Mira, turned around, grabbed Mira's arms, squatted, then flipped Mira over her back, straight onto the shelled surface of the alley. The candelabrum fell to the ground. Mira was winded from the fall and didn't move. Natalia quickly sat on Mira's legs, and held her arms down until Emma could return to help.

Cecelia, semi-conscious from the attack, lay crumpled in the alley, motionless. Together, Natalia and Emma flipped a writhing Mira over on her stomach, shoving her face to one side. Emma struggled against Mira's thrashing to pin both of her wrists together.

"Do you know if there's duct tape or anything anywhere we can use to wrap up their wrists and ankles?" Emma asked Natalia.

Natalia jumped up and ran to the garconniere. Emma heard her banging open cabinet doors and scrambling through the layers of junk in one of the cupboards.

"Found something!" She ran out with a roll of moving tape and began wrapping it around Mira's wrists and ankles.

"Don't you dare. I'll call INS! You won't be able to work here or anywhere else in this country." Mira struggled, trying to pull her ankles away from Natalia.

"If you call INS, you'll be calling them from jail." Emma pulled Mira's arm a little tighter. She nodded at Natalia. "We need to tape up Cecelia too. She could come to at any second."

Emma and Natalia wrapped Cecelia's wrists and ankles. She woke up and began struggling against the tape.

"You can't do this. You're on my property. I'm going to bring charges against you for trespass and assault. You'll be sorry you ever stepped foot on this place." She was flushed, red-faced, the veins on her neck bulged.

Emma nodded at Natalia and put her hand on her shoulder. "Thanks.

That should do it until the police come." She walked through the courtyard and entered the back door of the temple, which Natalia had left open. She picked up the kitchen phone and dialed 911. Then she walked to the front porch and collapsed on the steps.

Cecelia and Mira were bound up in the alleyway when Ren found them fifteen minutes later. Not known for their swift response, two squad cars' of uniformed officers arrived fifteen minutes after Ren. Emma brought Ren and the officers out to the back of the temple and showed them the syringe Cecelia had attempted to use.

Ren put on a pair of rubber gloves and retrieved the evidence, placing it in a plastic bag.

"Officers, this woman accosted me." Cecelia nodded toward Emma. "And she was trespassing. When I asked her to leave a few minutes ago, she turned on me. She hit me and kicked me too."

Ren walked over to Emma.

"Let's talk a minute." He moved closer, turning his back on the uniformed officers. "Are you okay? You look a little beaten up. Your face and your neck are red." He frowned as he touched her neck, moving her so that he could get a better look. "What happened? I think we need to call an ambulance. And what's this about trespass? What's going on here?"

"I did get a little beaten up. I'll explain that in a minute. But I didn't actually trespass. I just walked down the passageway between the houses back there and checked out the Lincoln. It's there, by the way."

"Great. And then what happened?"

"Mira and Cecelia saw me there. Apparently, they have a security camera back here somewhere. Anyway. They attacked me. And Cecelia tried to inject me with whatever's in that syringe." She nodded toward the bag Ren was holding. "I suspect it's another dose of ketamine laced with fentanyl. I'd bet it's a lethal dose. Natalia intervened and helped me. So I'm okay. No worse, really, for all that happened."

"What about the ambulance?" Ren said.

"I'm fine. I don't need one. She didn't hurt me. She scared me more than anything."

"I'm calling one anyway. You need to get checked out. And things are about to heat up here." Ren and Emma began walking toward the front porch.

"What do you mean, heat up?"

"We've had a joint raid planned for some time, and since you called 911and reported another incident related to the temple, it escalated. We've been working together as a task force all along. I couldn't talk about it. Not even to you. NOPD and the Feds. Narcotics, homicide, the INS, the Department of Labor, and the FBI. Warrants have been issued. They'll be here any minute."

Just then, three police cars, four black unmarked cars with government tags, and an FBI lab unit pulled up. Police officers and officers from the INS and Department of Labor made their way to the front door of the temple where Emma and Ren were standing. One of the officers held a warrant in his hand.

"We have a warrant to search this house. Are you the property owner?"

Ren stepped up. "I'm Ren Taylor, a detective with the New Orleans Police Department." He showed the officer his badge. "The owner of this property, Cecelia Crosby, is out back. She's been detained for threatening Ms. Thornton here. But go on in. I'll be joining you shortly, as soon as I make sure Ms. Thornton is okay."

* * *

After the EMTs released Emma, she drove home. She'd called the dean and had taken the rest of the day off. Ren stayed behind to participate in the search with his homicide unit.

The run-in with Cecelia and Mira had taken her by surprise. She was shaken and needed some time to collect herself. Her throat was sore from Cecelia's choke hold, but she didn't expect that to last long. She felt blind-sided by the assault and thankful Natalia had pitched in.

The phone rang.

"Hey, babe. Guess what?"

"What?"

"Brenda finished up the sketch."

"That's good. Does it look like anyone?"

"Yeah. I'm pretty sure it does."

"Really? Who?"

"It's a dead ringer for Cecelia Crosby."

Chapter Thirty-Four

Emma scooted her chair closer to the balcony railing and looked over the banister. It was getting late. She watched the sun as it descended over the horizon, the sky turning shades from blush to violet, oak trees, and church steeples silhouetted against the colorful backdrop. The dogs were asleep at her feet. The twins were upstairs, quiet for once. They each had big projects due and, as usual, had waited until the last minute to complete them. Emma had decided to order dinner out. A small treat to herself, not anyone else. She was distracted. Antsy.

Ren should be home any minute. It had been two days since the task force had completed its inspection of the temple, the garconniere, the cars on the property belonging to the Japaprajnas, and the shop. He said forensics should be ready any day, but forty-eight hours was the usual turn-around.

She heard a door slam. Then keys rattled. Ren walked through the door.

"Hi, sweetheart." She got up to give him a hug. "I'm sitting on pins and needles over here."

Ren smiled. "Yeah? Well, we got some feedback."

"Okay." She paused. "Can you talk to me about it?"

"Someone from the DA's office should be calling you soon. So, it's okay. Let me get a beer, and I'll join you."

Ren popped the top of his can of beer as he walked out to the balcony, and pulled a chair up to the railing. He peered over the banister.

"Pretty night, huh?"

"Okay, okay. Enough suspense. What's up? What did they find?"

"They found another syringe in Cecelia's desk drawer, and the contents of this syringe, as well as the one she intended for you, both contained approximately 2.5 milligrams of fentanyl, which is a lethal dose. It also contained about ten cc's of ketamine."

"Did they test it and compare it to the compound found in James Crosby's body?"

"Yep. It seems to be from the same batch."

"That's huge."

"Yes. They found an empty syringe with James' fingerprints on it, too."

"Why would she have kept that?"

"I guess she didn't know what to do with it." He grimaced.

"Anything else?"

"They found Angelina's hair and fingerprints in the Lincoln. There was some DNA there too. Apparently, there was some blood loss. There must have been a struggle in the car."

Emma nodded. "Right. She was fighting for her life. Any information about who might have driven the vehicle the night she was killed?"

"Cecelia's fingerprints are all over it."

"What about Mira's?"

Ren shrugged. "It looks like Cecelia was the only person who drove the car. The only other fingerprints in the car are Angelina's. Mud from the back alley, the alley behind the shop, and the alley behind the pizza shop are there. And some of the footprints from the alley behind the pizza shop match boots in Cecelia's closet. But there were a couple of other surprises."

Emma picked up her wineglass from the balcony floor.

"A pair of surgical gloves were found in the trunk of the Lincoln hidden on the inside of the spare tire. I'm not sure what they were used for. Maybe Cecelia used them when she entered the shop to start the fire. And it looks like the same substance that was used to set the fire at the shop was also found in the trunk of the Lincoln. So was the black hoodie with 'The University of Idaho' printed in gold on the upper left side."

"Wow. What was used to set the fire?"

"Kerosene. And fibers of the same rag used in the fire. We found a large bin of kerosene in an old shed out back. Looks like it was used to store garden stuff. Someone could have poured kerosene from that bin into the smaller container they found in the storage closet at the shop. There was a funnel next to the larger container, too. They also stored other flammable stuff in the shed. Gasoline, lanterns, paint."

"Yeah. People used to use kerosene lanterns during hurricanes when the power would go out."

"I'm sure they still do."

"What do you think all this means?"

"That Cecelia was determined to kill a few people. I'm not sure why yet."

"What about the fact that I found the Lincoln keys on Mira's desk?"

"Could just be a spare. Especially since we didn't find any other fingerprints in the car. We'll have to ask Mira."

"I knew Cecelia was going to inherit half of the estate upon James' death. But there wasn't much of an estate left. Maybe that was the point. Maybe Cecelia killed James because there still is money-making potential at the temple, and with him dead and not such a financial drain, they can still make money. I'm guessing Angelina and Raphael saw Cecelia coming out of the broom closet door after she killed James. So she killed them to protect herself.

"What I don't understand is Mira. I'm the victim of a crime she committed. No law prevents me from speaking to her, although she's under no obligation to see me. I'd like to try."

Ren nodded. "I was thinking of doing the same, but why don't you try first. There's a better chance she'll open up to you."

* * *

The next morning Emma traveled to Central Lockup and asked to see Mira. She wasn't sure she'd show. A deputy brought Emma into a small conference room.

She'd waited about fifteen minutes and then heard a shuffling sound and saw a small figure leading two deputies down the hall. Mira's long dark hair was in a ponytail. Her hands were shackled in front of her, her eyes downcast.

Mira hesitated at the entrance of the room.

"Thanks for coming, Mira. I'm glad to see you."

Mira kept her eyes on the cement floor and continued walking. She sat down at the metal table, then looked up at Emma, not saying anything.

"What happened, Mira? What made you and Cecelia attack me the other day?"

Mira covered her face with her hands, but Emma could see that tears were rolling down her cheeks. She stood up and began pacing the room, wiping her eyes with the shoulder of her jumpsuit. She sat back down.

"I don't know. I mean, I know what happened that day. But I don't know how it got to that point."

"Why don't you try to break it down. Maybe that would help."

She sighed. "Oh, I don't know." She sniffed. "James didn't have many principals, but I always thought I did. James was manipulative and conniving. He lied all the time. But mainly, he was an addict. Cecelia was worse. She was the one with all the rules, the one who wanted to control everything. And she would have done anything for money. People meant nothing to her.

"I got into drugs with James, then I got pregnant. You know that story. But my choices seemed limited after that. I stayed with him because of Jimmy. And I guess because I was so unhappy, I got into the drug thing more and more. More than I wanted to admit. So you could say I'm an addict too." She wiped her nose on her sleeve. "Ketamine makes you feel good if you don't overdo it. I lived for Jimmy and to do a hit of K when I could.

"James said we needed more money, so we opened the shop. It didn't take long before James decided it made sense to sell drugs, too, because we had a built-in clientele. I knew some guys at the tracks who could help, so I put James in touch with them." She stood up again and started pacing.

"James started using ketamine in his sessions, and I started using every day. I guess I got even more hooked, if that's possible. I mean, before, it was like, weekly, maybe. James encouraged everyone to use it all the time. And then Cecelia found out that I was using.

"I told you once that even though she was James' wife, she would only get half of his estate under the will because of Jimmy, and that Jimmy would get the other half. And that I was to be the trustee of the estate. Cecelia really hated that. She and James argued about that a lot. She thought she should take everything under the will. And I know she hated being humiliated by James and his womanizing with the girls at the spa. She pretended to ignore it, but she saw everything. And she kept score. I knew that someday she'd do something, and it would be big.

"When she found out I had a drug problem, she told me she would have me declared incompetent to manage the trust. But even worse than that, she said that if I didn't do exactly what she asked of me, she'd call the state and have Jimmy taken away. And I knew she'd do it." Mira wiped a tear from her face.

"So she asked you to burn down the shop?"

"Moonstone called me on the day it burned and told me that you and Raphael were at the shop, in the back. Moonstone was good at reporting everything. Keeping her job was important to her. I was angry and said something to Cecelia about it. Then Cecelia asked me to call Moonstone and tell her to go to the post office to pick up a package. I had Natalia make the call. After that, Cecelia asked for my keys to the shop. I didn't know what was going to happen." She shook her head. "Poor Raphael." She blinked, and tears ran down her face.

"Were you aware that there were financial problems with the temple? That the temple had received a foreclosure notice?"

"Yeah." She nodded. "Things had gotten so out of control. The house repairs were crazy. And we bought a lot of ketamine. James sold some, but not enough to pay for what we took and what he gave out at the temple. And I think he was probably starting to take more than half of the product."

"So Cecelia wanted to gain control of the estate."

Mira shrugged. "I'm sure she would have liked to cut Jimmy out of his share, if she could have figured out a way to do that."

"Was she trying to get herself appointed trustee?"

"Yes. That was her goal. And, of course, there was the Stacey issue."

"What Stacey issue?"

"I overheard Cecelia and James talking about her once. I know Cecelia asked James to leave Stacey out of the will. And I always wondered if Cecelia set Stacey up to take the rap for James' murder. Maybe she put the syringe in her room. I'm sure she did something."

"That's an interesting idea. You can't disinherit a child in Louisiana unless there's an extenuating circumstance of some kind, like murder. A murderer can't inherit from the victim," Emma said.

"Cecelia must have known that."

"If Stacey isn't convicted of James' murder, she can contest the will and claim her rightful child's share. But that's for another day. The interesting issue is whether Cecelia set up Stacey. But it probably doesn't matter much at this point. It looks like they've got her on other evidence."

Emma reviewed her notes. "I do have another question for you. You said that on the day of the murder, you got to the temple around five o'clock, entered through the side door, and then walked up the stairs to your office. You said you didn't see anything in the courtyard at that time. But did you? Did you see James' body on the fence through the kitchen window when you got home?"

Mira nodded. "I did. It was all I could do to get Jimmy up the stairs without him seeing anything. That's all I was worried about. I didn't want Jimmy to see his dad."

"Why didn't you say anything about it at the time? Why didn't you tell the police or me what you saw?"

"I guess at first I thought it was a terrible accident. And then when the police came back the next day and said it was murder, I suspected Cecelia. It seemed obvious to me. But I didn't want to say anything because I didn't have proof and because I couldn't afford to make her angry. She'd just turn that anger against me and Jimmy." She sighed.

"Did you see anyone else in the house when you walked in?"

"Yes. Angelina was there, in the hallway, and so was Cecelia. They were both by the closet next to the stairs. And Ralph was in the hallway too, but he was closer to the stairs."

"I see. Do you know anything about the entrance to the hidden staircase through the broom closet?"

She nodded. "Yes. I used it occasionally, although Cecelia wanted to keep it a secret. I saw her using it one day, and when she wasn't around, I used it too."

"Could Cecelia have used that hidden staircase to enter the second floor, kill James, then escape back down the secret passageway?"

"Sure. That would have been entirely possible."

"Did anyone know about the hidden staircase other than you and Cecelia?"

"Not that I know of. I didn't tell anyone else about it. And I'm sure she didn't."

"What were you doing the other day when I was out by the car. Why did you attack me? Why were you working with Cecelia then?"

"I didn't think Cecelia was going to pull out a syringe. But I was afraid not to back her up. At this point, she's got me so scared. I'd do anything to keep Jimmy." Mira continued pacing the room. "I don't know what to do anymore. More than anything, I don't want to jeopardize Jimmy. Then I ended up doing just that." She sat down, put her head on her hands.

"I know this is tough. I'm sure your attorney knows what advice to give you."

Mira shook her head. "I don't know how I can go on without my little boy."

"I'll go by Stacey's today, and I'll make a point to check on Jimmy. Isn't he staying with your dad and Harry?"

Mira nodded.

"I'll be happy to tell Jimmy I saw you and give him any message from you. I know he needs you, but he's being cared for as well as your dad cared for you when you were small. You know that. This will be over before you know it." Emma shuffled through her purse. She never had a tissue when she needed one. But she had an old unused napkin from the coffee house. She offered it to Mira, who accepted it gratefully, and blew her nose.

She reached her hand out to Mira, who grasped it.

"You're going to get through this."

* * *

Emma drove out to Stacey's and knocked on her door.

"Any news?" Stacey asked.

Emma could smell something delicious coming from the kitchen. Marinara sauce? Something Italian for sure.

"It's time to celebrate." She walked into the kitchen.

"Why is that?"

"Because the police found evidence which completely exonerates you, and charges will be dropped this week."

Stacey's eyes filled with tears. "What? Just like that? I can't believe it!" She sat down at the kitchen bar and propped her elbows on the counter.

Smiling, Emma sat down next to her. "Stacey, did you know the broom closet hid a secret passageway?"

Stacey sat up. "What? A secret passageway? No!"

Emma reached over and squeezed Stacey's arm. "Yes! I recently got the affidavits the witnesses completed right after James's murder. Raphael and Angelina both mentioned they saw Cecelia standing next to a closet close to the stairs on the day of the murder, and Angelina said it was around four-thirty when she saw her. That's what got me interested in the closet, which was where I discovered the hidden stairway.

"I suspect both Angelina and Raphael actually saw Cecelia coming out of the closet right after the murder, although their affidavits don't spell that out. With a little encouragement, I think they would have told that to the police. And I believe Cecelia feared what they may say, which is why she killed both of them. But there's enough evidence against Cecelia to prove she killed both Angelina and Raphael without going into motive.

"Wow, that's amazing." Stacey smiled.

"Then Moonstone admitted that someone from the temple asked her to buy the syringes of ketamine for them. We even think Cecelia set you up to take responsibility for James' murder. There's evidence linking her to all three murders."

"This is almost too much information to take in at once." Stacey blotted her eyes with a tissue. "Thanks for everything you've done." Stacey beamed at Emma.

"I haven't called your mom about this. I'm sure she'd want to know, but I'll leave all of that up to you. Binh said you're welcome to stay here as long as you want. He said you can take your time to think and decide what you want to do."

* * *

Later that evening, when the twins were fed and upstairs doing homework, Emma and Ren sat on the balcony. She'd set out a bucket of ice and a bottle of champagne. It had been a long day. But the night was theirs.

Emma wrapped her arms around Ren's neck and kissed him softly on the lips. "You did some good work, Detective."

She sat back in her chair and watched Ren uncork the bottle. She felt content. All of her worries about things not working out with him seemed far away. She could see them together into the future now, and it didn't scare her. They were good for each other, and they both knew it.

"And I commend your work as well, Professor. It was good to let the ADA know you wanted to drop all of your assault charges against Mira. The only person who should be charged with anything in the James Crosby and Angelina Diaz cases is Cecelia. Even she could see that. But Mira might be implicated in Raphael's case. She could get out of it, depending on what kind of evidence she is willing to produce against Cecelia." Ren poured two glasses of champagne and handed one to Emma.

"Right. I would bet that there will be drug charges leveled against Mira and charges for harboring illegal immigrants, indentured servitude, and conspiracy." Emma ticked off the charges on her fingers. "Cecelia will be on the hook for all of that too. They're tough charges."

"They are. But I think the brunt of those charges will fall on Cecelia."

"What about Moonstone? She wanted immunity from prosecution for her role in this and was willing to testify against Cecelia if she got it. Any word on that?" Emma took a sip of her champagne.

"Yes. The DA seemed to understand that Moonstone was pressured into getting the drugs, so he's going to cut the deal she wanted. So, if she testifies against Cecelia, the DA won't revoke her probation. Plus, her testimony against Cecelia really helps."

"And what about Natalia? She's here illegally. I was afraid about what INS was going to do with her once they found her."

"They cut a deal with her, too, which was pretty cool. They said they'd give her back her visitor's visa status if she'd testify against Cecelia and the Japaprajnas and explain what she'd undergone for the past two years."

"I'm glad to hear how well that worked out. I spoke to Binh and Harry when I went by to chat with Stacey. They were happy I'd dropped the assault charges, but understand that Mira may need to serve some time. They wanted Mira to go through a drug rehab program, too. I'm hoping that could also be a part of the sentencing. They have one in mind that's not far away. They could visit Mira there with Jimmy. And then they have a place for her to stay when she gets out. She can always stay in the big house if Stacey decides to remain in New Orleans and live in the carriage house, which was an option they offered to her."

"What's going on with her?"

"The DA should drop his charges against Stacey this week. She will probably stay here a while and then decide if she wants to go back to New Mexico. Stacey needs to get her life back on track. She needs to go back to school. Her mom's offered to help her with that, at least.

"Stacey had been looking for a safe place. That's what she thought the temple was at first. I always thought sanctuary was about a place of peace and comfort, and it is. But it's also about being with the people that make you feel that way. I hope Stacey can find that."

Ren turned to look at Emma. The setting sun reflected in his eyes and gave his skin an amber glow. "You're my sanctuary, Emma. Home is where you are. But something's missing."

Emma looked at Ren, raising her eyebrows in surprise.

"I want to make our life together official. I've wanted that for some time now." Ren slid off the wicker chair he'd been sitting on and put one knee

262

to the ground. He reached into his back pocket and pulled out a small box, and handed it to Emma.

Emma gasped. "Ren! We said no rings!"

"Emma Thornton, this is the second time I've asked you this. I know you've had doubts. And I know that sometimes I can be fussy, but that's only because I worry about you. I love you more than I could ever have thought possible. And I always will. Will you marry me?"

Emma blinked and took a deep breath. "Of course! I've already said yes once!"

"But I need you to give me a date this time. I need this to be legitimate. The real deal. No pussyfooting around."

Emma hesitated. "Okay." She grinned.

"And will you put that ring on your finger?"

Emma slowly opened the box, took out the ring, and slid it on her finger. She brushed tears from her eyes before she slid her arms around Ren's neck.

Ren wrapped his arms around Emma's waist and stood, taking her with him.

"How about next week? I don't think I can wait."

Author's Notes

1. P. 42 Neutral Ground: The neutral ground is what most people would call a median, or the middle of a boulevard. It gets its roots from when the French Quarter was occupied primarily by the French and the downtown and uptown areas were occupied by Americans. Canal Street was the barrier between the two cultures, and the median there acted as the neutral ground where they could discuss their differences.
2. P. 157 "Take Back Your Life: Recovering From Cults and Abusive Relationships" by Janja Lalich and Madeline Tobias (Bay Tree Publishing) 2nd edition, 2006.
3. P. 205 The terms 'lakeside' and 'riverside' essentially replace north and south in New Orleans. Lakeside means you should move away from the Mississippi River to get to your destination, while riverside means you should move away from Lake Pontchartrain. These terms are used since the city is built along the curve of the Mississippi River.

Acknowledgements

New Orleans continues to be my muse. The city has a beauty like none other. It's also a great location for a murder mystery with its dark corners and ancient architecture. This story takes the reader to tree-lined Esplanade Avenue and the lush Bywater District, through the French Quarter and down to verdant Bayou St. John.

I would like to acknowledge Brian Swanner again for his beautiful photography for the cover. Brian is not a professional photographer. Instead, he is a talented architect who takes time from his busy schedule to take stunning shots of New Orleans architecture for my book covers. Thanks to Brian.

Thanks again to Mari Ann Stephanelli for her thoughtful edits, and guidance, and for her review of *Sanctuary*. I always appreciate her wisdom.

I would also like to thank the following individuals and beta readers for their help and guidance in reviewing the book: Jodi Langevoort, Liz Humphries, Rip Sartain, Pat Pennington King, Mary Sutton, Mally Becker, Carolyn Jarboe, and Steve Halpert. I'd like to extend a special thanks to Steve Halpert, a man who practices criminal defense law in the state of Texas on a daily basis, for his time, his thoughtful critique, and invaluable advice.

Thanks again to the women in my writing group, fabulous writers, all: Dawn Abeita, Katherine Caldwell, Nicole Foerschler Horn, and Dawn Major. Their insight is priceless.

I'm grateful to Harriette Sackler and the team at Level Best Books, including Shawn Reilly Simmons and Verena Rose, for guiding me through the publishing process yet again. They are a talented trio, and I realize more and more each year how very lucky I am to be involved with this group.

Several people have also read Sanctuary, have reviewed it, and have prepared blurbs for the book cover. I'd like to thank authors Roger Johns, Bruce Coffin, Mary Sutton, and Annette Dashofy for their time, and their willingness to read and comment on this work. Their kind and encouraging words are so appreciated, and their talent and dedication to their craft will always be an inspiration.

About the Author

C.L. Tolbert grew up on the Gulf Coast of Mississippi, a culturally rich, beachy stretch of land with moss covered oaks and unforgettable sunsets. Early in her career, she earned a Masters of Special Education and taught for ten years before entering law school at the University of Mississippi. Licensed in Mississippi, Louisiana, and Georgia, C.L. practiced law for thirty-five years, concentrating on insurance defense, and corporate litigation. She also had the unique opportunity to teach at Loyola Law School in New Orleans where she was the Director of the Homeless Law Clinic, and learned, firsthand, about poverty in that city. The experiences and impressions from the past forty years contribute to the stories she writes today.

After winning the Georgia State Bar Association's fiction writing contest, C.L. developed the winning short story into the first novel of the Thornton Mystery Series, Out From Silence, featuring the Emma Thornton. In 2021 C.L. published a follow up novel, The Redemption, a mystery set in New Orleans, which Kirkus Reviews called an "engaging and unpredictable whodunit." C.L.'s love of New Orleans and murder mysteries continues in Sanctuary, the third book in the Thornton Mystery series.

C.L. lives in Atlanta with her husband and schnauzer, Yoda. She has two children and three grandchildren.

SOCIAL MEDIA HANDLES:
www.facebook.com/cltolbertwriter
www.instagram.com/cltolbertwriter

AUTHOR WEBSITE:
www.cltolbert.com

Also by C. L. Tolbert

Out From Silence

The Redemption